This is a tale of the [illegible] brought low the Lord of Hell. In my cell here alone, I can tell it only to you, the clay tablet a guard has smuggled me, and hope you will retain the story until the time is right for its retelling.

Is it convenient to know that I was called Homer, that I wrote in a weak and piteous age of a better one, and from my work men drew the truths of their convenience and inspiration for every kind of sin?

My stamp is on the corpse of every warrior to come here, the Welcome Woman said to me. As if they all wouldn't have made the Trip by other means, as if all the Alexanders and Pattons and worse of history wouldn't have come to their fates some other way.

I met a man, while I was with the Dissidents sworn to bring the Devil low, who had fought in a war so terrible its weapons razed whole countries, boiled seas, and made the very air rain char.

And there too I met Alexander of Macedon, who looked upon me with tearing eyes and said that it was my work that had guided him to his greatest moments, my influence that made of him what he was.

My influence. As if there had been no Troy, no black ships on the beach, no Odysseus and Diomedes, no Helen who raised her skirts to tumble men into war.

But I digress. I mean to tell you a simple tale, a tale of afterlife and what it holds. I have paid a great price to be witness for the damned. . . .

THE LITTLE HELLIAD

Janet and Chris Morris

Come, Muse, sing to me not of things that are, or shall be, or were of old; but think of another song.

—Hesiod

BAEN BOOKS

THE LITTLE HELLIAD

A Baen Books Original

Baen Publishing Enterprises
260 Fifth Avenue
New York, N.Y. 10001

First printing, May 1988

ISBN: 0-671-65366-0

Cover art by David Mattingly

Printed in the United States of America

Distributed by
SIMON & SCHUSTER
1230 Avenue of the Americas
New York, N.Y. 10020

To David Drake

For his acuity, support, and encouragement,
without which this book
would never have been written.

Prologue

This is a tale of the horrors of love and how it brought low the Lord of Hell. In my cell here alone, I can tell it only to you, the clay tablet a guard has smuggled me, and hope you will retain the story until the time is right for its retelling.

What is love, and where does it abide but in the sinews of man and the passions of conflict? This I dared to write and no one would heed me—not here, not in Hell. In Hell, as in life, truth is judged not by men's minds but by their glands, and must pass the test of convenience.

Is it convenient to know that I was called Homer, that I wrote in a weak and piteous age of a better one, and from my work men drew the truths of their convenience and inspiration for every kind of sin? Is it helpful to observe that from my tales of mighty souls and mighty passions skewed by love into mighty errors, men learned nothing of caution, nothing of wisdom—learned only to pit themselves against one another more fiercely?

I'm here in Hell, so I am told, because I am responsible for the 'Homeric' tradition, for the heroic model that spurred so many fools to murder and death. I'm here because my work was perceived as a treatise on the art of fighting with spear and bow, of chariotry and covert tactics—because I made war beautiful and glorious.

My stamp is on the corpse of every warrior to come here, the Welcome Woman said to me. As if they all wouldn't have made the Trip by other means, as if all the Alexanders and Pattons and worse of history wouldn't have come to their fates some other way.

I met a man, while I was with the Dissidents sworn to bring the Devil low, who had fought in a war so terrible its weapons razed whole countries, boiled seas, and made the very air rain char. I met another sure that truth was the single most potent weapon of destruction in a world powered by lies.

And there too I met Alexander of Macedon, who looked upon me with tearing eyes and said that it was my work that had guided him to his greatest moments, my influence that made of him what he was.

My influence. As if there had been no Troy, no black ships on the beach, no Odysseus and Diomedes, no Helen who raised her skirts to tumble men into war.

But I disgress. I mean to tell you a simple tale, a tale of afterlife and what it holds. I have paid a great price to be witness for the damned. I have met an angel, a single emissary of Olympian grace, who has agreed to smuggle out the story.

It is a tale of truth. It is a tale of sorrow. It is a tale that cannot be told here in my cell nor in the whole of Hell itself, where only the damned abide. This tale must be told on the living land, where the sweet wind blows and the winey sea rolls dark and bold. It must be told in my homeland and in all the homelands of men who live and breathe, so that they will cease hastening here in all their numbers.

It must be told so that I, who meant one thing and accomplished another, can make peace with every soul here on my account.

This time, I add a preface so I cannot be misunderstood. I say to you, clay tablet and custodian of my endeavor, that if all the men of the world can learn what I have learned since last I wrote, then they will know better things than how to strike a killing blow up through a man's bladder. They will learn that the price of passion is to be its everlasting slave. They will learn that what is done in life is forever, and what is given there will be received, manifold times over, in afterlife.

And if this tale does not teach the lesson, then I cannot teach it. And if we do not learn it, then death and destruction eternally is our lot. And so, since I cannot find an ear here, among those who have nothing left to save, I have struck my bargain with the angel.

It is for you, soft clay of infinite memory and infinite strength, to take this tale of self-made folly to those who may hear it, whose ears are not closed with the wax of arrogance and whose eyes are not sewn shut with the thread of sins. For on Earth, not in Hell, there is a chance to change the future. In Hell, there is no future, only the results of chances untaken and opportunities lost.

Everything that I tell you here is true, tablet, as everything I told before was true. It is up to the angel and fate and your faithful self to make sure that this time there is no misunderstanding.

* * *

Now, when the Devil himself came to me and said, "Homer, tell my story," I was unmoved by the honor. There is no honor in Hell that is not dishonorable, I learned that long ago.

So I was not surprised when the Devil added, "My joy has left me, and taken with it all hope for the damned. As awful as existence has been, for all the teeming souls consigned to me, they have had better than nothingness. If my *joie d'apres vivre* is not returned to me, there will be only nothingness. I cannot lose what does not exist." The Devil bared teeth sharpened on countless souls. His moon-gold eyes shone bright as sunrise; his flaming fury steamed his breath. He was larger than a man of any realm, and dark of skin, with a bold tail and horns finer than a Minotaur's. He was sitting, during this audience, in a chair built out of human skulls and thigh bones, an ivory of yellow caste.

And when I did not reply, he clacked his black claws on the skull of his chair's armrest, a skull frozen in an eternal scream, and said, "Well, Homer, will you do for me what you did for the minor lords of Troy and your querulous Achaean princes?"

"Do what for you, my lord?" I said. It's hard enough to get any kind of publishing arrangement in Hell that my soul ached to say yes and be done with it. But that was what the Devil wanted, obviously—for me to commit to a project for which I had no feeling. Worse, to commit to a project impossible of completion. "Write something that will bring your joy back to you? You are the Supreme Power here, not I. Surely there is nothing a scribbler can do that You cannot do."

"Damn you further, Homer, don't talk back to me. Only say you will undertake a chronicle of My Majesty in Hell. An enspiriting epic, a tale that will lighten the weight of eternity and ennoble my struggle. I am tired. I need to be revivified, to regain faith in the power of Hell itself. I no longer revel in the suffering of the damned; I no longer love the lessons of Hell, nor their teaching. I no longer love the glory of war, though it is all about me. I need, in short, to be the hero in an epic of Homeric proportions—to see myself as the Magnificent Antichrist once more. For this, Homer, you are eminently suited." The Devil, grinning, snapped his claws together and the sound caused my teeth to water. "You, who made a paragon of the snivelling Achilles, can create a mirror in which I can regain my love of eternal vengeance! Like that!"

My soul, brave as it was in the face of dissolution, was also canny. It was I who had given face and form and mind to Odysseus, remember! So I said, "Sire, I will undertake such a task, but only under certain conditions will it be the story you need to inspire your flagging sense of duty."

The Devil growled, "You made songs for the Dissidents without conditions."

"But they are only Dissidents—the underdogs. They were easy; you are the Fallen Angel, the ruler of Hell. I need to acquire the vision fit to your grandeur, to encompass the whole sweep of Hell."

"That's what you want—safe-conducts? Move you freely about then, throughout my realm, and see what you will. And now, about the deadline—"

Out stretched the Devil's hand and in it appeared a contract.

I shuddered and drew my own hands against my chest. "No deadline, Sire," I said. "A work of greatness cannot be done to deadline. If you wish hackwork, get Dante, or Borges, or Dickens or—"

The contract in the Devil's outstretched hand began to blacken and shrivel at the edges. It smoked; its center crackled; it turned red and gold as it flamed.

"No deadline," agreed the Devil, who was also flaming now. "But when I come to you and say present the tale, you'd best have at least some parts of it ready to read to me."

"Of course, my lord," I said to the Devil who was flaming away, crackling and shriveling and grinning through the noxious smoke as he burned. And that was my mistake—the one that got me in this prison from which I write, furtively, waiting for an angel to come and smuggle the real story out. But I get ahead of myself. . . .

Chapter 1: The Encounter

Fat Confucius and a blond, beautiful angel called Just Al were sitting together in the back of Hung Hing's noodle joint when I got there. Each had a fortune cookie in his hand and, as was the custom in New Hell's Chinatown, there was an extra cookie on the plate.

I sat down when Confucius smiled at me and the angel offered me the extra cookie. I hesitated: no fortune can be good in Hell. Surreptitiously, I looked around. The noodle joint was almost empty. The ancient souls at the two other occupied tables were unlikely to be Agency's spies, I told myself: too much blue opium smoke was wafting upwards from the basement. The Agency, like all other arms of Hell's proliferate government, hated drugs: drugs made the natives content, gave them fleeting relief, and dulled their suffering.

When I looked back, Confucius had already opened his fortune cookie: "If a man has nothing, he has nothing to lose." Confucius made a face. "I could have done better two thousand years ago. I don't see why my applications as a fortune-cookie-writer are always turned down." He crumbled the cookie in his fat fist and then, thinking better of discarding it, started eating the crumbs.

"Because," said the handsome Just Al, "you *can* do better." The angel smiled. Just Al, a/k/a Altos, was Hell's only volunteer angel. His ministry was vast, failure was his lot, and yet his face was young and unlined. Dressed in a dirty white robe, he was a stinging reminder to all who saw him of what had been lost, whether or not he was manifesting his great white wings.

Today his wings were not in evidence. And yet my eyes did see them, as a poet's eyes may sometimes see what is not yet manifest. These eyes, which had been blind by the time of my death, see many things others miss: they were given back to me after my third resurrection in Hell. Some said this gift was a simple error, made by the Devil's Undertaker, who resurrects the oft-dying damned, fresh for new torments, but I think now the Devil knew exactly what he was doing. What use would a blind poet have been to a Devil who wanted his story told?

When Confucius heard the angel's voice, tears came to his eyes. They welled onto his fat cheeks and meandered downward. The Oriental shook his head sadly and the tears flew. One landed on a fortune cookie, and one on my hand. It stung, as tears sometimes do in Hell.

I rubbed my hand and both of the others looked at me. Confucius said, "And how are you faring in the House of the Devil, revered Homer?"

Without thinking of how my revelation might affect poor Confucius, I leaned forward and whispered,

"Come closer, and I will tell you both a story the Muse has never dreamed of." And when they did, I whispered, "The Devil came to me himself and asked me to write a tale of His Glory, a chronicle of Hell, and for it, I have safe-conduct throughout the empire."

The angel frowned. Never before had I seen Altos frown. I had seen this angel in the Dissidents' camp when the Devil called in an air strike upon the helpless rebels, and even then he had not frowned, but been pacific of countenance.

Now he was frowning fiercely.

"What is it?" Confucius asked. "The lo mein? The oyster sauce?"

"Yes, what?" I demanded, a suspicion growing in my belly to gnaw upon my joy.

"Writing a paean to the Devil—Homer, you must not do this thing."

A silence hung over our table that did not end until Just Al picked up the plate with its one remaining fortune cookie and again offered the cookie to me.

I took it, filled with foreboding, and cracked it open. It said, "Beware princes bearing gifts."

And of course, I had just received a gift from the Prince of Darkness: my safe-conduct to travel throughout Hell.

"Let me see," Confucius demanded, and when he'd read it, balled the little strip of paper into a wad and threw it on the table. "Talk is cheap," he growled, putting his pudgy hands in his sleeves.

But the angel picked up the crumpled wad and smoothed it, read the fortune. Then he looked straight at me, saying again, "Homer, you must not glorify the Devil."

"I have agreed to make a journey, to report what I

see," I told the angel stiffly. "I will tell of Hell, as it truly is, and of what the Devil's nature is. You will not find it glorious," I promised the angel before I knew what I was saying. I promised him because I was frightened for my soul's sake; I promised because I could not look into his eyes of sky-blue goodness and lie. I promised because, I thought then, what was glory to the Devil would be shame and derision to an angel.

But promise I did, and Altos sat back in his chair, relief exuding from him in a sweet smell that made even wise Confucius smile.

"Good," said Altos the angel. "You will tell a true tale of Hell and all its horrors, all its woes. You will write what you see and what you learn, and when it is done, I will smuggle it out of here, so that living men may learn the truth about Evil."

I was shocked. Confucius was so startled that he belched. Never had anyone proposed such a thing before. We were, all three Dissidents in Hell, part of a struggling movement always near extinction. But no one among the Dissidents had ever thought we could get a message *out*.

But then, no one had ever been commissioned by the Devil to make him a hero. And no one had ever asked the angel anything but how to get out of Hell and into Heaven, in the flesh.

I realized then that I knew nothing of angels, nothing of Altos' God whatsoever. I muttered, "Don't we need a Judge for that?"

There was a saying, a rumor perhaps, that if you found your Judge, your case could be reopened, that there was a way out of Hell through litigation. Of course, this was believed only by those who had never been embroiled in a lawsuit. . .

The ancients at the other two tables got up and left the noodle joint. We were alone, but for the proprietor behind his screen of beads and incense.

"A Judge, beyond myself, is not needed. Sometime, perhaps, I will tell you about the Judges in Hell," said Altos the angel. "For now, you do not need to know that. You need only understand that you and I have a bargain, and that, because of it, you may ask a favor."

"A favor?" My mind was reeling, my spirit soaring. The angel had a hunger for the truth; this was going to be a much better story than some insipid glorification of Satan. From somewhere in my soul, unbidden by my mind, words reached my lips and came forth: "The favor I ask is this: I wish to find my characters of old, to sit and talk with them, all whom I labored to immortalize when I was alive: Odysseus and his kind, all the brave fighters from the long ships."

"This is a foolish waste of a perfectly good favor," said the angel in his melodious voice. "You were in the Dissident camp when Achilles and Diomedes invaded it; you did not speak to them then."

"The time was not . . . propitious. On this trek, it will be. And I must seek the nether hells, all human hells, for my story to be complete. Say yes, Altos, and our deal is made."

Confucius was shaking his head so that his long mustaches swung. "No one can guarantee the future. The handles of the cooking-pot are not yet forged. It is too soon to argue over what is for dinner."

The angel said, "Homer, Confucius is right. Are you sure you will not reconsider this condition?"

And before I could answer, Confucius said, "Have you never heard the story of Wo Chen and Su Li?

No? Then I will tell it to thee, while you are reconsidering your answer."

And Confucius began to tell the following tale:

Wo Chen and Su Li

In ancient times on Earth, when the Dragon had not yet forgotten what to do with his fire and the mountains and the heavens knew their accustomed place, lived the prince Wo Chen in a woodcutter's hut.

The prince was young and fair and he had been given into the care of the woodcutter because his mother had died by poison and his father, the king, had taken a second wife, who became immediately with child.

On the day of the second wife's birthday, the king had occasion to call his astrologers to the palace, and they, one and all, agreed that evil would befall the unborn child at the hands of its half-brother.

"What shall I do?" wailed the king. "My son is but a baby and his mother is dead. My new wife is as dear to me as the sun in heaven, and her baby is innocent, as yet unborn."

The chief astrologer said to the king, "Good king, you must separate these influences, one from the other. Taken apart, neither is evil. Taken together, woe will befall us all."

"What? What do you mean? Speak plainly!" demanded the king, pacing before the astrologers' cauldron.

"I have spoken plainly," said the chief astrologer, who wore a robe with stars and moons embroidered upon it. "The son of your first wife is a firedog; the child of your second wife will be a woodtiger. These two influences, if left on their own together, will destroy the kingdom."

"But still you are not telling me what do!" declared the king, and wrung his hands. "Begone, evil creature. I will consult the assistant chief astrologer in your place."

No matter how the chief astrologer protested, the king would not listen to him anymore. He was hustled out between angry guards, who had orders to put him on a boat for the end of the empire, and to take away all his rank and privileges, and make sure he never again predicted anything in that king's country.

Unfortunately, the guards misunderstood the degree of euphemism employed by the king, and they took the chief astrologer down to the river, where they tied him to a boat which was leaking and set him adrift. Before the boat had sunk to the bottom of the deepest part of the river, back in the palace, the assistant astrologer raised up his eyes to the king and said:

"Your wife is with child and a great child it will be. But your other child, your son by a previous marriage, is in danger from this. Perseverence brings misfortu—"

"Stop!" cried the king, tearing at the sleeves of his robe in distress. "Your predecessor prognosticated evil in this situation, and I have banished him from the country."

"That may be," said the young man who was the assistant chief astrologer, "but the portents cannot be changed."

"Yours can," threatened the king. "If you value your life at this court, you will tell me what to do to change these evil omens and make my house a happy one."

"Words can be changed; deeds cannot be changed. The omens may be changed, but fate cannot be changed," said the assistant astrologer. "Whatever you do to me, I will tell you only the truth, and the truth is this. . ."

"Yes, go on," said the king impatiently.

"If you were to take your eldest son into the forest and find him a home, he will grow up happy. If you were to leave your wife in the palace, she will be happy and her child, also. But if the second child is not the eldest child, neither will be happy. In the end, misfortune comes." The assistant chief astrologer shrugged his shoulders. "That, my king, is what the stars foretell."

"But it is a riddle!" shouted the king. "I hate riddles, and riddlers. It is an insult to tell your king a riddle when he needs good counsel. Begone." And: "Guards! Take this man to the river and see that he, and his wealth of fey riddles meant for my enemies, never darkens my sight again!"

The assistant chief astrologer was hauled away by the guards, who misunderstood the king's orders and put him, his pockets bulging with jewels and coins from the royal treasury, on the next boat to the kingdom of Wen, where he would live a long and successful life as astrologer to the ruler of that country.

Meanwhile, the king in the palace was questioning his single remaining astrologer, the assistant's apprentice. "And what should I do," demanded the king, "to save the peace of my kingdom and the lives of my children, born and unborn?"

The chief assistant astrologer's apprentice was a simple man, perhaps a simpleton, but he understood what the king wanted to hear.

"Do as the chief astrologer told you, my king, and send your eldest son to live in the forest. Heed the chief astrologer's assistant's warning, and do not let your wife think that hers is not your eldest child. Then the eldest will be saved, because he is not a prince; the younger will be the eldest, and all will be right in the kingdom, so long as the firedog and the woodtiger do not meet."

Now the king clapped his hands together and said, "This is just the advice I have been wanting to hear! I shall fake the death of my eldest son and spirit him off to the forest, where there is a woodcutter who will shelter him; I shall treat my second wife's child as my eldest; and we will all live happily ever after."

"And me?" said the apprentice.

"You?" said the king.

"Me—I have told you what you want to hear— how to cheat fate. What is my reward?"

"I will make you chief astrologer of the kingdom," said the king. "Never let it be said that I do not pay my debts."

And so it came to pass that the prince was spirited into the forest and left on the doorstep of the woodcutter, who took him in and fed him and raised him as his own.

It also came to pass that the king's second wife believed the lie she was told, that the prince had died in the night, and she bore the king a daughter, who was raised as if she were a son.

When the daughter was born, the king tore his hair, and rent his garments, and paced in his chambers, saying, "Woe is me, I had a son but I declared him dead and sent him to live with a woodcutter. Now my eldest is a daughter and for all I know, she will rule the kingdom."

But he could not tell his wife he'd lied about the death of his son, for he remembered the prophecy. And he was being attacked by the kingdom of Wen, the country to which the chief assistant astrologer had been mistakenly deported. And because the astrologer knew everything about the king's country, the war went badly.

For twenty years the war went on, reducing the wealth and breadth and people of the embattled king's country. For twenty years, he tried to beget upon his second wife a son, but he got only daughters.

In the twenty-first year, his wife died and his daughter, Su Li, roused the people against the king and overthrew him, promising an end to war with Wen.

Su Li put her father, the king, in a dungeon and she called in the chief astrologer, saying, "How may we win the war with Wen?"

And the astrologer said, "Bring back my teacher, the former chief assistant astrologer, for it is his counsel which gives Wen its advantage over us."

"How is it that the former chief assistant astrologer of my kingdom is aiding the foul dogs of Wen?" demanded the fiery queen, Su Li.

So the chief astrologer, who, remember, was something of a simpleton, told Su Li all about the circumstances in which the astrologer had been mistakenly deported.

When she had heard the tale, Su Li said, "Bring to me this woodcutter's son, this purported eldest son of my father's, so that I may look upon him, and show him to my father, the king who has lost this kingdom through his fear of fate."

Su Li's soldiers scoured the countryside looking for the woodcutter's son, who was happy in the forest. When they came to the woodcutter's hut, the woodcutter told the boy he had taken as his own, "You must go to the palace. The soldiers of the king are waiting."

"Why?" said the young man, now tall and strong, who was called simply Wo, since he was a humble woodcutter's son and not the son of a king. "I am happy here with you, cutting wood."

"You will not be happy here, cutting wood, if those soldiers think you are refusing to obey their orders. You must go with the soldiers, my son," said the old woodcutter with tears in his eyes.

So Wo went with the soldiers to the court of the king.

And when the king, who was a woman, after all, saw the woodcutter's son, she became very angry. She roared like the woodtiger that she was and she decreed that the woodcutter's son be thrown into the same dungeon that held his father.

"When the former chief assistant astrologer returns to this kingdom," she pronounced, "we will find out the truth of the matter."

But she never did. Her soldiers were caught trying to abduct the former chief astrologer's assistant from the kingdom of Wen, and the king of Wen became so angry that he launched a final offensive against her and her country, and he overcame her defenses, and made all her people his slaves.

When the army came bursting into the palace, with the King of Wen at its head, the king said, "Where is the woman who was king here? I will make her a handmaiden in my palace!"

But Su Li had known, that if he won the war, the king of Wen would make her a handmaiden in his palace. She had also stolen down into the dungeons and heard her father crying, begging forgiveness of his son, and seen them with their arms about one another. This indignity was too much for her to bear, and she had gone to the river and weighted down her robes and poled out to its center and jumped to her death.

Thus the soldiers of Wen could not find the woman king. "Fine," said the king of Wen. "Then bring me the old king, who is in the dungeons."

But the old king could not be found. The old king and his son had escaped, with the help of a faithful guard, in the chaos of the final assault upon the palace.

The father and son fled until they reached the old woodcutter's home, where they asked for and received shelter from the woodcutter, who was overjoyed to see the boy, Wo, again.

The old king watched the love flowing unhindered and true between the old woodcutter and the son he could have had, and he wept at how cruel fate had been to him. And although the woodcutter and the king's son protected the old king for the rest of his days, the old king never recovered from the loss of his kingdom to fate.

"And that," said Confucius with a flicker of a smile, "is the end of my story. Do not forget its moral, Homer."

"Its moral," I replied, "is too inscrutable, even for Hell. I don't see what it has to do with my condition, and no—I will not reconsider it: I must have access to all the nether Hells, including Ilion." My heart pounded at the thought, but no one could tell. "And that is that."

"As you wish," said the angel, and held out his hand.

I took it and the touch of that flesh was like the touch of Grace itself.

Then I said, feeling selfish and insensitive in front of poor Confucius, "But come with me on my journey, Confucius. I had forgotten what a good teller of tales you are. And you may join us too, Altos—"

But Altos was not there. The angel, the one men called Just Al, had disappeared. And on the chair where he'd been was a map, folded and old, which said on it, NETHER HELLS.

Chapter 2: To Nether Hells

Confucius and I were a day's journey down the west road out of New Hell, when we came upon a man buried up to his neck in a pile of dung by the side of the road.

We were well out of sight of New Hell, near a village of thatched huts with whitewashed walls that seemed deserted, but for the man craning his neck to eye us from his dung-heap.

Confucius looked at the man and said, "Who are you, honorable sir, and what are you doing buried up to your neck in that dungheap?"

I pulled on Confucius' arm, whispering, "Come away. That is probably a Mediterranean village there, and many Muslim sects bury offenders up to their necks. Then the whole village comes out to spit upon them and kick their heads and. . ." I broke off, not because the story of what Muslims did to offenders was too horrible for telling, but because the buried man had begun to speak.

"Who are *you*," he said in Classical Greek, "to

demand my name?" His nose was long and bony, rather like my own, and his stringy long hair was fouled with dung. Flies buzzed around his mouth as he spoke. "What right do you have to come upon a man at his ablutions and disturb his meditations?"

"Ablutions? Meditations?" Confucius repeated, shifting the pack on his back. Confucius' pack was heavy, filled as it was with egg rolls and rice balls and dried mushrooms and fortune cookies.

I myself had brought only bread and wine . . . and parchment and clay tablets and stylii ink and quills, of course. And the map of Nether Hells that the angel had given me. I swung my pack from my shoulders and took out a skin of wine, swigging from it before the buried man's eyes. Then I said, holding it out, "My friend's Greek is rudimentary, let us speak English. And if your English is rusty, here's just the stimulus for your tongue—fine Attic wine."

I walked toward the man in the dungheap, offering the gift, for I was curious, too, as to what he was doing there. And yet something about him was naggingly familiar. . .

Up out of the dungheap jumped the shitty man, gesticulating wildly: "Shoo! Shoo! Get that noxious stuff away from me! Don't think you can come upon a man minding his own business meditating in his dungheap and force spirits down his throat! If you knew anything about anything, you'd know that dung is the best thing for dropsy and a hundred other ills, and that wine is the worst thing for the constitution of a man with a working mind!"

Confucius, too, had taken off his pack. "Tea, then," he said mildly, brushing clots of dung from himself. "I have a ting in my pack; we can make a fire, have tea, and read the leaves, honorable—"

"Shoo!" said the irascible, shitty man, picking up a

handful of dung and raising that hand threateningly, as if to pelt us. "I drink only water, and that sparingly!"

By now there was a cloud of flies buzzing angrily about his head, and the stench of him, mixed with the dung, was awful.

One of these stimuli, either the flies or the stench or his irascible nature or his pronouncements, helped me remember what I had found familiar: "Heraclitus!" I said with some certainty, pointing at him. "You are Heraclitus, who said, 'The dry soul is wisest'; who buried himself in dung and shunned the company of men in favor of children."

"Really?" asked Confucius suspiciously.

"Really," snapped the man impolitely, and cast the dung he was holding toward Confucius, who stepped neatly aside despite his bulk. "And since you have no water and are not children, then get you from my sight! What are you doing on this road, anyhow? The only people who come this way are those on their way to. . . Oh."

"That's right," I said, putting the cork back in my wineskin and the wineskin in my pack. "We're on our way to the Nether Hells."

"You'll never make it," warned the philosopher from Ephesus, rubbing his swollen knees. "There are demons aplenty, and evils of the night, and there are hungry rivers and all the gods of war. . ."

"We will make it, honorable sir," said Confucius, who had decided to make tea in any case and was lighting a portable bunsen burner from his pack to boil the water. "We have a safe-conduct from the Devil himself. We have not yet introduced ourselves. I am Confucius, perhaps you've heard of me. And this, Homer the bard, of—"

"Homer?" said the irascible man, an eyebrow arched

in disbelief, his eyes looking me over for some kind of trick, his dirty hands on his hips.

"Guilty as charged," I smiled. "And since you know who we are, you know that such men as we are like children. Thus you can sit with us and have tea, since we are strangers in your country, and tell us any stories you might know which will help us find Lost Ilion, or other Nether Hells worth visiting."

"Ilion? Ilion's not lost. Nothing is lost. Everything that is, was, or will be is an ever-living fire, with—"

"—portions of it kindling quicker than a bunsen burner," Confucius growled, because the water was slow to boil and yet the ting's handles were becoming red hot. "May I offer you a fortune cookie, Heraclitus?"

"A what?" said the Ephesian philosopher, but sat crosslegged, groaning at the pain from his joints.

"Cookie with a prognostication inside," I explained. This Heraclitus was, in my estimation, the best mind of his time, although he was sour and sardonic. "If the prognostication is favorable, and if you can tell us one tale worth retelling, then you'll be welcome to travel with us into the Nether Hells, where perhaps you can find some children to keep you company." I looked around in exaggerated fashion. "Once long ago, I wrote that 'children are a man's crown, towers of a city.'"

Heraclitus looked up and in his long face, his dark eyes gleamed. "Children, yes. That would be nice. My village, as you have surmised, is deserted. Everyone grew up and moved away."

"That is unfortunate," said Confucius, handing Heraclitus a handleless cup of tea and a fortune cookie. "But tell me why you crave the company of children."

This was a blunt question, one a Greek would never ask.

But Heraclitus said, "Because men are less wise than boys."

"I will drink to that," I said. "What is it like down the road? What should we watch out for? Surely you've heard some tales of life beyond the rivers?"

The rivers that separated New Hell's environs from the Nether Hells varied. Here, it was the Lethe.

"Well, one forgets, you know. The waters have that effect. But if you can cross the Lethe, then you will be well on your way to somewhere, certainly, as sure as Cephalus himself was when he came this way, chasing the Teumesian fox with his hound; or Chimera herself was when she came this way, chasing that swift steed Pegasus and his vain rider, Bellerophon; or Satan Himself when he came this way, chasing that Trojan woman. Or Theseus himself, when—"

"Ah," said Confucius, "we have not heard those stories. And we are collecting just those sorts of stories. Before I give you your fortune cookie, tell us the tales."

"The tales? Four tales for a mere cookie and a cup of tea? 'One tale worth retelling' was your first offer, was it not? One tale is all you'll get, although the Lethe holds many tales that men have forgot. Then, if I travel with you, you may hear others. . ." Heraclitus looked at me. "What shall I sing, Bard?"

And I had a feeling there was a trick to the question, for I was in the company of the Riddler of Ephesus, but I answered anyway, "The tale of Satan and the Trojan Woman, for I know that the fox and hound were turned to stone on the Lethe's far bank—I can see them from here." I pointed to the river's marshy distance, where two boulders faced each other,

jaws eternally agape. I'd heard the Earthly version of
that story from Hesiod, and not forgotten. "And as
for Theseus, there are more tales of him than there
are sinners in Hell." And I grinned nastily at the
philosopher, adding, "Or stories men have forgot
because they drank the Waters of Lethe."

Heraclitus squatted down by the cookfire where
Confucius' ting wafted pungent smoke heavenward,
and rubbed his hands over the fire. Those hands
were dirty still, but stronger now than they had
been. In fact, his whole person was gaining sub-
stance, or seeming to, as if a god had come to abide
in him. His neck grew thick, his chest grew hair and
his sinews emboldened, even as I watched, and all
while he told this tale:

SATAN AND THE TROJAN WOMAN

Long ago when Hell was new and the Earth just
born from Ether, when the Devil was a haughty
angel with nightblack wings that spread across the
damned sky and all things lived in his shadow, Satan
came to this poor village disguised as a mortal soul.

He was long of eye and broad of back and went
unremarked among the refugees and deportees who
camped here on the Lethe's banks, hoping for either
the blessing of Forgetfulness or passage across the
river, to where their countrymen congregated. Either result would ease their loneliness, the worst
plague upon souls newly come to Hell.

And although no one knew who He was, everyone
could feel how lonely the newcomer felt. The agony
of isolation exuded from his flesh, so that no one
could sit near him and drink frothy beer in comfort.
So wherever in the camp he went, to the long tents
or the cookfires, the Devil was shunned by men.

He was the most alone of the refugees, the most lifeless soul of all, and he made a circle of emptiness wherever he would sit. No one would come close to him, except a simple barmaid who'd been a Queen of Troy, a comely wench as they had in those days, with honey between her thighs and proud breasts that never drooped.

This woman was unashamed of her flesh, for in her time no man had ruled over her kingdom, or hidden her sex from view, or made sins of the passions women know. She had come to Hell for displeasing a jealous goddess, whom she'd denied the sacrifice of a harvest king.

The goddess to whom the harvest king had been promised was a goddess whose name is not known anymore, a goddess whose symbols were eyes and whose temple was adorned with bull's horns and bull altars. To this goddess, at the death of the year, the queen's consort of the previous season was customarily sacrificed to guarantee the return of the spring.

But the queen's heart had softened unto her year-king, who was but a boy. They had made a girl child together, and this child the queen proposed to sacrifice in his place.

Thus the sacrifice of the girl child was duly made, but the goddess was not satisfied. Instead of a man's organs upon her bull altar, there was but an infant girl, and this was not enough. Worse, the queen was scandalously happy with her king that she had saved, and all through the town the Trojan women were looking at their men with proprietary eyes, thinking to save them and keep them from danger and hold them close to the hearths.

So the goddess became wroth with this queen and she said, "Thou who will flout the law of Heaven, the way of Nature, the nature of the seasons, will be accursed of the gods. Your women and your men, your town and your lands and crops, your children who are raised on those crops, all of you will suffer eternally, for you have denied the harvest king to the gods." And the goddess was increasingly angry, every night in heaven she spent alone, without the new year-king who should have been sacrificed to her glory.

So she went to the rest of the Trojan gods and she turned their faces from the Trojan people, saying that this queen was lawless and a sinner, and decreeing eternal curses upon the town, just as she had threatened the queen. From that day forward, no woman of Troy could keep her eyes from a comely man, and no man of Troy would ever stay by her hearth, and no son grew of their loins without a thirst for blood in his heart.

This curse came down from heaven and it smote the queen and her king where they lay in her bed, and he girded on his swordbelt and went off raiding, taking with him all the other Trojan lords.

They raided among the Achaeans and they raided among the peoples of Naharin. They raided all spring, and the women had to labor in the fields in their stead. And when the men came home in autumn, to women worn with toil, the angry armies of their enemies followed after them, for the men had brought home spoils and slaves, strange gods and implements of war.

All this while, the Queen of Troy had tried to pretend that nothing was amiss, not with her husband or with her country. But when the men came home bearing captive women full of sins, and slaves full of guile and wiles, she knew that the curse was full upon her.

She went to the goddess and begged forgiveness,

but the goddess did not listen. She went to her knees before the bull altar and prayed for a sign, a way to make amends.

And the goddess appeared to her, standing upon the empty altar, and suddenly the bull altar was piled with the bodies of foreign women and dead Trojan men.

Shaken and tearful, the Queen of Troy went home to her hearth, and there upon her bed lay her year-king, for whom she had brought suffering upon her people, in the arms of a foreign woman, engaged upon a fertility rite.

The queen picked up her husband's javelin and put it to his throat. She called upon her priestesses, and they came running. And they grabbed the foreign woman and the year-king and took them to the bull altar, where the queen herself sacrificed the pair to the angry goddess, as she had been instructed in her vision.

With tears in her eyes, she skewered her own harvest king, whom she had saved at the expense of a daughter of her loins, and the harlot whom he had brought back from foreign lands.

Then she turned to her priestesses and said, "All of you who have men who went to war instead of to the fields, who brought back foreign women and slaves, bring them hither and do as I have done, or the country will forever be accursed with foreigners and wars."

And the priestesses did this, amid much wailing and rending of garments, for they loved their men even though the men had learned to love war and its spoils better than home and hearth.

The Trojan bull altar ran wet with blood, and corpses piled up upon it, and at their pinnacle could be seen the goddess, treading upon them as a woman treads upon grapes in a vat.

But lo and behold, the goddess was not smiling a smile of forgiveness, but a smile of vengeful satisfaction. And from her mouth came these words: "You have heaped evil upon evil, women of Troy. You have taught your men to covet the spoils of war above all things, and have murdered the lords of your fields. You have brought home to your country jealousy and foreign gods. Now you must make husbands of your slaves and teach them to bear arms, for war and blood eternally is your lot. Your queen, who cared not for the fruitfulness of the fields or the fruitfulness of her loins, but cast those aside for selfish love of a year-king, has brought ruin upon you, and all your descendants."

At this, all the priestesses fell to their knees and broke out wailing, tearing their hair and beating their breasts.

But the goddess continued, "Troy has made its choice and sealed that choice in blood. Your town and your country shall be sacked and destroyed, until there are none of you left. By women, it will fall, over and over, until you are a people no longer. Every time your descendants build the city again, enemies will come and destroy it. All because of her, who denied me my rightful consort, to keep the man for herself!"

Then the priestesses turned on the Trojan queen and ripped her limb from limb, tearing the heart and liver from her body upon the bull altar consecrated with so many dead Trojan men.

This, of course, did not soften the heart of the goddess. But it may have saved the queen a worse fate, for she was killed by the priestesses before the first armies from Naharin and Achaea came to take revenge upon the people of Troy; before the women freed their foreign slaves to fight the enemies, and before the town was overrun for the first time.

But not for the last time. Troy, her women and her men, was sacked and sacked and sacked again, and soon it was necessary to crown a king who was a warlord, not a mere harvest king. And so no successor was named to the Queen of Troy, for the rule of the town and the country fell out of the hands of women and into the hands of men. And these men, being foreign men on the whole, knew nothing but war and cared for nothing but spoils, and set the women who had once been their masters to work in the fields ever after, and to be the servants of warriors now needed to protect them from the depredacious armies who came every spring to sack the town.

And all of this, it was said, was the fault of the Queen of Troy, whom all women ever after cursed in their prayers, and who came to Hell because of her love for a harvest-king that lost the rule of Troy to women forever and brought eternal war upon the sons and daughters of their loins.

So it can be imagined that the Queen of Troy, even in Hell, was lonely, nearly as lonely as the Devil who sat alone by the cookfire, right here where we are sitting now. She was so especially lonely because, in those days, sinners were fewer and everyone knew everyone else's business. Everyone knew how the queen had come to Hell—knew that she had lost to women their rule over men, and brought shame and low estate upon all her kind, as well as causing her country to be accursed.

Thus the men in Hell continually taunted her with their bodies, trying to see if they could turn her head as had the harvest king on Earth. For she and all subsequent women of Troy were famous for the sin of loving too much, of giving up all things for the touch of a man.

And she, for her part, was trying to turn away from men, all men and any man. She lived in constant fear of seeing the harvest king again, and she spent her nights alone whenever she could.

But the loneliness of the Devil drew her like a magnet. She could tell in her heart that this great-thewed man had lost as much as she, or more. She could see in his long eyes, as he drank, such torture as only she had known. And though she was the lowliest of barmaids in Hell, in her heart she was still a queen.

She walked like a queen and talked like a queen and when she served the Devil his beer she flourished it as a queen might bestow a regal favor upon a worthy subject.

The Devil could not fail to notice the queenly sinner, whose thighs promised honey and whose breasts were unbowed. He had lost his kingdom of heaven, and he was not yet accustomed to the torture of ruling in Hell. He still strove to lighten his burden; he still thought, in those days, that he could make a go of it here, make a place more fair and true than God had made.

And he looked upon the Trojan Woman and said to himself, "If I had this woman for my queen, my burdens would be lightened. If I had such a queen, all Hell would rejoice at her beauty, and souls would take heart that such happiness could abound in my heart."

As I have said, this was very early in the Devil's reign. Very early it was, too, in His punishments, for Satan sinned the vast sin of pride, thinking he could

go God one better, and God set him many lessons to
learn.

This Trojan queen was one of the first. When she
brought him his next round of beer, in the flicker of
firelight, he mistook her pity for a finer emotion, and
he reached out a hand to her.

All around the fire, men looked up. Conversations
stopped. Meat remained unchewed between tight-
clenched jaws. The Devil had reached for the woman
in a way that souls do with lowly barmaids, and as
was her custom, she threw his beer into his eyes and
ran from the fire.

The Devil roared and chased after her, and behind
him he heard men snicker, saying, "Well, there's
another fool gone after the Trojan queen, who has no
heart for a man to melt, for she left it on a bull altar
when she died."

But the Devil paid no heed, and he chased the
woman all the way to the Lethe's banks.

On its shore, he paused, for she was poised to
jump where the riverbank is steep and the Lethe
runs deep. "Come any closer," she threatened in a
quavering voice, "and I will jump into the Lethe.
Then I will forget you, and whatever sorrow you
bear in that blackened heart of yours. And if you
chase me there, you will forget what it was you
wanted with me, and what good will your horrid
passion do you then?"

The Devil paused, feeling lonelier than ever. The
snickering of the men came back to haunt him. The
laughter wafting from the town seemed to him to be
all at his expense.

He stood up straight and tall and said, "But I am
the ruler of this land, the Lord of Hell, the King of
all, and I will make you my queen if you will but
come to me and ease my loneliness."

"A king?" she laughed bitterly. "What good is a king to me? I was a queen, before. I had no need of such kings as you. I thought you were a lonely man, a kindred soul, a sufferer. I despise all kings, and men who grab for my thighs with no regard for my wishes."

"But you are a woman," the Devil protested, "and a barmaid to boot. A sinner come to Hell to suffer. How can you stand there and threaten to jump into the river of forgetfulness rather than suffer some companionship offered by the Lord of Hell?"

"I care not for lords, of Hell or otherwise," said the former Queen of Troy. "I care only for my harvest king, whom I have lost. And I do not believe any longer that you are lonely and in need of companionship, if—"

While she spoke, the Devil had been inching closer and closer, and now he sprang. He caught the woman, grabbing her back from the brink just as she tried to throw herself into the river.

"I have you," he said. "I have you now, and I will teach you respect and what it is to honor the Lord of Hell."

The Devil was shaking with rage. He was so angry that his loneliness meant nothing to him, even though he held in his arms the only woman he'd ever met who could chase that loneliness from him.

She struggled and he pinned her under him. And in their battle, a rock had fallen from the bank and Lethe water had splashed up and landed upon his lips, where it made him forget what a bad temper he had.

The Devil forced the woman, who was the only woman in all of Hell, past, present or future, whom he might have loved, to do his bidding. But when the act was done, he was lonelier than ever he had been before.

The Trojan woman lay under him with a tear in her eye and a snarl on her lips, and the words she spoke were these: "Cursed am I," she said to him, "to have come into the arms of the most hateful creature in all of Hell—a rapist. You are less than a man, you are a beast of the field. You are foul and if my curse can be shared, then you will share it: loneliness and lovelessness forever are your lot, evil one."

With that, she closed her eyes and refused to respond to him, no matter what it was he did to her. So eventually the Devil stopped doing anything at all and lay there, panting.

And then he began to repent. He repented loudly, and then softly, but the Trojan woman would pay him no heed.

When, exhausted and lonelier than ever, the Devil arose from the woman, saying dispiritedly, "I thought you were a woman who knew the pain of loneliness and would welcome another soul to your bosom," and walked away, another man came sneaking out from the bushes.

And the Devil saw this man, a man who had once been a year-king, a harvest king of a country and a town known as Troy, go up to the lonely woman who was sobbing quietly on the Lethe's bank, and take her in his arms, and wade down into the river with her, where he bathed them both in the Waters of Forgetfulness, so that the curse between them was forgotten.

When they came out of the river, on its far side, they were holding hands and brushing hips and their laughter was so full of love that the Devil's heart hardened as never before. It hardened to the very sound of lovers; it hardened to the tiniest chance that a soul could find respite from torture in Hell.

that well-told tale of Heraclitus', that I began to work on the *Little Helliad,* which was what I had decided to name the Devil's book.

It was also at that moment, with the help of Confucius and his ting, as later that night we read the leaves, that I learned I could as easily seek Ithaca as Ilion among the Nether Hells.

For it was surely possible to find the Ithaca of my Earthly youth. Men do one thing consistently: they make the same mistakes in Hell that brought them here. So there would be an Ithaca, and there would be men of my kind there, and there would be more second chances than repentant sinners to take them.

And there would be good Confucius by my side, with his spare and appropriate wisdom; and Heraclitus, the wisest eye ever to fall upon the natural world, to tell us tales the Lethe made men forget, along the way.

Oh yes, I had forgot. Sometime that evening, Heraclitus opened his fortune cookie and in it was a slip of paper that said, "Being faithful to a trust brings its own reward. An unapparent connection is stronger than an apparent."

Chapter 3: Ode to Lucifer

When the Devil showed up, our little party still had not crossed the Lethe. Confucius and I had just convinced Heraclitus to let us build a bonfire out of his beloved dung chips, that we might hail the ferryman tarrying on the river's far shore.

The dung burned hot and high, and the smoke from it was acrid. It billowed in low-flying plumes about our heads. It seeped into our mouths; it stuffed our noses; it stung our eyes until the tears ran.

This blue-gray, awful smoke wound itself around our heads as if it were possessed by the soul of a hungry python intent on our suffocation. A wind whipped up from somewhere, one of those keening winds that carries with it all the moaning of the damned; in it, speech was impossible.

The wind mated with the smoke and multiplied it; the fire in the dung heap grew brighter and fiercer, reaching high into the sky, licking toward clouds that seemed underlit by the blaze. The fire took on shapes and out of it sprang demons as bold as gods, who danced about us as we coughed.

Heraclitus fell to his knees and started crawling toward the water. Confucius covered his head with the skirt of his robe and sank to the ground where he stood. Around him, shadows thrown by the horrid fire danced and then seemed to rise up, alive. Flame-headed harpies came out of it, and dragons with open mouths and burnished scales; and on the backs of these were fiends with bloody teeth, and in the eyes of the fiends were all the torments of the underworld: Rape was there, despoiling men and women with a wide and gaping smile; Murder was beside her, wild of eye and covered with gore; Theft and Treachery went arm in arm, in a chariot driven by souls whose skin was flayed from their bones; Avarice followed behind the chariot, drooling, and Betrayal, smirking and rubbing his bloated belly, brought up the rear, riding astride Cowardice, who bawled as she came on.

All of these rose from the smoking dungheap, and their eyes were white-hot coals; behind them, the river turned cobalt, and its tides wrought snakes upon the shore. Then the snakes rose up, growing legs like men, and battled among themselves there and then, striking each other with their fangs and darting tongues, and with their new-grown arms into which the weapons of man had come. And into their midst waded the demons born first of the bonfire, who grabbed up the fighters in their multitude, and carried armloads of them away into the flames and smoke, while the warriors themselves took no notice, so intent were they upon slaying their brothers.

All this time Heraclitus, headed for the riverbank and crying for water, crawled through the midst of their battle, crushing some alive and toppling piles of their dead as he went.

And I, who stood alone, could not come to the philosopher's aid. Nor dared I turn to help Confucius, hiding and quaking in the tent of his robe. You must remember, I was blind for much of my life. The fear of darkness in me is ingrained. Because a man overcomes a curse does not mean he has beaten it; the threat of sightlessness, of groping in the dark, of dependency on others, of being denied the world of color, the 'simple' pleasures of reading and of writing—what could confound a poet more?

I thought sure, there and then, that the last sight I would see in Hell was that of the dung-fire's horde, with their electrum bones and their cobalt eyes, with their ivory, blood-splashed teeth and their hair smeared with viscera. The smell of feces had liberated itself from the heap, and all around me was that odor most associated with death and overpowering fear.

By now, my vision was so blurred by the fire's foul smoke, which would not rise, that I did not at first recognize Satan when he strode out of the blaze toward me.

No man who has seen the Lord of Hell has failed to be impressed, but consider my position: moments ago, I was sure I was going blind again, this time for eternity. So it was not simply the Devil's winged aspect, his midnight skin over muscles of wrath, his eyes burning with the fires of hopeless hubris, which caused my knees to weaken and me to prostrate myself before the Lord of Hell.

I was grateful to be seeing anything at all. Yes, I was grateful to the Devil, and full of fear of his power as I had never been before. I abased myself. I dropped my forehead to the ground and there I quaked.

Thus I did not see the disposition of the fire-spawned warriors, or anything else but his carboniferous, horny feet as they stopped before me.

Claws scraped close, then halted, tapping upon pebbles like a stylus on a slate. Tap. Tap, tap. Tap, tap, tap. It was the cadence of a frustrated tutor, the impatience of an angry slavemaster, the promise of discipline to come that rode those simple, repetitive taps which made me raise my head, which made my teeth water and my soul shrivel.

And then I was staring into the eyes of Lucifer, whence all the carnage on the riverbank must have come. Must have, because, now that he was here in full manifestation, all of that was gone. There were no snakes turned to men in their hacked and bloody masses, no livers on pikes or pink swords drenched with arterial blood in twitching hands. There were no ophidian heads with stuck-out tongues or throats pulsing over gaping cuts.

There remained, on the riverbank, only Heraclitus, who had reached the water and lay there, his head sideways in the shallows, one hand splashing desultorily like a child's; and Confucius, his tented robe pulled fast down over hunched shoulders, cradling his belly tight with firm, crossed arms, before a dung fire burning low, burning out at last, passing final wisps of smoke and steam like farts into the sullen air of the riverbank.

And myself, before the Lord of all Lords of Hell, on my knees with my buttocks stuck up in the air like a bath slave.

I remembered my dignity, then. Now that the smoke was not choking me, the air not black and biting, now that snake-men did not wage war upon the shore, it was mine for the taking. Cowardice is a curse of thinkers; doers know it not, I told myself, and straightened up.

At least I was upright before my two companions—willing to eye the Devil, not hiding in the Lethe or under my own skirts, I consoled myself.

At least I dared to look Hell's master in the eye. And say, "Satan, my lord, what brings you out among the damned?" First, I wanted to call the words back, so shallow and foolish did they sound. Secondly, I reconsidered how they *did* sound and found them arrogant and vain. Thirdly, I knew with misery that there was no "right" thing to say when you've been caught unawares by the Devil himself. Thus I added no disclaimer, or any qualifier; neither did I attempt to restate myself in any way, just looked up at the Devil from my vantage on my knees.

"Up, fool, up," said Satan with a flick of his tail.

I scrambled to my feet. Out of the corner of my eye, I saw Confucius peek out from under his robe. Down by the riverside, Heraclitus raised his dripping head from the water, stared in puzzlement, then let his head fall back.

Even with the Devil before me, I knew what I must do. I mumbled, "Excuse me, sire," as I edged by the mighty winged lord. Then I scrambled down the bank to pull Heraclitus from the water.

Heraclitus didn't help. He didn't understand. He looked at me queruously from half-vacant eyes. And there was Lethe water dribbling down his chin. My heart wrenched as, with my sleeve, I carefully wiped the waters of forgetfulness from the Ephesian philosopher's lips. From his chin. From his gullet where it had dribbled.

And I whispered, "Oh, Heraclitus, why did you do it? Why? Nothing is as bad as losing yourself."

But the man who barely recognized his name did

not understand my question. Like a child he took my
hand and his face clouded over, as if he might cry in
the face of my rebuke.

No horror of hell, not the whole battle of the
transmuted snakes, had ever hurt my heart like the
sight of those once-wise eyes gone vacant and young.
No threat, even that of blindness, compared to the
reality of Heraclitus with no more mind than that of a
child. I led the bony philosopher past the Devil,
whose claws were again clacking in his impatience,
to Confucius.

Before the sage I stopped and tugged Heraclitus'
hand toward the fat man who peered at me from
under his robe. "Hold on to him," I said. "Until the
Devil is through with me. He's drunk the waters; he
can't be left upon his own."

I put Heraclitus' hand into Confucius' and turned
away.

The Devil was not pleased with me, I could see.
But I thought I saw a tinge of amusement pull at
those purple lips over the tragedy of Heraclitus.
Behind me, the philosopher now sat crosslegged with
Confucius, playing with the sandy soil as if he'd
never made a castle out of mud before.

Ahead of me, the Devil was demanding, "And
what of my saga, Homer? My tale of glories, my
wondrous story? Where is the first chapter? Where
is your outline? Where is, as you promised, a tome
to raise my spirits?"

"I. . ." Abashed, I could not meet his eyes. Rather,
I sought the tumult-muddied riverbank, where the
ruts and bloody pools of battle still remained.

"You what?" said the Devil, taking a step toward
me, his wings rising until they blotted out the glow
of Paradise completely.

In that inky shadow, it seemed as if I had been cut

out of reality, excised from the phenomenal world. There were only the Devil's glowing eyes and his voice, louder than a death knell, wider than Hell in all its reaches, coming from everywhere and anywhere, sprinkling sparks of rufous stars among the blackness it transformed.

The voice was a thing upon its own, like the voice of a muse or the voice of conscience. It uprooted my senses and posited them in a firmament such as I hadn't seen in Hell, where only Paradise and the clouds of stained souls mark the way to heaven.

There I thought I saw the gods upon their mount, and they were frowning. I surely saw a comet with a tail like a wild horse running, and its face was that of Mephistopheles. I saw, too, the very faces of the gods—every one whose hymns I had written: I saw Dionysus and comely Demeter; I saw Apollo helping Paris upon the battle plain, bow in hand; I saw Hermes laughing at my plight and Aphrodite pulling up her skirts in the forest, while a stag rubbed his velvet on her arm. Ares too, I saw, and realized that he had overseen the battle on the Lethe's bank, for all the fighters who had died there were heaped around his feet. I saw Artemis, sister of the far-shooter, with her Melian horses, and Aphrodite bathing on a Cyprian beach. And Pallas Athene, guarding the mighty city, and golden-throned Hera backlit with Zeus's lightning. And Hermes and Pan, goat-footed and horned, with his snowy shock of hair, cavorted round her, there on the Olympus I had never glimpsed in life.

Nor thought to glimpse from Hell. I shook my head; I rubbed my eyes. And when I opened them, the Mount was still before me, created out of the Devil's blackness, amid his white-hot stars. And Hephaestus lived in the mountain, making things, teaching men, dwelling in the stars themselves. And beneath him I glimpsed Poseidon, shaker of the earth, of the fruitless sea, the dark-haired master of the depths.

And Poseidon looked upon me with the Devil's eyes. I closed my own at this, and when I opened them, Zeus the all-seeing was before me, son of Chronos, ruler of time without end. And he, too, looked to me as the Devil had, with mighty thews and beetled brow.

And all of these spun together, pointing at me with all their fingers, which became the Devil's own clawed digit, which held steady upon my person as those mighty wings came down, taking Olympus and the stars away with them as they folded to his back.

I whispered wonderingly, "So it is not far from here to there, or any different place at all, but only your power holds me here?"

The Devil said, "There are ways out of Hell for those who earn them. Write your tale for me, revered Homer, and . . . who knows?" At that, he grinned, and his face changed around the grin, lightening and shrinking until the Devil was very much like a man.

There were no wings on him now, but the Devil in any garb is still the Devil. And he continued to speak, as if his wings and tail and fangs had not been replaced by the baldric and javelin and shield of a warrior of my time: "Show me progress, or you'll never take another step toward the fate that might be yours."

He meant the Mount, just as I had seen it, the Mount that whispered, in my memory, that there was a heaven very near this hell, and a way from here to there.

So I said, "I began to work upon the Little Helliad

at the same time that I commenced, with the help of
Confucius, here, and poor Heraclitus, to trek for
Ilion and Ithaca in the Nether Hells. To continue
that, sire, I must get across the river. And to do that,
I need Heraclitus."

"You have him," said the Devil slyly.

"I have his husk. He has drunk of the Lethe, and
what he knows is lost, unless. . ."

"He must earn it back. And you must earn your
own way. There is a Judge for you, Homer, and it is
I." The Devil bowed like a courtier.

Everyone has heard the rumor of Judges in Hell—
find a Judge, the authority responsible for that soul's
eon, and a commutation of sentence is possible, if
the case is strong enough. But to have the Devil as
my Judge was the same as having no Judge at all, I
thought. "Sire, you are the same in aspect as
Hephaestus, just as Hell, in some way, is the same as
Heaven. This you have shown me. And I shall write
a tale for you that you adjudge sufficient, and true
and fair. But you must give me back the guide I had
in Heraclitus."

"If you want something in Hell, Homer, you earn
it," said the Devil, crossing his warrior's arms. "Now,
the tale, or some part of it."

Thus I came to compose, on the spot, the *Ode to
Lucifer*, while reminding myself that I had just seen
the Devil in every god of my youth, including the
jealous and treacherous, tricky masters of Fate.

"Hark, clear-voiced Muse," said I, closing my eyes
and looking pained, "I begin to sing of Lucifer, chief
and great god among the Underworld, all-knowing,
lord of all, the Transgressor who reaps the harvest of
mankind's labors, who sinks men's hopes like ships
upon the rocks of sin. O accursed one, be kind unto

the servants of the land, having one mind over all of us, and bestow grace upon my undertaking."

I cleared my throat. The Devil's arms were still crossed; his eyes were closed. I hadn't another thing to say.

He cleared his throat. He stamped his foot. He said, "Well, Homer, go on, I am waiting."

I took a deep breath and said, "Unto these endeavors, allow success to come. Success is yours, O Satanic Majesty, not a humble mortal's. A hundred offices of damnation have the gods alloted you, and because of it, your Majesty is unaccompanied. None can share it. None can partake of it. . ." And with less trouble than I'd anticipated, I segued neatly into a retelling of the Trojan Woman story I'd heard from Heraclitus.

Half-way through the tale, the Devil chose to sit. A throne appeared under him. His head sank to rest on his massive fist, and his golden eyes, glaring even in his human face, seemed to dim. He sat that way until the tale was done, and by its ending, he'd become again that winged creature meant to make men quake.

And quake I did, for I had told the Devil how a woman had flouted his passion, how he'd been brought low and thwarted in love by a mere mortal.

He might have punished me there and then, I knew the risk. But I had no other story ready, and this was a research trip—I must make that clear, or I was sure I would not be allowed to continue. And I must continue, now that I knew, somewhere—reachable because I had seen it—was the great mount of my heritage, wherein lived the gods I had labored so hard and long to please.

All the Devil actually did, after the story was told, was to raise his head and say to me, in a voice that seemed flat and distracted, "I will be back, Homer. And if your vignette is not accompanied by some sign of your so-called genius, if you haven't embarked upon the glorification of My Majesty, I will cast you into a Hell so deep you'll never see a glimmer of your Olympus again."

"But sire," I pleaded, aware now that Confucius and Heraclitus were listening, hot all up the back of my neck at the way the Devil had reacted to my work, "I must work hard to develop sympathy for your cause—to make your case. To set up context wherein your mighty exploits have—"

"Homer, fool, scribbler, dolt!" said the Devil thickly, for he was already beginning to disappear, "I want my epic, and I want it in good time. I want it in a style that appeals to me, and I want it to contain nothing abhorrent to my nature. If I find you cannot do the job. . . ."

The sentence remained unfinished, for the Devil had ceased to be. I felt in my pocket, under my robe, to make sure my maps and safe-conducts were still there. This commission had turned into something new, now. The Devil was threatening me, and every threat he left unvoiced had more power than a dozen lesser penalties.

Don't get me wrong, I was fully intending to write the epic glorifying Satan, as I had agreed. But I wanted it to be a true reflection of Hell, and now that I had seen Olympus in the Devil's wings, I was no longer sure that I understood Hell well enough to begin such a task.

And, too, I had failed to help poor Heraclitus, who was making drawings in the sand and goo-gooing at them while Confucius tried to keep the childlike philosopher's fingers out of the fortune cookies.

Disheartened, I joined them, suggesting to Confucius that we make tea upon that shore. Across the river lay everything I needed. But I didn't know if I had the heart to go on, looking at Heraclitus who looked back at me with uncomprehending eyes.

Confucius understood all of what *he'd* heard, though he hadn't seen Olympus. Or so he said, when the tea water was boiling in its ting.

"But perhaps I understand some little thing," said the fat man, "that you do not. Look." He pointed across the river and I gazed that way.

Now, in response to our cookfire, as it had not to the great dungfire, the ferryboat was coming. Surely coming. The ferry was getting larger; it was drawing away from the fox and hound in stone on the far bank, heading right toward us.

Confucius looked at Heraclitus, who seemed to be growing younger by the minute, as if his mind controlled his flesh's age, and asked me, "Shall we take him? He is but a child, now."

"If we did not, with whom would we leave him?" Behind us was only the deserted village where we'd found the philosopher. "Anyway, it's my fault that he's like this—the Devil uses him to teach me a lesson, to make me write what is in his soul, not in mine."

"And can you do that?"

"I don't know," I admitted. "Part of the time, yes," I bragged then, in case the Devil could hear. "But its wrongness—the forcing of a tale into a shape it should not take—is the very iniquity of Hell itself. The Devil's *true* story must be told."

Confucius nodded, making three chins out of this one. "I thought you would say that. There are tales within tales, and tales that can be told two ways. If you do not lose your temper, you will have success. With intractable people, one teaches by example."

I was polite. I answered yes, of course. But to satisfy a creature like the Devil, who listened not with his ear but with his ego, and who patently had my punishment in mind from the outset. . . I was not sure that I could ever write an epic that would please him. Not when the subject was his Satanic Self.

However, the ferryman was drawing near, the water in the ting was boiling, and the child-Heraclitus was clapping his hands at the "pretty boat, look!"

So I looked again, and realized that, for whatever purpose, the Devil did want me to labor in his behalf. Otherwise, the ferryboat would not be coming unerringly toward us.

What I didn't realize, then, was who the boatman was.

Chapter 4: Things Forgotten

I could not banish the image of Olympus that the Devil had shown me. It preoccupied me as the ferry approached; it made my tea tasteless and even overwhelmed my sorrow for the squeezed grape that had been the sharp-edged mind of Heraclitus.

I daydreamed, there on the shore of the Lethe. I dawdled. I ignored even the portents of Confucius' fortune cookie ritual. Though my crumbled cookie revealed the message, *Resist temptation*, I could not come to grips with its import. Thus was I tempted by the Devil: I could not see the beacon of Olympus as temptation. It was salvation to me then, though one who had written what I had written, of gods and men and life, should have seen what the Devil was trying to do.

But I did not, and as the ferry made its way to shore, I ambled toward it like one in a dream, not asking who and whither, or even why.

Heraclitus was transported with excitement, jumping up and down on the sand and clapping his hands

in glee. Confucius had his own fat hands full, what
with the childlike sage in our care, the ting and the
backpack of supplies to get aboard.

I barely noticed the ferryman. My head was still
among the clouds, where Athene abided, where Zeus
held sway, where all the desires of my youth could
be fulfilled. Thus the fact that the ferry had a bottom
of glass, a deck of clearest nothingness, seemed in-
consequential to me.

But not to Heraclitus, who went immediately to
his knees, whooping in delight. And not to Confucius, who slipped on its slickness, lost his balance,
and fell inelegantly upon his ample rump as the
ferryman, without a word, poled the boat from shore.

It was not until he'd exchanged his pole for oars,
not until we were embarked upon the waters of
forgetfulness, that I thought to look at the ferryman's
face, hidden beneath the cowl of his robe. The Lethe
grew deeper under us. The cries of Heraclitus, the
oohs and ahs of childlike awe, mixed with the slap of
the oars and the heavy breathing of Confucius, who
sat on the deck, staring between his legs. Still I paid
no attention to anything but the wonders in my
head.

Perchance, I could win Olympus for my own. Perhaps the Devil would play me fair. I, who had sung
the praises of my pantheon, who loved all the gods of
Greece only slightly less than their progenitor, God
himself, had earned the right of heaven, if any had.
Chronos had given me a glimpse of salvation, I told
myself. And like my ancestors, I must simply seize
the moment, win my day.

All this prattled of its own accord inside my head,
the mix of muse and man that hope calls daydreams,
and I was far from where I sat, in a glass-bottomed

ferry with a cowled guide, no matter how ominous was the shore our craft approached.

Thus I remember little of the first half of that boatride, nothing worth reporting until my dreams of Olympus faded, until the cries of Heraclitus penetrated, until the sight of Confucius, bent as double as his belly would allow, brought my mind down to matters at hand.

And 'down' was where Confucius stared; 'down' was where Heraclitus was, prostrate upon the deck, his nose pressed to the glass. Finally my gaze saw past my muddied feet, through the terrible clear waters of the Lethe, to the detritus there upon her floor.

There, in the river's mud, was everything that man forgot, everything that had been lost to Hell and mind. There, in a torment beyond any I'd thought to glimpse, were cities and armies, chariots and horses, strange machines gliding hither and yon, and souls.

Souls staring up at me. Souls in fine habits; souls naked as new morning. There were the souls of babes in search of mothers' teats; there were the souls of grieving widows who could not recognize their husbands; there were the souls of architects and artisans, stranded on half-completed amphitheaters. There were the souls, in fact, of all Atlantis, for I knew the tales and the city there was surely that one.

Her walls were high and golden boats lay wrecked on them, like birds impaled on spires high in the air. Her palaces were hung with wrack and jeweled with barnacles and starfish. Her carriages, tiny from this distance, were drawn by mantas and their sides were grown of coral. And every soul I saw there never thought to look up.

Not a one peered up to find the source of the

shadow that marked our passing. No one paid us the slightest heed. They were about their business, everything from a battle on the reefs with strangers riding sharks, to the burial of what must have been a king.

Our black shadow passed over the burial procession as if on cue, and it was no more, to them, than a cloud crossing sweet Ithaca's moon. As it did, I saw a blacker shadow, then two, then three—shapes like men with webbed feet and tentacles sprouting from their mouths; shadows with misshapen backs, leaving trails of bubbles.

Not even these, in the middle depths, disturbed the mourning train below.

As we passed on, beyond the midpoint of the crossing, over a ridge of reef that nearly scraped the boat's glass belly, I felt the first stirring of fear. And that fear chased the last of my dreams away. Were we to founder on that reef, so far from shore? How deep the sleep, when the mind has lost its place in time? How sad those creatures far below, once men, who breathed water now instead of air and did not know enough to miss what they had lost.

The glass beneath our feet became a treachery, a fearsome thing and frail, too frail to go unnoticed.

I slipped from my seat onto its slickness, and slid to Confucius' side. He was staring as if mesmerized as the boat passed over the reef and another kind of city gleamed far below.

This one was a city of skeletons: skeleton galleys and skeleton barques; skeleton triremes and skeleton barges; skeleton warships sporting cannon with cankers of rust and colonies of coral and barnacle nations living on their tortured metal. Also were other ships there, gray ships and long, with sprouting masts of wire and crooked crosses on their hulls,

I
hor
fall
tun
spit
"
The
wor
back
us,
sure
I
bank
were
I l
to th
us. V
the I
see t
dock,
distal
No
and c
towar
An is
one ir
I ha
not tc
were
tower
sight c
would
Confu
boat.
"Ho
that wi

ships with whole convoys of trucks and more upon their decks; ships with sailors who might be dead, corpses waving at their posts; or alive, and living like the Atlanteans in our wake.

Some ships were moving, through the deep waters, and these had no lights or decks beyond a single poop. While we watched, they catapulted stones at one another; when one was hit, a soundless flash of light and bubbles split its hull and took it to darker depths, out of sight.

I cared no longer for these creatures of the depths; I was concerned for my own self. Young Heraclitus was pounding the deck in his excitement. I reached past fascinated Confucius and grabbed Heraclitus' hands. I wrenched him upright by that grip and, as if he were a boy in truth, slapped him backhanded. "Sit still. Don't pound. Don't move, in fact."

The youth who was once a wise philosopher was increasingly younger; even his long nose was shorter as his body shook off age with wisdom. Perhaps he was twenty, now; for certain he was a danger.

He'd lost all his collateral of personality already. Confucius and I still had ours at risk. I snarled at Heraclitus and his eyes grew misty, hurt, then resentful, like any child's. He struggled to free his wrists, but I held them firm.

The ferry beneath us began to rock as the boy philosopher pulled harder and I, in my turn, pulled back.

Confucius scrambled to the boat's center and planted his bulk there, trying to catch my eye. When he managed, I looked into those fat-enfolded orbs and saw a warning there.

"This is no time for teaching lessons; this is a time for holding firm. In the center lies salvation."

"Right," I said, and let the youngster go, deter-

mining there and then to throw Heraclitus overboard if I had to, rather than risk being dumped into the Lethe, where everything knew nothing of itself, where all that mattered to a man like me was lost.

Lost as everything that should have mattered to Heraclitus had been lost before he'd boarded. The boy said huffily, "How come you grabbed me like that, old man? I was just lookin'."

I peered at Confucius, and he at me, and Confucius said to our friend whose face was now smooth and unlined, "Sit quietly, Heraclitus. All that lives so far below is less than abides on the shore we seek. If you rock the boat, we'll never reach the land."

The boy subsided, hugging himself, squatting beside Confucius, who offered him another cookie, and occasionally skewered me with an accusatory stare. But I had other things to look at.

I had chanced to glimpse behind me, and now I alerted Confucius to do the same. The shore we'd left, where the deserted village had been, was no longer a huddle of whitewashed cottages clinging to the riverside. There were great gaps of cloud and colored wind, as if time itself were on display, between us and that shore, but one thing was certain: it was New Hell teeming there, or some other awful city. Right down to the shoreline it hulked, black and filthy, wrapped in a pall of its pollution like an old wife in a shawl. It stared back at us with a thousand eyes and each was baleful. It owned its sky, and that was red and purple and grey and brown, depending on where one looked.

And from it jets rent the sky, and night shone down in slivers, and flame gouted, as if a war was underway.

"What's that?" demanded Heraclitus, once he saw what Confucius and I were looking at.

By then I was not certain; I'd never seen a place so horrid, not even New Hell. For New Hell did not fall in upon itself; its buildings did not shiver and tumble, sending up great gaping clouds of dust, or spit out flame, or host warring aircraft in its sky.

"New Lebanon," said Confucius, "or some such. There are hells for warriors, Heraclitus, which are worse than anything you know. If we were to turn back now, that would be our fate. Like that beneath us, it is one inferior to pressing on. And that, I am sure, is the point."

I looked again at the ravaged city on the Lethe's bank, and it was as far across the water as if the river were a sea.

I looked the other way, at last, past the ferryman, to the shore from which the boat had come to fetch us. When the ferryman had set out, the far shore of the Lethe had been so close it was no feat at all to see the boat, the stone fox and hound beside its dock, and expect our bonfire to summon it so short a distance.

Now the Lethe was like an ocean, dark and broad and carrying us in its palm. The shore we headed toward was shrouded, misted round, like an island. An island, I realized, was what it was indeed, and one increasingly familiar.

I had spent too much time in the west of Greece not to realize where the Lethe and the ferryman were taking us. I saw the citadel; I saw the light-tower with its wood-fueled fires of home. And the sight of it struck me with foreboding that somehow I would never make that landfall. Once again, I bade Confucius keep the boy still, in the middle of the boat.

"Homer, if you get your tail wet, there is nothing that will further. But this fox here is young; he will

cross the great water. So will I. So will you. The
Devil will not give you up so easily." Confucius smiled,
a beatific smile that chilled me.

Seers have always troubled me; if a Pythia speaks
your future, you are bound to it. Without the inter-
ference of prognosticators, man's will is freer. It is
the gods alone who have men's fates in their minds.

I almost said this to my friend, in my disarray, but
Confucius was again soothing Heraclitus, who had
spied mermaids on seahorses in the water below,
and a dragon who struck the boy with terror.

Seeing young Heraclitus cower against Confucius
for protection from a serpent of the sea made me
braver, and I looked again to the island shore.

Sweet Ithaca, or I'd left my memory back on the
beach with Heraclitus'. And I spied something else,
now, that horripilated my skin and made me wish I
hadn't taken comfort in Heraclitus' fear.

The ferryman's hood slipped back. From it, eyes
gleamed in a broad and grizzled face. I looked closer,
and I saw how wide were the shoulders that rowed
us to our destination. I saw legs knotty with muscle
and sinew; I saw a scar upon one knee, a gore that
wriggled up the thigh. And I saw hands that had
shaped my lifetime, strong and long-fingered and
callused.

The shore wind was blowing up. If the oarsman
did not break his stroke and hold his hood, it would
blow right off.

Somehow I knew he would not stop his rowing. I
was entranced by the pull of his shoulders, the ripple
of his arms. Yet I wanted not to look, not to see that
face if the hood should blow back completely. I was
not ready to confront him.

I searched in his form and his silent progress for
something amiss. It could be a demon that rowed us.

It could be a trick of the Devil's. I wanted it to be a quirk of chance, a vicious ploy of Satan's, a mistake on my part—anything but proof of the certainty growing in me of who it was who rowed us.

I caught his eye and said, "Ferryman, how long to Ithaca?" boldly, to show I knew where I was going, to challenge him, to make him speak.

"Before dark, we'll reach shore," he said in a voice as old as my cradle and as familiar as the blood in my veins.

But how could it be? What Hell would waste a man such as the one before me, ferrying commuters across an uncertain deep?

But then I recalled all that I had written, and how much of this man's trials had been by sea.

My eyes misted. My vision swam. My senses reeled. My heart felt fear and pity, honor and dishonor, rage and grief. And then, after all other emotions, came embarrassment. Trepidation. Intimidation.

How else to feel, before my ancestor, mighty Odysseus? My heart ceased beating; my mouth went dry. I was clumsy where I sat. This was not the creature of my imaginings, the shadow of my family tree; not the grandfather whose scent of oil and leather was all I recalled, but for those massive hands.

This was the man himself, the damned soul, Odysseus, son of Laertes, seed of Zeus; resourceful Odysseus, friend of Agamemnon's—on whom all I had done of consequence in life was based.

And what did he think of it, my life's work? Did he even know of it, or me, or care? The man for whom the gods held back the dawn might disavow such a descendant as I, a weak scrivener, a chronicler who lived at the sufferance of warriors and kings, a creature wracked with words, not deeds.

I looked upon Odysseus and I cried. I cried shamefully, trying to hide my tears, hoping they would pass for irritation from the wind. I cried from fear of slights worse than death. For this man, I had labored year upon year. For his glory, I had sweated. For his tale, I had sacrificed so much.

Had he even read it? Could he read? If he could, would he deem it fitting? Or pathetic?

I wiped my eyes with the back of my hand and determined not to announce myself. He had not. He was a ferryman taking me to Ithaca because the Devil had arranged it so.

Oh, I knew it was the Devil's work. Emotion such as tormented me now could be no less. I found in myself a coward, that day in Hell, that I had never known existed—or never admitted was within me.

Cowardice of deeds is one thing, of spirit, quite another. I could not bear to hear that Odysseus despised me. All authors fear their critics, but no other poet, I was sure, had been faced with the abyss that Odysseus represented.

If he hated the Odyssey, then I would throw myself into the Lethe, I decided. If he even guessed who I was, I would flee Ithaca like a wraith in the night.

All this, before the hood blew off in a gust of infernal wind. All this, wringing of hands and shrivelling of soul, before those eyes plumbed mine, before the wide brow furrowed, before Confucius said, "Ithaca, is that where we're headed? A fine omen, boatman—my friend Homer seeks the inspiration of his earthly epics, the ancestors of—"

I kicked the sage, hard. I looked into the eyes of Odysseus and I saw there nothing but the glow of kingship—no disgust, no disavowal. And no welcome.

But I saw puzzlement, over the kick. And Heraclitus, who was bold in the way of children, had seen something on the shore.

"Look! Look! Horses, chariots! A party! A picnic!" And the fool stood up in the glass-bottomed boat, rocking it so that both Heraclitus and I dove to pull him down.

Some Lethe water sloshed over the boat's low sides. Confucius quickly tore a strip from his robe to sop it up.

The mighty strokes of the ferryman did not slacken. When we'd mopped up the water and tossed the rag over the side, our guide said to us, "The water's safe here, so close to shore. Full of salt, is all."

"I . . . thank you," I said.

Again he looked at me, and asked, "Whose house are you seeking? Whose guestfriend will you be?"

"I'm . . . Homer, as my friend Confucius said."

"A bard, yes. But whose ancestor do you seek?"

"I'm . . . not just any bard. I'm of your line, if you are Odysseus. I'm a poet who wrote of you, in life. A child of Telemachus."

"A poet, son of Telemachus?" The boatman's shoulders hunched. Then his head tilted. "I am Odysseus, as you say. And since I am, you may guest in my house, for Telemachus is not at Ithaca right now."

Then I felt my soul dwindling. This revered hero had not even heard of me; he didn't remember my babyhood with any fondness; he had never heard my poem. A life's work, turned to ash in an instant.

I hugged my belly and leaned forward, colder than the shore spray would warrant as he rowed us in past the jetty.

Nothing more was said until we made landfall, and then there were indeed chariots and horses, for there was some sort of game being played on the beach.

As Odysseus unfolded himself, beaching the ferry

before we were even out of it, I tried to console my muse: he was as big a man, as fine of head and imposing of form, as I'd said he was.

He was, in fact, very much as I'd imagined him. Too much, perhaps.

For when we'd all scrambled ashore and his household came down to greet us, as we were walking up the beach to fabled Ithaca, in its prime and glory, he looked at me out of one narrowed eye and said, "You're the one who wrote that story too long to be told after dinner?" and shook his head with amusement.

If I could have left then, I would have. Only Confucius' comforting hand, and the need to watch the cavorting philosopher who'd been Heraclitus, got me through that first night in Odysseus' palace.

Chapter 5: My Ancestor

It was not simply Telemachus who was not at Ithaca. Ithaca herself was not at Ithaca; the citadel in its prime that loomed as we had climbed the leaf-trembling slope was just a husk, a joke of Satan's, a lure.

This place was a shade of Ithaca, a hell of remembrance full of empty beds and echoing memories. I should have known it would be so, for this was not escape from Hell, but adventuring deeper into it.

Still, I was shocked and full of pain. No Penelope kept house and hearth here, though the place was full of brawling suitors. No loved ones were here, in fact, at all. Odysseus was alone among a multitude of enemies, of wraiths and sirens and dead men come to life.

The retainers of the house took no orders; the cooks were as likely to serve up head of man as whole roast pig. The halls resounded with women's cries but women there were not.

Even the hounds and horses were all aliens. No

Argos, no wetnurse to comfort the heart, no joy was anywhere in this Ithaca.

Yet all of history was there, and I have never closed my eyes to that.

Once the first night was past, a lonely night full of footsteps in the halls and latch-thongs creaking and Heraclitus sobbing in Confucius' bed, I resolved to confront Odysseus and have his story.

There had been no time at dinner, what with all the strangers there—men from isles I'd never heard of; men who wore their helmets to the table; men whose brooches showed crests of unknown lands. Among these men the talk was all of current troubles, of invasions from the "sea."

Men spoke of the sea-dragon that Heraclitus had seen, or of his brothers, ravagers of ships. Heraclitus had attested to seeing the graveyard of the long ships, and there had been a lengthy silence after that.

When asked, we'd explained judiciously how we were searching through all the hells for certain men, among whom was Odysseus, our host.

The tension this evoked soon ended idle chatter. No one trusted any other here. Eyes darted in heads and hands caressed hilts worn to dinner for more than cutting haunches of well-roast pig.

Confucius' countenance alone evoked sly whispers, and halfway through that meal I pled exhaustion for my party. Better to sleep hungry than to mix in what we could not understand.

One thing I understood about that dinner was its nature: a war council was under way; these black and brown and pale men awaited only our leavetaking to go to work.

A good guest sees to the health of his welcome. I took my friends up cold stairs and there we slept, among the memories and ghosts.

Ithaca was not so great or proud as I remembered; the suitors had raged here for a thousand years or more. A woman, I told Confucius, could set the place aright.

He shook his head and told me bide until morning, for what was wrong here was nothing a maiden or a marriage could fix. And Heraclitus asked why all the men were so dour and old, why there were no children or youths here.

Confucius ruffled the Ephesian's hair and put him to bed without an answer, which might be why the boy philosopher had bad dreams and had to crawl into Confucius' bed like a child.

Confucius had said, "Heraclitus has found the child he sought; now he can seek the man."

No more of that evening do I recall but the constant grinding of my mind's wheels, as I cogitated plans to get Odysseus alone.

I need not have bothered. In the morning, the hero came to my door and invited me to walk with him before breakfast on the battlements.

The wind there was blowy, and we had to put our heads together to talk. Thus we had no fear of being overheard by the sentries on the wall, who leaned on their long spears and never once looked at us as we passed.

"What brings you here, Homer? A bard who offers no song at dinner is rare indeed."

"I came as a guestfriend," I protested, stiffening. "Not to sing for my supper, but to see my ancestral home."

"There is no home here, nor comfort. This is Hell, in case you have forgot."

"I . . . wanted—still want—to find those men whose praises I sang in life. You are the greatest of those—"

"Was."

"Lord?"

"Was the greatest. Now I am embattled and embittered more than in life. You see we have no gentlewomen here, just the odd creature of the kitchen. You are a warrior's poet; you know the signs of siege preparations when you see them. Guestfriend, you are welcome to stay when the horde overruns us, but I counsel you—depart while the way is clear."

I shook my head, no.

"Then there's more here for you than curiosity, or you would not risk your life—or your friends'."

"You are Odysseus. I have . . . questions."

"Then ask them." The big man stopped, where the battlements overlooked the sea.

"Ah—" The questions I had in mind were all too prying; one cannot interrogate an ancestor, not one with thews like trees and eyes thirsty for the blood of any enemy who might declare himself, not atop his own battlements. What was I to say to this crafty man, this lord of lies? Where is Diomedes, your close companion? Where is Achilles, your nemesis? Where is your son, your wife, all the peace that Zeus the aegis offered you? I could not speak a word of that.

Rather, I looked upon Odysseus, into eyes like the wine-blue sea of home, and my words withered upon my tongue. Might I explain the Devil's commission to this Odysseus, ripe with war, whose gaze glittered like bronze? This man whose Hellish age was unknowable; whose willful mouth was curled with impatience, whose forelock stirred in the breeze like a stallion on Neritos—of this man, might I ask penetrating questions and survive?

"Yes?" said the lord of Ithaca, crossing his arms. "I'm waiting. Men do not come here without fated

purpose. I've ferried no one to this place who did not
have his reasons. Come, Homer, what are yours?"

"To ask you questions. To learn what I can of how
my . . . ancestors . . . fare in Hell. To meet, if I can,
men I never met in life. Yourself, Achilles, Diomedes,
Menelaos, Agamemnon. . . ."

"Agamemnon." Sharply spat, was that single word.
In its syllables were all the frustration and rage of a
warrior betrayed by his gods to hell. "Agamemnon is
obsessed with Ilion; he has nothing better. Look
there for him, not here. And keep away from bath-
tubs when you do." Humor glinted in those eyes so
deep they had no lids. One hand went to his hip.
"Next question, gold-tongued Homer of the indefati-
guable word."

It was an insult and I knew that. As far as a host
could push a guest, Odysseus had shoved me with
that slight. He wished to be rid of me, because he
understood my purpose here as meddling of the
Devil—or because he didn't. Whichever, I was angry.

"Where is Penelope?" I blurted.

He closed his eyes. He shook his head. He said,
"The underworld has taken her from me." His voice
was thick. "Ask a different thing."

"Why did you not wed the wench Nausikaa of the
Phaiakians?"

"Who says," said Odysseus as a crooked grin flashed
across his face, "that I did not?"

"It's history—I mean, I said that you did not,
because so was it told to me. So Telemachus had it
from your own lips."

"Think, man. Was I not then newly reunited with
loyal Penelope after twenty years away? What should
I have said? That I spitted every filly who crossed my
path? That the Phaiakians pressed the wench on me,
and she stole into my bed and blandished me with

caresses, so that my need came hard upon me? That the Phaiakians had no intercourse with other men, I *did* say. The child-bride I left there was sure to make no outcry; her father knew the way of it. If there was an heir from that union, he would claim only Phaiakian inheritance, being of a reclusive people who thought themselves too good for other men. As for me, I got my ship and transit home . . . the rest was as the gods allowed."

He grinned that crooked grin again and his head lifted, a worldly lord regarding a bumpkin of the meadows.

"Oh," I said, hot to the ears. "Of course. As for Penelope, if I knew the circumstance, perhaps I could be of help. I have safe-conducts good throughout all of Hell, given to me by the Devil himself. I will gladly accompany you on a search for her, if that would please you," I offered thoughtlessly. Partly to wound him back for lying a lie that lived for centuries, a lie that trapped me into declaring it a truth. And partly to show him I had power, too. I was not simply a long-winded bard who told stories too long and complicated to be told between the boar and cheese-laced posset. I was a man of resources, my own self.

His smirk was gone. The wind had taken it. He scowled now down on me through eyes wholly black and did not say a word.

I added, nervous: "I am gathering tales of my old heroes, after all. . ."

"From the Devil, you say?" Odysseus glowered, a look not meant for a guestfriend. "You come from the Evil One, who has turned all the gods of Ithaca against me?"

"The Devil hates lovers most of all," I said to calm him. "Now, quick, the story of Penelope. Did she ever come to Hell at all. . . ?"

I wasn't sure it would work; Odysseus was a man of towering rages, but also one of infinite resources. If the ploy failed, I was certain, the next thing I would see would be the rocky shore far below as my helpless body hurtled toward it. Then would be the pain, and the Undertaker who presided over the oft-dying damned, and my unending misery: to be murdered by my ancestor. Meanwhile, Confucius and Heraclitus would be trapped here, without safe-conducts, amid an Ithaca preparing to war against whatever Hell provided. It was too cruel. I closed my eyes, then opened them when rough hands did not seize me.

Odysseus raised his head once more and looked out to sea and proceeded to speak as if his muse was with him:

PENELOPE

Perhaps you think you know the fate of those the gods immortalized, the story of my Odyssey, my twenty years of wanderings and my return, but if you don't know this tale, you know nothing, since a story is not a story until you know how it ends.

I had a son by Circe, named Telegonus, a creature of power if you'll recall his mother. While I struggled homeward, he grew up fatherless and angry, and set out looking for me.

Once Penelope's suitors, every one who now sits at my war councils in Hell, had been buried by their kinsmen, I sacrificed to the Nymphs and set out for the isle of Elis.

It wasn't so much that I needed to inspect my herds there, but that the walls of Ithaca closed in on me, after so long adventuring, and though I loved

Penelope, Athene once more put the wanderlust into my heart. I was given a mixing bowl as a gift on Elis, and had adventures suited to my nature, before the thongs of marriage forced me home.

There I gave Penelope the bowl, a fine gift, and performed more sacrifices to the gods because my wife was clinging to me, telling me how cruel it was to leave her, how much love she had for me, and all the rest of those things that women say that drive their men away.

Like a bull to a wild herd I was drawn to venture seaward; like a herdsman she drove me from her the harder she tried to make me stay.

Don't get me wrong—I loved Penelope, but I had blood in my veins and I had memories of my youth to chase. I had other sons than hers, beloved Telemachus, and other women who bore them.

Athene was my patron, and she too was a love of mine. The grey-eyed one came to me one day, appearing like a vision, and stirred my heart to war. Among the gods, there was a blossoming of old feuds, and some of these had me at their center. So for the goddess, and for my loins' sake, and to outrun the shadow of age looming over me, I agreed to go.

War was I promised, if I set sail—noble contests and spoils as befit a victor. We would share out the booty and the women of the vanquished, and I would bring home to Penelope, who loved me too much, who kept weaving suffocating shrouds of kindness over me, spoils to heal her hurt and loneliness.

So I made my bargain, and so Athene agreed. I went to Thesprotis, and there I found Callidice, their queen. I married her, to give her comfort and a warlord—and because she was fine and new to me, not yet acting like a wife.

The war broke out—we helped it—between the

Thesprotians and the Brygi on the mortal side, and between my patron, Athene, and Ares, who backed the Brygi.

Ares routed us once in mortal battle, and the heroes on the battleplain bled out until the gods dimmed their sight. Athene came to fight with us the next morning, and she engaged Ares upon her own, and the carnage of that warring was the worst that I had ever seen.

My noble queen Callidice came to the battleplain in a brazen chariot, saying she was pregnant, and wept wifely tears upon the shiny reins of my horses, saying I should make a peace with the Brygi for our son's sake. At the same time, Apollo separated Athene and Ares, and a truce came down upon the land.

Callidice bore me a son who'd looked upon bloody battle while still in his mother's womb, and then she died. I gave this son my blessing, let him succeed to the kingdom, and returned to Ithaca, tired and worn, sick of war, looking for a living wife to warm my bones.

But when I arrived on Ithaca, I found that Telegonus, Circe's son, had come looking for me there. Not finding his father, he had ravaged whatever he could of the island and was still sacking it.

So I had no peace there, which I had come to find, but rather violence from my own blood, and the spawn of my loins. There was nothing for it but to ride out to meet the despoiler of my country. I could not say to Penelope, "Look, this man is a son of mine, and we must take him in, treat him with respect, anoint his wounded heart with the oil of familial love, and make things right with him." She, after all, had a son of her own to put forward, a son as much a wanderer as his father.

By now Penelope was graying. I thought to ride

out against the marauder, engage him in close combat, and reveal myself. What I thought I would say
to a man of such prowess who ravaged my country
because I had been no father at all to him, I don't
remember.

Out I went, to stop him one way or the other,
thinking that when we saw each other, blood would
have its way and we would find ourselves in glad
reunion, but it was not to be.

Bold as a god in his fury, angry at the whole land
of Ithaca, which he thought stole my love from him,
Telegonus, my son out of Circe, struck me down and
killed me there and then, as I hesitated, before I
could form my name upon my tongue.

Then, I have heard, there was mourning and
wailing. Telegonus claimed, I was told, that he killed
me unwittingly, that he never would have killed his
father. I know these things from the mouths of those
who sat about my corpse in lamentation, because
Athene willed that my ghost tarry there.

Or the Devil did. We did not know, in those days,
of evils worse than Hades. I had no glimpse of this
Hell where I now abide. Nor did I wonder which of
the Olympian host were evil, or if the Devil worked
through heavenly meddlers on occasion. In those
days, some gods took your part; some did not. The
lords of Olympus quarreled, and their sides were
taken, their points made, by men who loved them. It
was a simple world I carried with me out of life, fully
expecting that Athene would guide me to my well-
earned rest eventually.

At worst, I was sure, I'd wander with ghosts I'd
met before on my visits to Hades for a time. I did
not expect to wander in the world, a helpless ghost,
while my wives and children tampered with my fate.

Telegonus, my son, and Penelope, my first wife,

and Telemachus, her son who was returned from Pylos, made a plan that even Athene could not forestall. They all proclaimed, wailing over me, that they did this for my soul, but you have seen what became of that.

They took my body to Circe's island, and my wives faced one another. My sons faced one another. And my ghost faced these mortals but could not stay what was to follow.

Telegonus, son of Circe, begged his mother to make immortal all of those who had come to her: Penelope, Telemachus, and Telegonus, since he had done as Circe asked and returned her lost Odysseus to her.

Now, you remember Circe. She was not bound by the laws of men. Once, perhaps, she would have looked upon my corpse and felt pity, remembered love, and raised me to immortality in a true sense, so that I could walk upon Olympus with the rest.

But Telemachus was there, fine-formed and brave, the image of me in the flower of my youth. And her son was there, who, though he had slain me in fair battle, still habored hatred in his heart for the father who had deserted him. Thus this was the bargain that Circe offered Penelope and Telemachus, my first and foremost family:

Penelope would marry Circe's son, Telegonus, for Telegonus wanted that revenge upon me more than any other. Circe herself would be the wife of Telmachus, finest spawn of my loins, and he would never leave her as I had done. For this, all would be made immortal, including myself.

But Circe forebore to explain what immortality she offered me, a dead and powerless shade already—the immortality of life in Hell. As for those others, my faithless wife who married my son, and my other son who married my once-wife Circe—all of them reside on Olympus.

Thus Circe finally got the best of me, and paid me back in the manner of jealous women everywhere. So do not look for Penelope, or Telemachus, in Hell, not even in the misty mires and quarries of Hades, nor in the Mourning Fields or anywhere else that you or I, Homer, can reach. And do not talk to me of lovers in hell, or what the Devil wants. The only life left to me is war, and the lovers I find in Hell are those who, like myself, played others false in life, so that love is no love at all, but only another kind of battle.

All the time Odysseus had been talking, I had been watching the shore, thinking of my own poor mother, Epicasta, who mourned her lost husband, Telemachus, and never knew the truth of it. Meanwhile, out of the water, black shapes had scrambled, shapes with tentacles streaming from their mouths and misshapen backs. These were making their way from rock to rock, up the beach, unnoticed.

Were they an advance party of the enemy Odysseus was expecting? I did not know whether to point them out or not. There were sentries on the battlements, and since Odysseus himself was there, it was not my place to make assumptions. Guests do not insinuate themselves into the matters of their hosts.

Anyway, I was too shaken by Odysseus's story. I had met separated lovers in Hell, and those who had grown fond of one another, but never had I realized what Hell might do to the heart of a man like Odysseus. And I was reminded of the matter of the Trojan Woman, and how the Devil felt about lovers.

But I knew I could not explain to Odysseus that the events he'd retold to me were not entirely his fault. If I tried, only ill would come from it. You cannot shake a man from his beliefs, whatever ones he has made to comfort himself.

Now I understood the hollow hearth of Ithaca. Now I understood what the second chapter of the *Little Helliad* would be. Who knew how many times the Devil had interfered in the lives of men and women? Who knew how his wrath seeped into the souls of the unwary living and kept love from bearing fruit, or rotted that fruit upon the vine?

Looking at the hard face of Odysseus, bitter but never repentant, the face of a trickster who had been tricked, of a man the gods had treated ill and who treated all the world ill in his turn, I knew I had written him wrong.

So I lost a loved one there, too, that day on the battlements of Ithaca. I had met an Odysseus who deserved his fate, as the hero I had written did not. I had made his clever lies and his tarryings and his hard-held wrath at man and god into a tapestry of heroism, into fine attributes for a wise and canny warrior—and by that means, set into the consciousness of man an admiration for certain kinds of evil that now, if I could, I would erase.

I had set Odysseus up an equal to Diomedes, a straight man and a great-hearted one; I had made dishonor equal to honor; I had allowed subterfuge and selfishness to be glorified in the guise of implements of war.

I was sorry now. I understood why Odysseus was in Hell now. And I wanted to get away from there before I stayed long enough to find out, first-hand, in what battle Odysseus was now engaged.

For there would be one. By his own will and his own hand and his own words, there would always be one. This man needed adversaries as he needed blood in his veins; a sword in his hand to hold back black introspection; an enemy without, that he might not confront the enemy within.

Perhaps we all do, but it is a reason for Hell to be our fates. Men who strike out and do evil unto others out of fear, out of the need to be shown larger and stronger than they are—these men make bravery a synonym for cowardice.

And I? Might I be one of them? Or was I simply fooled, a victim of the sirens' song that legend is? I consoled myself that, even in my day, such exploits as Odysseus' were not fitting for men anymore.

And I said, to the man staring out to sea, "Well thank you, noble host, for your hospitality and that fine tale. I will get my compatriots and we will be going, before your war begins, if we can but borrow a boat to take us."

"What?" Odysseus had all but forgotten me. Now he turned from the vista and said, "Go? If you can, storyteller. If you can. Ask those coming up the beach, and perhaps they will help you. We haven't a boat to spare but the ferry, and I won't have time for ferrying for a while."

I glanced again at the black shapes mounting the slope. They were coming to the east gate of the citadel. I left Odysseus there, staring down at them, his mighty hands curled over the fenestrations of his defensive wall, and went to greet the strangers.

Chapter 6: Wings Over Ithaca

As I was descending the citadel stairs and smiling at the sentries, who were nervous and quick to draw their blades at the slightest sound, a shadow passed over me.

I thought it was a hawk, at first, and didn't look up.

Again it circled, and this time, the shadow hovered over me. I craned my neck and peered into the bright sky above Ithaca, and there I saw a winged man—a glowing form, silver and gold.

It circled twice. It seemed to reach out an arm, to wave. Then it caught an updraft and the spell was broken.

I knew what I'd seen, though: the angel, Altos, on the wind. It was surely him, no demon or misshapen bird. No other white in all of Hell was as brilliant as his robes.

I hurried down into the cool blackness of the palace shadows, blinking until my eyes smarted, trying to adjust them to the dim.

So I stumbled upon Confucius before I saw him.

"Homer," said Confucius. "I was just coming to find you. Hurry. We must leave this place. Inferior men are on the rise here. Heraclitus has come to me with a tale of imminent war, and—"

"I know. Get the Ephesian and meet me at the east gate."

I didn't know why I'd chosen that meeting place, now that the angel was about. Seeing Altos flap his wings above Ithaca was no guarantee of salvation, and Odysseus had said to ask the black creatures coming to the east gate for help. But it was too late to change my mind, unless I wanted to shout: Confucius was already moving away with a speed his bulk belied, into the west wing of the citadel, muttering to himself.

And I had the long and difficult staircase down, yawning before me like a black maw, as treacherous to my eyes as the black shapes from the water whom I hurried to confront.

I have not spoken of the brazen beauties of this shadow citadel. It had silvered columns and walls into whose cypress had been carved all the myths I'd ever told. It had friezes of Odysseus' labors; it had wide benches at the foot of every staircase.

These were made of stone, and on one I sat, to catch my jagged breath, before proceeding through the doors toward the east gate. My head was reeling from my exertions, and from all I heard high on the battlements. I wished I'd never come here. The Devil knew his heinous work, sending me out to find that all I loved was lies.

I felt sorry for myself, and this weakened me, as it always does with men. But then, the heart that kept me moving from gueststead to gueststead in life spoke up, saying that I must find more of my heroes, that

not all would disappoint me as the crafty Odysseus
had. Should I find noble Agamemnon, or Diomedes
of the wise counsel, or even bold Achilles, I would
find the men who matched my vision.

So cheered by the wellspring of hope, I rose up
and headed through the tall doors of the palace, out
into the bright light of the courtyard.

And there before me were the black, misshapen
creatures, slick with salt and wrack. They were taller
than I by a head. They had seaweed dripping from
their arms and single, baleful eyes. Their mouths,
however, were like men's mouths, and from them
came men's words.

The tentacles I'd seen now dangled at their chests,
and they were shrugging off their misshapen humps.
One said to the other, "Oh boy, do you see what I
see?"

And the second replied, in that flip American English I'd learned in New Hell, "One more Old Dead
in a bedspread. So what?"

The first cyclops stepped forward, its hand held
out to me.

I backed up a pace, then another. Then I halted,
for the one who hadn't come forward was removing
his whole hideous face, and a man's face was underneath it.

So I stepped forth and took the hand of the first
beast, while the second became ever more manlike,
stripping off his black skin and stepping out of it a
man.

The one who had his hand out now took off his
face and clear human eyes regarded me. "Homer,
isn't it? Sir, it's a pleasure to meet you."

"*Sir?*" said his companion, as if the first had abased
himself before Zeus. "Who'd you say he is, Welch?"

"Homer is my name," I said, taking the black hand

of the first man, which felt like the underbelly of a shark, clasping it as he clasped mine, fingers around the other's wrist, then releasing it. "Odysseus told me that if I wished to leave Ithaca before the fighting starts, I should ask your aid." I looked into the clear eyes of the first monster, who had only partly become a man by then.

He inclined his head, rubbed his beard-shadowed jaw, and said, "Yeah, I'll try, but I can't speak for the opposition—they have their own timetable. You alone?"

Behind him, his companion was totally a man now, wearing tight leggings and modern weapons on his hip, and cursing softly, his face screwed up, in response to the other's words.

"Not alone, I have a travelling party of two—a sage named Confucius and a troubled philosopher—"

The second changeling came up beside the first, looking me over, saying, "We ain't got time for this, and you know damn well we—"

Without looking away from me, the first man said, "I'll find the time, Nichols. Like I would for you. You get about our business here. I'll catch up."

I wanted to make sure the friendly one won the agrument, so I said, "I have safe-conduct from the Devil himself, to travel wherever I wish in—"

The unfriendly one, who was passing me to enter the citadel, stopped in his tracks and said, "Oh goody. Well, why didn't you say that in the first place?" giving me a scathing look before he trotted up the stairs, discarded humpback in his hands, where retainers of the house waited at a safe distance.

The one left with me was stripping off his skin now. I noticed his webbed feet, dangling from his own discarded hump, and his tentacles. I asked, "Are you from Atlantis?"

He said, "No. We were doing some reconnaissance there for Odysseus, that's all. Where do you want to go, Homer?"

I hadn't thought that through. Anywhere would do now. But I couldn't say that. So I said, "Ilion." It was a reasonable choice, I thought.

The man straightened up, stuck his thumbs through his belt, and stared at his feet. He said, "I really don't want to go back there again," very softly. Then, louder: "That's a tough trip, old man." And suddenly switched to an oddly accented Greek that nonetheless was better to my ears than English. "If you seek a person, not a place, it's better to seek him elsewhere. If you seek Ilion, you'll find yourself amid a war worse than the one you flee here. The choice is yours. You have little time. Decide and I'll come back for you."

And he left me, running to catch up with his companion, flinging his black skin at retainers on his way.

I was still mulling it over when Confucius came huffing down those same stairs, without Heraclitus, looking pained.

"Where is he?" I asked unnecessarily. "That creature you must have passed, the one in New Dead clothes, has agreed to help us escape the brewing carnage. We—"

"—must find Heraclitus," Confucius gasped. "And quickly. He has disappeared."

Even as those last words spilled from Confucius' lips, the shadow of wings blackened the courtyard, and those wings circled over us, growing larger and larger as the angel descended into our midst.

He landed lightly in the courtyard, gusts from his silver wings buffeting us with the sweet smell of Paradise. He smiled at me, as if it were nothing

unusual for an angel to arrive in Ithaca, and bowed
to Confucius. Behind, the palace doors swung shut
as retainers retreated before him.

On the battlements, sentries stared, then sheathed
their arms and returned to their posts as the angel's
countenance shone upon me and Altos said, "So,
how goes the Devil's Temptation of Homer? Have
you traded all you hold dear for dreams of lost Olympus?" The angel's Greek was impeccable.

"I . . . must flee this place," I said. "And you, too,
Just Al—terrible battle is about to descend upon
Ithaca and—"

"And," Confucius interrupted me, "we can't find
Heraclitus anywhere. He drank the Lethe water and
became like a child, you see. He is innocent now,
and he's wandered off, and we must find him before
we lose our ride to safety—before the young fox gets
his tail wet. Can you help us?" Confucius always
came to the point. And yet some unspoken thought
clouded his little eyes, as if it had struck him as he
spoke.

"Do not waste yourselves," said the angel, "searching for Heraclitus. As you say, sage, he is innocent
now. More, he is pure. And the purity he always
sought in children, having become his, changed him
within and without. I chanced upon him high on
yonder wall, and his memories returned with the
sight of me. Those memories mixed with his childlike self, and were transformed. All bitterness left
him, all cynicism disappeared. His wrath followed
after, and when he touched my hand, we both knew
that he was changed. Born anew, bathed of all his
sins, and adjudged fit for manumission." The angel
smiled like salvation. Which, at this moment, he
was—at least to Heraclitus.

"But we haven't said goodbye," I protested.

Confucius was more direct: "How do we know you tell the truth? How do we know we aren't deserting him? Only a Judge can commute the sentences of the damned, and—oh."

Confucius and I looked at one another. Altos had come to carry Heraclitus up to heaven, to Olympus, to Paradise, to higher realms. And we were still in Hell.

But Altos was answering Confucius' question, while my eyes welled with tears of loss for myself, tears of shame that I had not been adjudged fit to join Heraclitus, and tears of joy for the philosopher himself.

"How do you know that I tell you the truth, Confucius? How do you know that you breathe? How do you know that there is a chance of heaven, but for me? How do you know that perseverence furthers? Through trust. Through your own nature. Through the grace of heaven, even here."

Confucius' hands were in his sleeves. His shoulders, strapped with the backpack, slumped. He asked, "Will Heraclitus remember us? Remember all that we shared together?"

"Everything, I promise. He is not half a man now, but whole and pleasing in the sight of God. He called upon supernal aid to save you both—and not himself—from the war brewing here at Ithaca. He is a spirit that my Lord is pleased to welcome."

Confucius said, "A superior man is true to his nature; he is not destroyed by evil, but transmutes it."

"All this being true, why are you still here?" I asked the angel, whose face was showing compassion for us both, two souls before him unready for salvation. I had not truly believed in the Judges. Now I stood before one, and knew I was not ready. I was hurt and angry. I thought of Odysseus on the battlements and suddenly he seemed no pathetic creature, but a wise one.

"I am here," said the angel, "to save whom I can of these foolish souls. As I went into the Dissidents' camp when you two tarried there."

I remembered the time when the angel came upon the Dissidents in New Hell, and guided many, us included, into sheltering tunnels while, above, the Devil smote the place with fire and brimstone.

"I recall that day," I said uneasily. "Two men, New Dead, have promised to help us escape—Welch is one, and he called his companion 'Nichols.'"

This news made the angel's face sorrowful, and he bowed his head. "You know I wish you only success, precious Homer, in writing the true story of Hell and its damned master. But these two men are Satan's trusted servants. Beware them."

"Beware them?" Confucius repeated. "But they're our only hope of escaping the destruction you yourself know is coming. Else why would you be here? Unless, of course, you, angel, intend to spirit us away as you did Heraclitus?"

The angel paused then, his face downcast, and said, "I cannot dispense salvation, only deliver it. It comes from each soul and from on high."

"Why do you tarry with us, then?" I demanded, full of foreboding.

"Only long enough to tell you about Welch and Nichols," said the angel and began to speak thus in his soft and wonderful voice:

"These two men, Welch and Nichols by name, came to Hell as all moderns do—from violence and treachery such as was not known in ancient times. Welch was a creature of expediency, who excused all manner of evils in the service of freedom's high ideals. He was murdered on his doorstep by enemies of his nation, wild America, whose covert actor he was. Here, he serves Authority, as he served it in life, making no differentiation between order from a wellspring of good, and order from a wellspring of evil. He is a creature of infinite duplicity, whose skills make the Devil glad, and of infinite honor, according to his own heart.

"This confusion of man's view of the world and the world itself, Welch shares with Nichols, a soldier of the greatest army man has ever seen. Nichols looked Armegeddon in the eye and then survived it, giving up his life over a woman whom he raped, and giving up salvation thereby.

"Both these men are willfully in Hell, and as irredeemable as their century could make them. They believe in nothing but their prowess; no god do they serve but their own good. This selfishness, which above all brings moderns to Hell, delivered them into the hands of the Devil's favorite Agency of torture. They are among the Devil's Children, and beware the prerogatives that they enjoy.

"Beware most of all the clear-eyed Welch, who knows not right from wrong, but only winning; who understands nothing of the nature of sin, or the joy of being, but only values actions, and the process of becoming. He is a spirit whose shifting shape can never be trusted.

"And his servant, the soldier of aggrandized war, the unrepentant Nichols, gave all for the god called Country, and never learned from any man he slew. They are the essence of Hell, and they are the modern minds of man which have forgotten more than Heraclitus ever could.

"They are here because the sea will boil and the sky will open fire upon the land. They are here, as they were in the Dissident camp, to oversee man's destruction of his brothers in numbers too great for counting. This is the thing about moderns that ancients cannot understand: no life has value but their own; no slaughter is too massive, as long as the end is won; no soul is counted worthy but the souls of allies; all enemies are like ants upon the table. But understand this: if you travel with them, you will see Hell's darkest nature, and why, when there is Paradise, there must be a Hell for such as these."

The angel took his eyes from mine, and I rubbed my arms on which the hair had risen as if a thunderbolt was about to rend the sky.

Thus I saw the one called Nichols, hands on his hips, shaking his head, and Welch coming up behind.

There was no way to know how long they'd been there, but Nichols said, "Boss, I'll blast this chicken-winged featherduster back to Paradise in a New York minute if you'll just give the word," as the one named Welch approached the angel.

"Altos," said Welch in greeting. "Should have known you'd show up here. You have some claim on these two? They're missing a member from their party. I'll leave them with you; it's all the same to me."

And the angel looked upon Welch with a sorrow I could smell as I'd earlier smelled sweetness wafting from his person. "Do as you will here, Child. But do not look for the missing man, for he has won his way to heaven."

"Sure, buddy," said Nichols, who was bearing down on the angel, shouldering Confucius from his path. "And I'm the Good Fairy. Scat! Go on, before we clip those wings of yours."

He reached out to Altos with an unfriendly hand and that hand closed on empty air.

The angel had disappeared in an eyeblink. He simply was not standing there.

A shadow from above crossed my path, as Confucius remarked on Altos' disappearance, and Nichols swore blasphemously and felt the emptiness.

I looked up and I thought I saw Altos, with Heraclitus hugged to him like an old friend. And both were waving farewell as they ascended high into the air.

Welch's words came short and clipped, silencing Nichols and Confucius both: "Let's go, girls. If we don't get down to the beach in time for the rendezvous I called in, we're going to be fried in our socks. Leave the gear, Nichols—these two are all we're taking."

Still I paid no heed. I was watching the dot ascending, the way to heaven, my friend who had found his judge, and the angel from on high.

Then Nichols shook my arm as if I were a child and pushed me rudely toward the east gate, where the unimaginable awaited.

I did not look back, or up, again. I was Homer, the bard. My task was to go abroad in Hell and write what no man had written: the true tale of damnation.

It had been foolish of me to think this would be easy, or that Satan would not try to skew the story in his favor. But I knew then that I would write of Heraclitus, the soul that found his way to heaven, and when I wrote it, I would weep.

Chapter 7: The Heart of the Dragon

On the sweet beach of Ithaca, waiting for I knew not what, the one called Welch asked me, "So, where to, Homer?"

And before I could answer, unfriendly Nichols said, "Look, Welch, I know this means something to you, but the best we can do is drop these guys, like any other hitch-hikers, somewhere on the way. Our mission in Thebes won't wait while you get personal. That's how we got this punishment detail, anyhow, you gettin' person—"

"Okay, Nichols; okay," said the clear-eyed Welch, so tall and straight beside me, watching the sea roll in.

Confucius reached back into his pack even as the querulous Nichols continued, "Okay if you're hearin' me, sir. Okay if Achilles gets to us before the U-boats start shelling this beach." As complaints issued from him, Nichols squatted down and began digging in the sand. "Okay if ol' Altitude's visit doesn't mean more trouble than we're set to handle, out here in the Nether Boonies. . ." Now he ceased digging, having found the six tied-together bottles he'd been seeking, and straightened up, offering one to Welch. "Beer?"

"Yeah. Homer? Confucius? A Knick?" Welch twisted the top off his bottle and offered it to me.

I took it, and drank of the New Dead's weak beer. Confucius, too, took one, and eyed me significantly.

Then I said to Welch, "Thank you. Did your friend mention Achilles—my Achilles?"

"I dunno that he's yours," Nichols said around the mouth of his bottle, his adam's apple bobbing as he drank and spoke at once. "Little red-haired rooster? More guts than brains? Bad temper? Same one you was cryin' over in the Dissidents' camp when we sprung him from the interrogation tent?"

Then I remembered this Nichols clearly. His square jaw and his empty eyes confirmed my recollection of that day when carnage struck the camp. He had begun it, with his modern weapons of slingshot death that roared so loud, and all of Altos' warnings now made more urgent sense.

"This place will go the same way as the Dissident camp in New Hell?" I thought remorsefully of Odysseus on his battlements. What use was courage against the weapons of the Devil, all the New Dead's apocalyptic toys of war that made a man as helpless as a blade of grass before a forest fire?

Welch answered, "Probably. These Old Dead lords have to be dispossessed every now and again, or they forget, down in these Nether Hells, that they're in Hell at all—hunker down in their power structures and get too comfy. A trip through the system, some time in New Hell . . . Odysseus will survive it. He has before." It was kindly spoken, gently said. The one named Welch was full of sorrow.

But Confucius intervened before I could say I understood. "If it is that Achilles you describe, then my friend and I will travel with you until you reach your destination." Implacably, Confucius held out his palm. In it were four fortune cookies.

"That right, Homer?" said Welch wistfully as he took his cookie. "Thebes will suit you? You're more than welcome."

"Achilles will suit me," I replied in the same English. "My quest is for men, not abodes, as you deduced." The pink slip in the heart of my cookie remonstrated me to bring order from confusion. That there was confusion in my heart, I could not deny. I wanted to run back up the beach and warn Odysseus. Even if my companions had permitted it, I was sure it would do no good.

Nichols wordlessly chose a cookie and cracked it between his fingers and read, "If chaos and darkness prevail during creation, one must appoint helpers." Then: "What the Hell does that mean?"

Confucius replied, "Difficulty at the beginning, where we now are—motion in danger's midst brings successes," as if that was what the fortune cookie he was chewing said, although he had not opened it, but popped it whole into his mouth.

Welch smiled wanly, finished his beer, and discarded it. Then he said, "Fine, that's settled. Homer, you and Confucius can ride with us to Thebes— not as guests, but as consultants."

"Consultants?" Nichols said, eyeing his leader askance. "What's this crap?"

"The fortune cookies. Achilles will buy that. Anyway, it's my damned mission."

"Damned, indeed," Confucius remarked, as he stared past me out to sea.

I followed the sage's gaze and there I saw a dragon

rise from the waters. It came out of the waves only part way. Its scales shined in the sunlight. Its head was pointed straight at us. And from it a small boat that had been riding on its back departed, headed right for us, roaring.

This boat had a steersman aboard, and the steersman waved as a voice came from the chest of Nichols, saying, "Yo, Nichols, you'd better swim out to meet us. We haven't got any time to lose."

Nichols reached to his chest and fingered it, as if surprised that another's voice had come from there. And he spoke in his normal voice to that one, saying, "Yeah, Tanya. On our way." Then, raising his head, spoke to us: "You heard her. Come on, Welch, let's move. You, Homer, Confucius—you can swim?"

This, because of the sage's face. I took Confucius by the arm and encouraged him, and down into the surf we waded.

There, however, the sage stopped, uncertain, until Nichols grabbed him by the elbow and said, "Come on, Fatso, strip off the pack and leave it. That's a good ball of lard. Worse comes to worse, you'll float and I'll tow your ass."

Welch had his hand on my arm, also, and the grip was not one of a friend, but of a captor. I kept looking over my shoulder at Ithaca, and my mind's eye covered the citadel in flames and roiling smoke such as the New Dead's weapons can inflict. But there was no arguing with the two men who had come from the sea which once was the Lethe. Their dragon awaited. Their henchwoman came ever closer; the boat roared in my ears.

Swimming was never the best of my skills, and my heart was moored to the beach already behind me, but I swam with the Devil's Children, away from the wrack-strewn shore of Ithaca, until we reached the boat which roared.

Into it Welch ignominiously boosted me, his hands upon my arse, and I lay there, gasping, as Confucius came aboard in a wash of salt.

The boat listed with his bulk, and that of the two New Dead, those moderns about whom Altos had warned me.

But ahead lay Achilles, bold Achilles, and safety from the fires of Hell.

My heart knew all of this, but it lingered on the beach long after, until I thought it would never come and rejoin my body, but perish there on Ithaca with Odysseus in his lonely citadel.

Yet as the boat roared and reared up on her stern, guided by a slight woman with sun-gilt hair, and made for the dragon and deep waters, I heard the awful sound above of chaos approaching.

Once you have heard this sound, like a thousand angry wasps swarming, like the sound of Haphaestus' furnaces—this sound of war on the wing, you do not forget it.

The others, too, looked up. I saw in their faces that they too knew what death rained from a sky that hummed such a song.

Welch looked at a disk on his wrist, and slipped away from us, back to the steerswoman, and kissed her cheek. Nichols watched over us like a hawk over prey. The sound above grew louder.

The dragon before us grew nearer. Spume licked its reared head and its glowing eye. And then a man popped from its mouth and waved us urgently forward.

Around us, the water was uneasy, and I saw other dragons glide below me, and beyond, where lines of froth betrayed their progress. A school of dragons was gathering, and these were dragons of war such as

I had seen when the Lethe gave way to this treacherous sea, over the reefs beyond Atlantis.

The dragons were so huge, so black, so cold and fascinating in their power, that I did not realize how close we were to ours until our boat's prow banged its side.

Nichols was up immediately, and Welch came forward, and we were pushed out onto the dragon's very back as Nichols made the boat fast with ropes that moved of their own will, and the man who had waved from the dragon's head held out his hand to me.

I took the hand of Achilles, of bold Achilles, and let him lead me down into the dragon's maw without a qualm. His red hair was braided; his eyes were shielded, his frame was small and lithe.

But in his company I feared not the gullet of the dragon, wherein were awful smells and humming sounds and spitting sparks and blinking lights. In his company, I made no outcry, no complaint, as we descended the dragon's staircase into its very heart.

Was this Achilles not the bravest of my heroes? Why should I fear if he were with me? Though he wore the black, legged shroud of the New Dead, though he had a strange crown upon his head, he was *my* Achilles, and I was glad to be beside him, even in the heart of a monster.

And there in that heart were couches, resplendent daises and Pythia's scrying bowls turned on their sides. There were the lights of the sky here, too, and a feeling like a temple. And among all of this sat a man made like a god, a boyish man of fine visage and perfect form in miniature, who waved a greeting before he turned back to his meditation before a glowing bowl.

Achilles' first words to me were, "Sit down, old

man; strap in; enjoy the show." He pointed to a high-backed chair all cushioned and inviting.

I took that seat, and soon Confucius was huffing in another chair, beside mine, wet and bedraggled and bewailing his lost backpack. "My ting," said he. "My ting, lost on yonder shore. How will we make tea now, Homer?"

And then the beautiful boy turned slowly toward us, his whole throne turning with him. "Homer?" His voice was flat.

"Homer," I agreed; "and this is Confucius."

"Not now, Alex," snapped the bold Achilles. "Let's get out of this war zone before we start sweating the small stuff."

From behind, a woman's voice said gently, "We've got tea, Confucius, and everything else we need— except time."

And she slid past us, dripping wet so that her clothes were stuck against her skin, and Welch followed, and Nichols too, and seated themselves before the scrying wall.

I call it this because it showed pictures of what could not be seen, as well as what could be seen. It showed the undersea, and it showed the view from above such as only an angel might see firsthand, and it showed the walls of Ithaca much closer than we were to them.

"Okay, you garbage pail, dive," Achilles said to someone, and then my ears felt oppressed, and my stomach began to quiver. From the side, Confucius' hand stole over mine, and squeezed.

His eyes were closed, I saw. I could not close my own. Each windowlike scrying bowl showed a different view of a sight so horrible that only my days in New Hell had prepared me. I saw the fires of Hell come down on Ithaca in silent scouring. I saw the battlements ripped asunder; I saw men and mortar melt. I saw stone come tumbling upon stone. And I saw the great stones that shot up from the water and arced high, to land on the very tower of the citadel where I had left Odysseus.

No, I could not close my eyes; I could not turn away. I watched the eery, silent, unerring flames of fated death come down on Ithaca. I saw giant wasps sting her; I saw the stones from the sea rend her. I saw wave after wave of flame overrun her until the very mount of Neritos lay bare in baleful light.

I heard Nichols say, "Damn, I'm getting an error message I can't track."

And, a moment later, Welch's voice came from his hunched form before me, saying, "Yeah, Tech Support, this is U-boat 666. We've got a tracking error, code T33, TRT, TUN. We're at five hundred fathoms and I don't need this grief."

And a voice unlike any belonging to our party came echoing from everywhere, "That's a new one, Six Six Six. I'll have to get back to you."

"Before lunch," Welch admonished. "We need to know whether we've got a problem or an anomalous message."

"Right; checking; over," said the voice from everywhere.

Welch straightened up in his chair and turned it, as the blond called Alex had, to look at us. "You two all right? Tanya, how about that tea?"

"You make it, Welch, I'm busy," said the woman at her scrying bowl.

The leader of the dragon's party got up, unbinding himself from his throne, and moved past us, squeezing my shoulder as he went.

This was meant to be a comfort, I knew. But not

until the voice from everywhere invaded the silence in the dragon's heart, did I know why.

"U-boat Six Six Six, this is Tech Serv. You want to run that error code by again?"

Achilles talked a gibberish of numbers and letters and strange English words to the ubiquitous voice, and it finally replied, "I don't know—you satisfied? Haven't a clue. You try something, it doesn't work, you'll know it's a real screw-up. Otherwise, we can't troubleshoot it—at least, not until something actually goes wrong."

"Not until," said Nichols in his unfriendliest voice. "Not until we're dead in the water at the bottom of this damned mud puddle, you mean? Not until we're drowned? Not until I come back to New Hell the hard way and feed you your diagnostics manual?"

"Whatever, sailor. No can do now, that's for sure." And the everywhere-voice went away with a crackle like the laughter of a sybil.

Welch reached over Confucius' shoulder with a mug of tea, and handed another to me. "Well, what did you think of the battle?"

It had to be said. "Dishonorable," I replied.

And the boyish one looked at me again.

Confucius sipped his tea and pronounced it good. "My friend Homer had ancestors on Ithaca," he explained as if my words had been insulting. "You must excuse him in his grief."

"I suppose," said Welch, "better introductions are in order. Achilles, Alexander, Tanya—this is Confucius, a Chinese sage of unparalleled wisdom."

"But not smart enough to keep his ass out of Hell?" said my hero.

"Nobody is," Welch reprimanded Achilles. "And this is Homer, the bard, the author of the Iliad and the Odyssey, who's anxious to get to know you, Achilles, on the trip to Thebes."

"If we make it," said the small red-haired hero sullenly, as if it mattered not at all to him who I was, or what I'd done in his behalf. Nichols muttered something to him and the small man slipped his crown off his head and ears and said, "Glad to meetcha, Homer," still using English.

I responded in our native tongue, sure that it was the English between us, nothing else, that made the meeting seem less significant than it should have been:

"And I you, brilliant Achilles, son of Peleus and Thetis, leader of the Myrmidons. What curse or trial brings you here, into the heart of the dragon?"

"Curse or trial, indeed, singer," he replied in Greek. "The evil counsel of our leader, the foolish and over-principled Welch, has brought down upon us all the wrath of Poseidon, and that of the Evil Lord as well."

Into this moment, for which I had so long waited, the handsome boy intruded, saying in an odd accent, "You *are* that Homer—my inspiration, my guide in life. It was you, beloved Homer, who made of me a king who conquered all the world. I carried your unparalleled works with me to the ends of civilization. I'm honored beyond Hell's ability to despoil—"

"English, everybody," Welch said sharply. "For the benefit of Nichols and Tanya."

Confucius, who had followed every word, tapped his mug against mine, saying, "Look, tea leaves. Perhaps the loss of the fortune cookies is not disastrous."

But it was not to read my fortune that Confucius intervened then. It was to give me space in which to compose myself, to catch my breath, and to think of a proper answer for Achilles, who seemed not to care one whit about me, and for someone named Alexander, who cared too much.

"You got a fortune there, Confucius?" Nichols wanted to know. "Anything that can help us figure out why we keep getting malfunction codes out of this pisspoor excuse for a submarine'll help. One thing I don't need is a watery grave."

"Hush, Nichols," Welch whispered, "don't scare them."

But I was not afraid, and neither was Confucius. If the dragon foundered on the bottom, all we had to do, I thought, was open up her belly and float to the surface.

It was not until Achilles explained to me that we were "too deep, old fool," that I began to sweat and help Confucius search the tea for an answer no disembodied voice or scrying bowl could give.

Chapter 8: My Admirer

I missed Heraclitus. My muse kept wondering what it was like where he had gone, beyond Hell's blood-stained clouds. I missed not only the wise counsel of the man, but the unwearied joy of the boy who had traveled with us. And I wondered what those reborn eyes would have made of the dragon carrying us to Thebes.

And of those who traveled with us. Confucius, more than myself, had studied the ways of the New Dead. Hell is as varied as man himself, and if a man wants no truck with some era's spawn, it is easy to avoid them. For a while.

As the clear-eyed Welch had said, if one does that, one can believe one is at home. Not since my time in New Hell among the rebels had I been so close to the machines of war.

I had never thought to ride inside one. Confucius learned to make tea the New Dead way, to use the instant ting belonging to the gilt-haired woman, Tanya, during that time we rode beneath the sea.

Achilles called it the Sea of Sighs, and he might have been right, though no map I've ever seen has shown the Lethe giving into that broad ocean. There were sighs aplenty within the wounded dragon in those days. Sighs from Achilles, and outbursts of frustration that silenced everyone on board. Sighs from the unfriendly Nichols, who felt the need to keep Achilles in his place.

If Nichols had known his Iliad, he would have realized there was no keeping Achilles from his ungovernable anger.

Thus I said to Confucius, and Confucius said to Welch, and Welch just raised his empty hands and told us that Achilles was worried for our safety, in the wounded dragon's heart.

Welch, too, was worried. His brow was furrowed; he sat long with the woman and they consoled one another.

This, of course, made Achilles all the louder, all the angrier. A woman for an audience, a woman in contention, and Achilles brayed like a randy stallion. With this woman there, I knew, things were not likely to stay quiet long.

After we had slept, Achilles came to Welch and proposed they dice for the favors of this woman, Tanya.

Welch's eyes were far from clear, then. He asked Achilles, "Where the hell do you think you are, buddy? *Who* do you think you are?"

With those words, faithful Nichols left his seat beside the boy named Alex and came to full attention and positioned himself between his leader and Achilles, watchful as a guard dog.

"Who I am's the only guy with any fuckin' chance at all of getting us out of this mess," boasted Achilles. "You think *you* can navigate this blind scow through this rift? You think you've got a snowball's chance of seein' the surface without me? Ever?"

Welch was about to answer, his face draining white as the angel's robes, when the woman herself spoke up. Her tones were soft and measured, her body sure as she slipped in front of Nichols and faced all three in turn. "I won't have this," she said. "You're all treating me as if I were a chattle. From Achilles, perhaps, I can excuse it—old habits never die in Hell, they say, just make life tougher. But from you, Welch . . . consider this," she paused for emphasis, "an operational necessity and *back the hell out of my personal business.*"

Welch put up a hand as if to fend her off. "Easy, Tanya. Everybody's jumpy. Let's all not do or say anything we'll regret."

For an answer, the woman turned on Achilles, stared him up and down, and put her hands upon her flaring hips. "And you, friend, let's see you do your stuff. Bring us through this crisis, back to the surface, out of this accursed submarine, so we can sleep on solid ground, and then come talk to me about sleeping arrangements. Until then, as far as I'm concerned, you're *all* talk." And Tanya brushed clumsily by me and Confucius, disappearing down a corridor that led to the dragon's hearth, whence we soon heard the whistling of the instant ting and the sounds of dinner being made.

No man spoke then; everyone was silent. Backs were bristled and spines stiff.

It took too long for Achilles to relax, to curse "the lot of you," and go back to his work. It took even longer for Nichols to unbend enough to begin poring over his living map, in its scrying bowl where it dwelled, of the submerged world around us.

It took longest of all for Welch to make his way

back to Tanya at her hearth, taking Confucius with him in search of tea, leaving the boy named Alex and me face to face.

"Don't mind Achilles, revered Homer," said Alex to me in an intimate voice as he came to take Confucius' seat. "He can't hear us with those muffs on his ears. And he's just as you delineated him, which must make you proud—so much that man, that not even eons in Hell could change him."

"The man I wrote about knew nothing of dragon's hearts, or jeweled scrying bowls, or New Dead machines."

"But he knew war, and to know war in hell, one must know its weapons. He's as good with modern weapons as any man born to it. He's as good with a submarine as with a long ship, with a helicopter as with an offering to Hera. And he's come a long way, for a village chieftain who died before he was twenty-five."

"Who are you?" I asked.

He flushed, his fine skin heating before my gaze. "I told you, I am Alexander—Alexander of Macedon. Alexander, you might recall, who was for a brief time the leader of the Dissidents' rabble army. Or was that for too brief a time for you to notice?"

There was something almost bashful in him; an unaccustomed emotion, I sensed, to a mind such as his, a mind sure of its primacy, a man sure of his greatness. "Macedon?" I asked, to avoid answering whether or not I'd noticed him among the Dissidents when I was there.

He snuffled softly, chuckling like a stallion about to paw the ground, waiting for his race to begin. "You wouldn't know even my nation's name, unless you studied what came after you. But you—I know everything said of you; everything said about your

works, man's finest, and even conjectured. I fought
with your man, Diomedes, here in Hell, and stood
upon hellspawned Ilion with Agamemnon's—"

"Diomedes? Agamemnon?" I could barely contain
my excitement.

"We left both behind in Ilion. Diomedes, I have
heard, set out for Argos, seeking home—he ever was
a wanderer. As for the rest—the Atreides, the fortress, the twists and curses of capricious fate that
wobbled there when I walked that beach . . . you
don't want to know. Your way was better. Your tale
told it all. What Hell does to men, all men see in
others, but no man sees in himself. Stay away from
Ilion, beloved Homer." Alex's eyes glittered with
tears unshed. He leaned forward and took my hands
in his and kissed them, then let them go.

I looked quickly over my shoulder to see if Nichols
had noticed this remarkable gesture of love from a
boy who claimed to have conquered the world.

Nichols hadn't; or if he had, he made no sign.
Achilles had one hand against the earflaps of his
crown and was talking into the diadem that curled
around his mouth from its apex.

And the one named Alexander still stared at me
with glowing eyes, with fellowship and eagerness
and—dare I say it?—yes, then . . . with love in
every fiber of his person.

"I cannot stay my wanderings from Diomedes of
the wise counsel, or from Agamemnon, foremost
among Atreides, young king: it is this task the Devil
has set me, to tell a tale of Hell in all its profundity.
And this tale I am basing on souls: the souls of my
heroes, and souls whom I will meet along the way."

"Souls you will meet?" There was something akin
to awe, and eagerness, in Alex's voice. "Might I be
one such soul?"

"Perhaps," I said, uncomfortable with the nakedness of his entreaty.

"You may call me simply Alexander; no titles need come between us two," he offered. "I will accompany you everywhere and anywhere, even to dread and maddened Ilion, if necessary. But I know I can help you find Diomedes, if you will but accompany us to Thebes . . . I have power there, and friends among the mages and the sages of mighty Egypt. There is more than one way to skin a cat."

"A cat?" I looked around me. Seeing no cat, I looked back at the youth who so loved my work that he mistook me for it. "We need no cats, or magic. If you would be part of my new books, the *Little Helliad*, then merely adventure with me, as you say. And tell me any tale you know of the Devil, or of what you have learned and lost in Hell."

"Tell *you* a tale?" The young king blushed further. "O inspired Homer, I couldn't . . ."

Meanwhile, he was batting his eyelashes, so that I knew he could tell a tale, but only awaited a second invitation.

This I made, and he sobered.

He sat up. His face grew pale and somber. The smile drained from his lips and his whole body stiffened. "What I have lost in Hell, dear Homer, is only everything. I lost the world, you know. I lost Hephaestion—my Patroklos. I came to Hell and found an Egyptian and a Roman who thought me unwhole, mere parts of their souls. And I lost Bucephalus, the saddest loss of all." His eyes were brimming tears now; his voice was trembling.

"Bucephalus?" I asked. "Who is Bucephalus?"

"Bucephalus," said the quivering voice of Alexander, "was my mighty warhorse in life, my closest companion. In death, he was my Judge. You know the Judges?"

It was my turn to fight back tears. I knew the Judges; I had seen Heraclitus raised to heaven by one. "Tell me of Bucephalus," I said.

And Alexander's muse began to speak, but in a choked voice I knew could not hold forth for long:

BUCEPHALUS

Bucephalus was my war horse; black and mighty was he. I tamed him when none could stroke his velvet muzzle. He carried me into countless battles, helped me form the Companion cavalry that made my army great. Together we remade the very art of war. Together we were invincible. Such love had we for one another as man and beast have never known, before or since. But a horse's span is not like a man's, and Bucephalus grew old.

I spared him, as best I could, once his knees began to swell and his back to sway. All the while, more and more of the world fell under the hooves of my army, and we went farther and farther from the green pastures of our home. One day, on campaign, after many mountains had been climbed and many battles won, he died among the horses of the army. Such a funeral I made for him as no horse has ever seen. As a god I buried him; and my heart went with him then and there, though I did not admit it. Once he went to heaven, the omens all went bad. And though I have never said it to another man, he spoke to me in dreams. He would arch his neck and launch himself at foes; he would nuzzle friends; he would come into my tent and paw the ground, anxious to carry me away from my enemies, back to Macedon.

And I should have heeded him, but I did not. There was ever more world to conquer, and my army to keep in line. If any man had shown me the faith that Bucephalus had, the unstinting love, and that wisdom, my life would have ended differently. As it was, Hephaestion died on me as well, and my heart was no longer tethered to the green earth. I took a wife who was a witch; I denied the omens; I buried Hephaestion with as much glory as a man could muster, but once I had buried Bucephalus, I had buried my luck.

When I came to Hell, I was more lonely than any man has ever been. I wandered amid the wild tribes. I made raiding parties with painted men and chalked men; I stayed away from citadels and men of bronze, to save my heart the pain. And all this time I was grateful to the gods, because Bucephalus had not come to Hell.

Then I went journeying with Diomedes, who found me one day and promised to take me to Achilles. And I was seduced by thoughts of the mighty heroes of the Iliad, so I went with him to Hell's Ilion, and there we fought a battle ten times worse than ten years on the beach. And Diomedes, perhaps the best of the Achaeans, was the finest friend I had there, until such time as the war was over.

Yet even he could not understand what it meant when Bucephalus appeared to us, a living omen on the beach. We chased him and at last I met up with him again. His muzzle was free from gray whiskers; his strength was in his fetlocks; his mane flagged out behind him as if he were a colt again.

And I wept with joy, to have him under me. I fought through to the end there at Ilion, because of Bucephalus, and when the war ended, he came to get me. We rode together on the beach and we were in our own world, and I was full of joy.

I did not know him as my Judge; I did not pity him for being in Hell, for we were reunited. I was so selfish to be glad, and though he bore me to the very halls of Theseus' palace and set me on the pinnacles of power, I never thought to wish that he were elsewhere.

I gloried in his strength; I never asked why he'd given up the neverending pastures of Olympus to be with me. That steed who could have munched godly clover and mounted the mares of Tros, I kept with me. And I did no good among the suffering damned I saw, but merely rode about, exultant.

And one day, Bucephalus' great hooves trod upon clouds, while we were riding up a mountainpeak, and the gods came to take him. They shook me from his back like a fly, because I was unworthy. They would not let me go with him.

Bucephalus was my Judge, come to bear me out of Hell, but I failed him, and the gods took him from me. They called him back to heaven and let me tumble through eternity to land in a deeper hell alone.

But I know that, somewhere, he is waiting until my soul has paid its tithe. That my Judge loves me more than love itself I have no doubt. No steed has the failings of men, and now I must only teach myself to love as unselfishly as he.

Every time Paradise sets, I look to the mountain tops, where one day I will see him again, neighing at the sky. And next time, I will not waste the chance. I will be worthy of Bucephalus, and he will carry me to Paradise on his back as broad as Heaven. I know it because Bucephalus has taught me that, to be worthy of salvation, a man must save himself with love purer than any I have yet felt.

When I can see that wedge-shaped head and cry for his travail, not my loss; when I can stroke that velvet muzzle without desiring anything more from him; when I can look into those liquid eyes no blandishment can turn, and not turn away myself, then Bucephalus will judge me ready, and bend his foreleg for me to mount, and the clouds will be our rolling fields. Forever."

Defiant, Alexander looked up at me. Tears rolled freely down his cheeks. "So you see, Homer, what the Devil stole from me: my chance of Olympus; the feel of Bucephalus between my knees. Thus I seek purification in Thebes. And I will have it. I wage war against the Devil. And that war, in time, I'll win. I am Alexander the Great, who conquered the world. Can Hell be any harder to subdue, even if its boundaries are those that lie in my own heart?"

I hadn't expected such wisdom from a boy. Or such passion. Or such pride. I did not say that, Judge or no, his very passion was suited for Hell alone, and never the Elysian fields. For this man had all in him that was noble in our race. For all his faults, he had won me to his cause upon the spot.

So I said, instead, "Alexander, for that is what you have graciously said I should call you, I will gladly go into Thebes as your guest, your bard, your friend, if Confucius is welcome also. Only say that you will help me in my search for Diomedes, and my eyes, my lips, my tongue and the muse in my heart—all are yours."

"Done," said Alexander, and held out a hand to clasp my forearm.

"Done," I agreed, and squeezed back hard.

"What's done?" said Welch, just coming up behind us with Confucius and a pot of tea. The woman, Tanya, was nowhere in sight.

"Surfacing's done, that's what," said Nichols in a triumphant voice, pushing his crown down around his neck and leaning back in his throne. Putting his booted feet up on the scrying wall's ledge, he added, 'Twenty minutes to zero fathoms; an hour or so to landfall."

"Great," said Welch. "Good work."

And Achilles, who was now among us, his crown also down around his neck so that his ears could hear, said in a surly tone, "Yeah, well, ask him where we're landing before you break out the Old Number Seven, Welch."

Welch did not, but said, "Anything's better than another night in this sardine can." He and Nichols exchanged pregnant glances.

"Well, Nichols don't know where in Hell we are, and you can't know for sure it's an improvement." Short Achilles got up, rubbed his hands, and added, "But I'm off to tell the lady we've met her conditions." And he grinned a feral grin before he left us, headed for the hearth with hips aswing.

"That bastard—" Nichols sucked his teeth.

"Did he help with the navigation problem?" Welch asked Nichols.

"If he didn't cause it in the first place, I guess you could say that," said Nichols, taking the tea Confucius was doling out.

"Homer," said Confucius, "come with me and sit. We must read the leaves for this new place. See what kind of men are there and how to proceed."

I sat with him, and we read the leaves, and they were noncommittal. Which was just as well. I wasn't sure I wanted to know what the fates had in store for us when we went ashore, wherever that shore happened to be.

I remembered Achilles' legend too well, and how he'd behaved over another woman, to look forward to an interim port, now that Thebes was on my itinerary.

Confucius, having read the leaves, said only, "Perseverance furthers," which, from him, was not the most cheery of omens for our landfall.

Chapter 9: Arabian Knight

As rosy-fingered Paradise climbed the vault of Hell, our dragon floated to the surface of the Sea of Sighs and lay there.

We climbed into her tethered boat and it began to roar, speeding to an unknown landfall. Twice Achilles looked behind him, where the dragon lay at anchor, and worried that we should have left one of our party with her. But no one stayed behind and the dragon languished on its chain, its hatches locked against the day.

Ahead lay a city, whitewashed and low against the dunes. Above it lay a smoky pall no morning wind could stir.

Nichols sniffed the breeze as we pulled the rubber boat ashore and said, "Diesel. Trains, by the sound of it."

And the sound he meant was deafening, whistling in my ears. I looked around for its source, and saw only the others of our party: Confucius, Achilles and beautiful Alexander; Welch, Nichols and the woman,

Tanya, who was dressed as were the New Dead men, in splotched shrouds and trousers, with weapons slung at breast and hip.

Beyond them stretched the beach, its rocks and grasses, wrack and jetty, where single-sailed boats were tied. These square-sailed boats were crude and had swathed men at their helms and tillers.

Welch scratched his head and said, "Arabs. I didn't think there was a seaboard settlement between here and Thebes."

"Between *where* and Thebes?" Nichols asked the unanswerable question. "Thanks to that hot-dog," he jutted his chin at Achilles, "we don't know where we are."

The reminder was not necessary; everyone among us knew we were lost, on foreign soil.

Achilles said, stepping close to Nichols, his little body straining to be tall as he bore down on the larger man, "You know damn well it's not as bad as that. Of course there's Arab settlements here—Thebes is crawling with Egyptians, ain't it. These're your basic Libyans, or Persians, or—"

"Persians?" young Alexander echoed, bending down to take a palmful of sand and let it run through his fingers. "My Persians? There's no place like this in Persia."

"You mean there wasn't, in your day," said Tanya softly. "But you're right, Great King—this is nothing like the East. What do you think, Welch? Take a guess; nobody'll hold you to it."

Welch mimicked Alexander, bending down to feel the sand. Then he stood and stared inland. "Gulf States, somewhere. Early Modern, from the look of it."

"What are you trying to determine?" Confucius asked. "The past is not real; only the future exists.

This place, whatever it is, is not some slice of antiquity, but a living home that men have made."

"Omanis, you think?" Nichols prompted Welch, ignoring Confucius. "Could be Aden . . . Afreet bin Aden—that's a town I've heard was down here, somewhere."

"Only way to find out is to go and ask," Welch said to him. Then he turned to Confucius. "You're right, sage—only the future exists. Whatever this place is, I want you—and everyone—to keep in mind that it's just a pit stop. Don't get involved. Maybe Nichols can get some 6066 chips for the boat, maybe not. We can reprovision, see if we're on course for Thebes. Maps are what we want. We need to know where the Nile starts."

"What if it doesn't?" This, from Achilles.

"Say again?" said Nichols; the two were still eye to eye.

"What if this isn't your Aden, but the equivalent of Alexandria?" said bold Achilles.

"That cannot be," Alexander said with certainty. "Alexandria—any of my Alexandrias—would be greater than this, by now."

"Alexandria!" I myself exclaimed. "Where the library is? Intact?"

"No," Welch quashed all hope with a single certain word. "I've been there recently, and it's nothing like this. You've got to remember, Alex, Homer, that large populations tend to set up settlements where they can maintain their way of life—*when, and only when*, enough of them died together, or with ideological ties strong enough, to found one. Otherwise, the groups are diluted by the system, the cultures spread. So whatever town this is, lots of one kind of Arab died around the same time, or for similar reasons, or lots died for those reasons year after year—

like the wars that created the Persian West—to found it. Whatever the group, whatever the reason, whatever they're into here, we don't mix in. We get what we need and get out."

Tanya wondered if there would be technology of the sort Nichols wanted for the failing dragon, and no one answered but Achilles, who leered at her and said, "That's not what I came ashore for."

Alexander kept himself between the woman and Achilles all the way up the beach, across the jetty, and into the bazaar that faced the sea.

There we saw ox-carts and ass-carts and stinking horseless carts and magnificent steeds that made Alexander catch his breath; steeds with tassled martingales and dished noses, whose riders were resplendent in voluminous robes.

And we saw other steeds, with nearly mule-long ears and narrow faces, ridden by pale men with shiny boots and flaring pantaloons who wore visored caps upon their heads and were protecting a chimera that Nichols called, "a train, a goddamned steam engine," that howled like a banshee and made the horses rear.

And I, with Confucius by my side, was astounded at the abundance of men and machines, at the racket and the smells and the veiled women and beggars by the score.

Our party separated, Achilles and Alexander flanking Tanya; Welch and Nichols going toward the chimera blowing steam and letting men out of its belly.

Confucius and I stayed where we were, asking passersby where maps could be bought, or merely viewed. The sage had his hands in his sleeves again, and his sleeves resting upon his belly. His little eyes darted everywhere, keen and all-seeing, but even he could not find a soul in that crowd who spoke either English or Greek, or understood the sign for "map."

So busy were we among the orange vendors, who understood coin and gave us change, and the date vendors and the veiled women, we did not notice when Alexander, Tanya and Achilles wandered out of sight.

But we noticed what sort of coins we received in trade for ours, along with the fruit we'd bought. These coins had English on one side and Arabic on the other; a queen's portrait in the silver made Confucius sure we were in a "protectorate of Victoria's—in Aden, wherever that may be."

This was of no import to me. I had looked up from my fruit in time to see a man come out of the chimera, and Welch and Nichols step into his path, between him and a group of dark men on swift-footed horses.

This man was an oddity, even here. He was pale, unlike those awaiting him, and tall like Welch and Nichols. Yet he was swathed in the white robes of the darker race, down to his feet, on which were shiny boots.

"Confucius, let us join them." I tugged on the sage's sleeve and nearly dragged him from the food stalls; he was loathe to leave before he'd bought all the provender he could carry, and another backpack. So I left him there, asking every vendor for fortune cookies.

When I reached Welch and Nichols and the stranger, Welch had a wallet in his hand and was holding it before the stranger's eyes, saying, "—Agency talks, Lawrence, you listen. Is that clear? I want some answers, and I want'em now."

The man in the hood had a sharp nose, a sensitive mouth, and Aegean eyes full of guile. He said, "Agent Welch, I am at your service, whatever that may be, my good man. Now if we can just step away from these others—" He turned his head and a torrent of strange words issued from him. The dark men on the horses bowed in their saddles, and responded, calling him "Aurens."

Beyond them, on the bigger, mule-like steeds, pale men in shiny boots fingered curved swords and rifles such as the Dissidents used.

There was enmity between these groups. It occurred to me, I know not why, that what held tempers in check here was this man who came along with Welch, away from the sighing chimera to a quieter corner of the bazaar.

"Okay, Lawrence, what are you doing here?" Welch demanded.

"—haven't the foggiest, old man," said the stranger, tossing his head so that his hood fell back and blond hair glistened. "I was minding my own business—" white teeth gleamed "—in New Hell, engaged in a little sortie on Julius Caesar's business, don't you know, when the hand of Providence swept me up and deposited me . . ." He turned and eyed the chimera. ". . . there. On the train, which of course was prey to what we English call 'banditti.'" Again, the smile. "Inshallah, don't you know. I'm rather pleased to be here. I dare say that wasn't what the Devil intended, but it's the truth. As long as you aren't about to tell me I must fight against the desert tribes, I'll gladly take your orders. There's no desk in those orders, is there, Agent Welch?"

Welch said, "You know where you are, don't you?"

"Certainly I know where I am. Is this a test of some kind?"

"We need a map," Nichols shouldered close to the man called Lawrence. "We've got a sub offshore. We're on our way to Thebes, chasing an apeman called Enkidu who's supposed to be headed there.

We've got technical problems. We need Six Oh Six Six chips, and someone who speaks the language. You're him."

"A guide, is it?" Lawrence said, and his gaze went to me for the first time. "I rather thought this venerable gentleman here was your . . ."

"Homer," Welch interjected. "This is T. E. Lawrence, an Arabist—a New Dead Brit in love with primitives and antiquity . . ."

As I began the English formula of introduction, the newcomer marched straight up to me, muttering, "My stars. I never thought that Hell would give me such a pleasure. Your Iliad, you know . . . I retranslated it, honorable sir, in what I hope was a style more true to your intent, to the valor of your heroes, to your genius." He held out a hand that quivered. His large eyes sparkled.

I took the hand and said, "Well met, Lawrence. I wish I knew as much of you as you of me," while behind him, Nichols muttered to Welch about "a goddamned celebrity, knobby knees and all."

Welch said, "Later, you two. Right now, Lawrence, let's get to finding maps and chips. This place looks like a tinderbox to me."

"Oh, quite right, Agent Welch. Quite right. Shall we gather your people and depart? I can commandeer horses for us in—"

"No horses," Nichols said, his warning clear. "We're not staying. We've got to find our—Confucius, come here."

Lawrence repeated the sage's name in childlike glee as the fat man waddled toward us, weighed down with provisions.

When Confucius reached us, while Lawrence sang his praises and pumped his hand, Nichols was trying to find out where the others had gone.

Confucius said, "Alexander, Tanya, and Achilles? I haven't seen them since Homer and I found the orange vendor . . ."

This news evoked quick action from the moderns. Horses were commandeered after all and we went galloping through the streets on small, beautiful steeds while, behind us, the pale men on big horses trailed in our wake, truculent and suspicious, but holding back.

"Separate," Welch called out at an intersection. "Nichols, go back toward the beach; take Confucius. I'll find the maps and see about the chips, and meet you there. Lawrence, tell your Brits to go with Nichols."

I hadn't realized that the pale men in shiny-visored caps belonged to this Lawrence, until he gave a signal, and they followed Nichols and Confucius around a corner and were gone.

Welch, Lawrence, and I went the other way, and soon were in the middle of dark riders who greeted Lawrence with bright smiles and made Welch uneasy.

And Welch, who sat a horse no better than I, who obviously was from a noble class more used to driving a chariot than riding astride, forced his wild-eyed beast next to mine and said, "Homer, Lawrence has a soft spot for you, but he's treacherous whenever he's among his Arabs. Goes native at the drop of a hat. So I'll need you to keep him in line."

I looked ahead; Lawrence was perfectly in line, the middle rider of three abreast down this white-washed street. It was Welch who had broken forma-tion, forcing one of the two dark men whose horses flanked mine to drop back.

I was about to ask Welch what he meant when our raiding party—for that was what it felt like, and might as well have been from the way pedestrians fled before us—turned a corner and a large building loomed ahead, with columns and arches studding its facade.

Lawrence and his dark men rode right up its broad staircase, and our horses followed, no matter what we did. At its head, with hooves ringing on marble and under the guns of the shiny-visored men that Welch called Brits, he dismounted and handed his reins to one of the dark men.

Then Lawrence swaggered up to us, his robes billowing in a sea-breeze from the harbor which this building overlooked, and put his hand on the bridle of Welch's horse. "Dismount, gentlemen. If there's a map or chip in town that you can use, it's in here."

Down we slid from those swift-footed horses, and the dark men beside us grabbed up their bridle reins.

Into the shadowy building we followed the robed man named Lawrence, listening to his bootheels crack upon the stone. Past a khaki-clad guard at a desk we went with a wave and a recitation of our names. Down corridors lined with stacks of books that reached up into the eaves of the building we continued, until Welch whispered, "It *is* Alexandria, then?"

"Tsk tsk, m'lord, no," said Lawrence. "It's just the library, that's all. And the provincial government offices, of course. The Devil's stashed this place out here where you'd least expect to find it—if you were looking, which of course, you're not. Every treasure of the Ancient Near East, an Assyriologist's dream, an Arabist's paradise . . . in the middle of a coastal village where everyone who died in the wars I fought has come to rue his days."

This, without slowing his pace. "I was riding a desk in the real Alexandria too long not to know it if I'd seen it. But you can get to the Nile from here, without a map, as your batman said you wanted, just by—"

Welch lunged forward, grabbed Lawrence by the shoulder, and spun him around. "How, man? Don't mess with me, you boy-loving faggot, or I'll . . ."

Lawrence's eyes were shadowed, but the hurt of this insult shook his whole frame.

Welch took a deep breath, bowed his head, and said, "I'm sorry. I've got a lot on my mind, and lots at stake here."

"So do we all, Agent Welch," said the blond man; "so do we all."

"If there's a way to the Nile from here, that's all I need."

"What of the maps?" I reminded him gently. "And the 'chips' which seemed so necessary before, to heal the dragon? What of Achilles and Tanya and—"

"The dragon?" Lawrence echoed. "Achilles? Surely not that Achilles?"

"The dragon," Welch answered. "The sub. The sub's got navigation problems, which aren't so great if we can head her up the Nile where there're landmarks. The maps and chips, you know about. As for Achilles—why not that Achilles? If Homer doesn't mind him, why should you?"

"Mind?" said Lawrence, while he pulled a volume from a stack and opened it. "My dear man, I don't mind. I'm intrigued. Here's your map." He handed the book to Welch and fixed me with his piercing gaze. "What do you think, Homer, of the soul whose earthly life you mythologized?"

I was taken aback. I struggled for words. "I have not yet sat with bold Achilles and heard from his lips an illuminating tale. This I will do on the journey."

And that journey was facilitated by Lawrence of the strange and wild eyes, who had showed Welch the book of maps.

When Welch had pored long over the map, he looked up at Lawrence, who was staring at me the way Alexander had stared at the proud-crested Arab horses, and the modern said, "I don't get it. The Nile's right here?"

"Only if you go out the back door of the library, which is *the* library—the one that was once in Alexandria, but in Hell is here, on Oman's coast. Down this corridor, turn to your left, your left again, and you're bloody well there. Out the back steps and down them, and you're overlooking the ancient harbor that this place once faced—Alexandria, the delta . . . the Nile itself."

"How am I going to get the sub in there?"

"You can't; you jolly well can't," said Lawrence with a sly smile that drew in his cheeks. "The Devil, or some gentlemen like yourself from Agency, decided in their, or his, infernal wisdom, that nothing like your sub can violate the antiquity of Egypt, or of darkest Africa, for that matter, unless I miss my guess. The railroad doesn't go anywhere near the river, not upstream; all is as it was, one may venture to say, in ancient times."

"That can't be," Welch said.

"I bow to your wisdom, Agent Welch, but I have told you what I know. Now, the chips you need, we should find upstairs in the Records section, if you don't mind stealing a circuit board." There was a wickedness in this man, a prankster, a dark soul that Achilles would have understood.

Up we stole, into chambers full of scrying bowls such as had been in the dragon's heart, and the two men gutted these with practiced hands after Welch showed his wallet and cleared the room.

Lawrence was as pleased as a boy with a new bow at these machinations, and Welch was taut at his tasks. "They're going to find out," Welch said, "that I have no jurisdiction here, not officially, and they'll be back. Damned mad, too."

"Her Majesty runs a tight ship, so to speak," Lawrence agreed solemnly, and from his robes pulled additional robes, which he called djellabas, entreating us to put them on and hurry, for he would sneak us out to safety.

When we did as he bid, Lawrence led us through labyrinthine halls and down a staircase and then another, and finally out onto a patio overlooking a harbor we had not seen from the dragon's back.

"The real Alexandria," said Lawrence with a sweeping bow, "or at least what Hell has made of it."

Here were more single-sailed vessels, crude and with hulls of baled reeds, and larger vessels that Welch called triremes, and a bustle etched clearly for about a mile and then shrouded in mist coming up from the water.

"Shit," said Welch. "I've got to get the others."

"The others?" said Lawrence as if this was a very foolish thing to ask. "Alexandria, my dear man, comes and goes. So does the Nile, I'm afraid. So do I, as you well know. You'd best hurry and collect them. I'll wait here. For all I know, none of this will be real when you return, and I might be back in New Hell, slaving away at thankless tasks." He held out a pale hand, first to Welch and then to me: "Noble Homer, it is a joy beyond Hell's ability to countermand, that I have met you." And, quick as a striking asp, he stepped forward, grabbed me, and kissed me wetly on both cheeks.

I staggered back when he released me, and felt Welch's steadying, cautionary hand upon my back. "Let's go find our traveling companions. If you can, Lawrence, stay here till we get back."

The robed Englishman was already turning toward the harbor, his feet on the path hewn from the living slope.

It took us too long to find Achilles and the rest. In the streets there was fighting between the pale men with the shiny boots and the dark men with the single-foot horses, as well as with other dark men in helmets whom we hadn't seen before. There was fighting all around the chimera, which wailed as if it could rend the sky.

In the confusion, we darted from street to street, dodging violence. My hands were clapped to my ears because there were so many reports from the sling-shotting rifles, sounds that made the horses scream.

Paradise was losing her fight with the clouds of Hellish darkness. Purple shadows lengthened, eating up the whitewashed streets, before we found the beach again. And there we found them, faced off over the woman who was kneeling in the sand—all but Confucius and Alexander.

Achilles had his hand in Tanya's hair and his weapon trained on Nichols. Nichols stood spread-legged in the sand, a rifle at his hip trained on the hero. In the waters beyond them, the dragon—if it was still there—was obscured by the darkness falling. Great mountains of clouds, like hills aflame, had lowered with the evening and the waters were all reflections, one with the sky.

Welch touched me and I halted. He got out his own weapon; a fearsome bang came from it, and the combatants looked up. "Cut the crap," Welch called. "We're leaving. Now."

"Fine with me," came Nichols' growl. "Alexander and Confucius have gone out to the sub. They took the Zodiac. You want I should get them, you keep this fool from jumping Tanya while I'm gone."

At the bang, Achilles had released the woman's hair and now Tanya scuttled away from him, straightened up, and ran toward Welch. Achilles' laughter followed her.

"Yeah, get them, Nichols. Now. Take one of those boats." Welch pointed to the single-sailed ships docked at the quayside which we'd seen when we first came ashore. "I've got the chips but we're not taking the sub." Welch caught the woman as she raced up to him, put one arm around her waist, and continued down the beach, his weapon trained on Achilles. "As a matter of fact," he amended, coming abreast of Achilles, "I'll come with you, and so will Tanya. Just go on ahead with Nichols, Tanya, and I'll catch up."

The woman gave Achilles a wide berth and even in the fading light of Paradise I could see her face was puffy—from weeping or fury or passion, I could not tell. When she reached Nichols, they set off toward the quayside without questioning their leader's orders.

Achilles did: "What's this action, Welch? What do you mean, we're not taking the sub? If you don't need the sub, you don't need me. I'll gladly stay be—"

A gunshot interrupted Achilles' challenge, a resounding blast accompanied by fire spitting from Welch's gunbarrel, a fire green and yellow and red.

Achilles howled then, and crumpled to the sand, cursing and moaning, a destroyed shadow in the dusk.

As I ran to the hero, I heard Welch say, "That's right, fool—if I don't need the sub, I don't need you. And I don't need your ass messing with my woman, or your arrogance, or your ugly self in my face. Maybe," Welch said as he strode by in the wake of his two companions, toward the single-sailed boats at the quayside, "if you don't die and take an express Trip back to New Hell, we'll pick you up on the way back. And maybe we won't. It don't mean squat to me what happens to you."

Welch's voice, fading as he followed his friends, told Achilles what sort of "negative report" Authority would receive of this misadventure.

Neither Achilles nor I was listening. I hardly heard Welch's caution that I wait here, if I wanted to go to Thebes.

I was not sure then that I wanted to go to Thebes, or anywhere, with the cold-blooded Welch, who had shot Achilles over a woman who was not even hurt.

My hero was lying on the sand, the thirsty sand that was soaking up his black blood. It gleamed in the deepening dusk, and I could hear his gritted teeth grind as I tore strips from my robe to bind his chest.

Finally, I took his head in my lap and stroked it. I kissed his sweaty brow and brushed the sand from it. I rocked him like a baby. Men who died in Hell returned to the dreaded Undertaker, in horrid New Hell, where they were tortured exceedingly before being reborn to this semblance of life that imprisons all us sinners.

If he died, I would never learn his stories, never find out what had become of him in Hell. And he would return to New Hell, combusting on the spot, in disgrace and the misery of death. He might languish long in the Mourning Fields, or be lost otherwise, before he awoke. And when he awoke . . . Achilles would hate New Hell and the Mortuary there and the Undertaker whose scalpel cuts us all.

I wept tears over Achilles while he shuddered, and I wished that Welch were lying there in his stead.

And eventually, the hero's blood stopped flowing quite so fast, and he murmured to me, "Thank you, Homer. That's better. It doesn't hurt so much. I'm cold, but that makes sense. And it's really getting dark, isn't it?"

I heard the fear in that last question, and I knew that the gods would close his eyes. So I said, "Tell me a tale of your time in Hell, Achilles, a tale you want widely known. And as I did in life, in death will I sing your glories."

This even a dying Achilles could not refuse. With bated breath, in a voice softer than I'd ever heard him use, Achilles told me this tale before he died in my arms there on the beach in the dark:

ACHILLES' LAST BREATHS

What men do not know of me, poor Achilles, the fated one whom the gods raised high and then destroyed, is greater than what they do know. So say this, noble Homer, in your poem. Remind men that I never wanted more than a good woman and a warm hearth, but even these the gods denied me.

When I was but a boy, my mother, Thetis, hid me from my foretold death. She hid me in Scyros. She dressed me as a girl and kept me there, where I met King Lycomedes' daughter and fell in love.

To marry her, I had to put away my skirts, at least in private. Then when bold Odysseus, having been told by a sybil that Troy could not be taken without me, came looking for me, he discovered my manhood, for I had fathered a daughter there.

Wise Odysseus convinced me to put on armor. He did not say my death had been foretold. My mother knew, but she did not warn me. So I brought my

Myrmidons in fifty ships to Ilion and there began the quarreling. I loved and lost both men and women, for I understood both minds, having spent so long as a girl.

All the Achaeans lied to me; their honor was beneath their sandals, Agamemnon and Odysseus worst of all. Once Agamemnon took my girl away because he'd lost his own and could command mine, I would not fight for him, but lay with Patroklos, my bosom friend, until I was tricked once more by fate.

Patroklos, bold Patroklos, put on my armor and my helmet and went to fight my battles in my stead. So did he die, mistaken for me, and I put on armor made for me by my mother's friend, Hephaestus himself, and strode out onto the battle plain to seek my death.

And found it there, as the gods decreed and prophecy foretold, and Thetis and the sea-nymphs mourned me better than any man. But even then I was not cross with Agamemnon. My ghost has been in Hades longer than any of that army's. I wandered alone in the mists until I found a way to warn the living. Yes, my ghost struggled long and hard to warn my living comrades of fates to come. I reached Odysseus across the veil, and Agamemnon, but nothing a ghost could say would they heed.

I struck a bargain with the lords of high Olympus that, if they would let my ghost warn Agamemnon and the army, I would come willingly to Hell, not fight to stay in Hades as a man with Thetis' blood in him had the right to do.

But when Agamemnon and his followers sailed away from Troy and I foretold their doom, not one listened to my shade. They thought me an undigested meal, a trick of dreams, an evil omen, nothing more.

Thus I gave my last chance of immortality to save men who would not be saved, and they died, every one, as I foretold, even Agamemnon who was murdered by his wife. Liars cannot recognize the truth when they hear it, and it was this that doomed them, not my ghost's misspoken cautions. I who have loved too much and loved the doomed say this to you: no man breathes who has not his fate within him from his first breath; no man who comes to Hell has another place to go.

So I came here, and did the work of the damned because of my mother, and did what few men have ever done—walked as a shade among the living; talked to Odysseus from beyond the grave—all this, because within me, honor lives. It did not die when my body did. It will not bow to convenience, or to circumspection, or to coercion. Thus I became the Devil's willing servant, and learned the dread, demeaning language of the damned. I mastered English, and all the engines of modern war. I even went again to Ilion, restless Ilion on its accursed soil.

And there I learned I had given up salvation for men who were not worth the price. The arrow Apollo loosed into my heel was nothing, compared to seeing doomed fighters on the beach again.

I have been everywhere in Hell, dear Homer, and I tell you this: there is nothing here worse than what men do to other men in life. If there was honor in men while they lived, there would be no Hell after they died. I was killed by a god and fathered by a Nereid for the very purpose of dying at Troy, yet I might have avoided all, if my mother had not made of me a woman to forfend it.

Thus it all comes back to lies. Tell them, you who talk to the living and the dead, that lies are chains of damnation, lies and nothing less.

When I went again to Ilion, I saw all the liars and the maddened monarchs, trading untruths on a land which itself had no truth of place. The rivers moved and the sea remade itself; Agamemnon made men into stone in his palace, and the Minotaur was loose upon the land. Hell is a mirror into which no man dares look, lest his lies overcome him. And whatever I have done, as man or shade or damned soul, I have owned to it, though I serve the Devil. In life I served the gods, and fared no better.

It is not the Devil who makes Hell horrid, but the men who come here thinking right and wrong are open to interpretation. Make not the mistake my mother made, dear Homer—know that a man is a man, and his fate is his fate, and no lie will save him.

Like Odysseus and stout-hearted Aias fought over my weapons before the cairn they made me, though my mother had spirited me away and my body was not there, men fight over the wrong things, leaving their honor behind like a robe to be put on again when there is no danger that might soil it. Odysseus gained my armaments by the contrivance of Athene, and from this, Aias went mad, destroyed the Achaeans' herd, and killed himself. And it was this lie, this treachery that brought a man to suicide, which condemned Odysseus to all that followed—to a Hell he'd earned.

So weep not for me, nor for my comrades. All of us are here because we've chosen unrighteousness over righteousness—chosen freely.

And blame not the Devil for our sins. For if there were no men, there would be no Hell to receive their shameful souls. I, who was brought up a woman and yet never learned better than to squabble over women, can attest to that.

*   *   *

Thus, in the language of his youth and not the English of his damnation, did Achilles speak to me before he died. And even in the dark, I looked into the indomitable eyes of that hero and saw that he told the truth exactly as he knew it. For Achilles, nothing had changed but the Fates for whom he labored, not in thousands of years.

The death of Achilles was a different matter—this was something I had never seen so close at hand. As his lips relaxed and his body breathed its last, his flesh began to warm. The head upon my lap grew heavier. It grew warmer. It grew hot.

I was forced to let the sand be his pillow, for though his chest was still, his weight seemed to be increasing.

I moved back from him, and as I did, his mighty frame began to glow. It glowed like embers; it caught like pitch; it blazed like a bonfire set to warn venturing ships of dangerous shoals. It lit the beach and licked the sky.

Farther, I drew back, retreating from the heat of it. And farther, as what had been the body of Achilles burned high, and then burned low. Thus in Hell he gained the flames his mother, Thetis, had denied him when she snatched him from the Achaeans' pyre on the beach at Troy.

I rubbed my arms as the blaze consumed the man, the soul, the flesh and the bones of Achilles, and then the fire went out. And as he asked, I did not cry. This hero I had rendered rightly; this man was as pure now as he had been in life. No tale I could tell of Achilles would limn him better than his own words, I decided, and I swore I would remember every one, and lay them into the *Little Helliad* unedited.

For by then I knew I would write two versions—

the one the Devil wanted, and the one the angel wanted. Until that moment, I had been fooling myself, thinking they could be one and the same.

On that night, I was still fooling myself, thinking I could write a book to make the Devil proud. For the honor Achilles found in damnation belonged to a simpler soul than mine. But I needed to tell myself, that night as I waited for the Devil's agents and the doomed souls who would accompany me to Thebes, that I could write myself out of my dilemma.

I had not yet realized that Hell itself has a will; that it, more than the Devil, determines its stories. But I was beginning to, I was beginning to.

By the time Achilles was a pile of embers upon the beach, my comrades had returned. Welch saw the coals and looked away; Nichols swaggered up to them and kicked the ashes, causing sparks to fly, while Confucius came to my side and stood there quietly and Alexander and the woman, Tanya, waited, arm in arm, for Welch to bid farewell to the captain of the square-sailed boat that had carried them to the dragon and back.

In that darkness, it seemed to me that the fabled shade of Achilles still hovered over me. I could not find words to greet Confucius, who murmured to me, "Dark and light unite: Peace. Be not sad; nature unites all things, even in Hell."

This I found distressing, but when I turned to chastise Confucius, he was holding out two oranges: one for me, and one which he cast with all deliberation into the ashes that were once Achilles.

I thought I heard the Nereids, the Muses, and even sea sprites chanting then, but no one else did, that was certain.

Welch was cursing his luck that Nichols had dismissed the Brits who'd accompanied him here, and calling everyone to order.

As we struggled up the beach, it was the un-friendly Nichols who walked with me, behind Alex-ander and the woman, who were in their turn behind Welch while Confucius brought up the rear, looking often over his shoulder towards the embers and the sea.

So I had occasion to ask this Nichols, "When we first met Lawrence, you said that you and Welch sought an apeman, someone called Enkidu, in Thebes. Tell me about this."

Nichols replied, "It's a wild goose chase, old man. Welch got into some trouble with the Devil—he didn't quite get his ass fired, but about as close as you can get. So we're going through the motions. Maybe Enkidu's in Thebes, maybe not. We follow orders." He shrugged, with as much emotion as I'd ever seen in the man, and spat over his shoulder in disgust. "Welch ain't exactly an outcast, but he's not exactly in tight with the Powers That Be, either. We'll be okay, though; ain't no use you frettin' about it."

It had never occurred to me that these agents of the Devil were being punished on this journey. I thought long about Hell, and what Achilles had said, and the nature of the men these agents had shown themselves to be, and decided that if Achilles was right, and not even the Devil was happy in Hell, then it followed that these men would have their own tribulations—that these agents of Authority could suffer a fall from grace.

Still, it was odd to look at them, who seemed as close to Lords in Hell as men could be, and think that they too were frightened, uncertain, that they too ran risks. And it was disquieting to think that Confucius and I might unwittingly have fallen in with fated men.

When we quit the beach, Lawrence's dark men were waiting with horses, and as we rode the rioting streets back to the library, I heard Welch saying to Nichols that "the way our luck's been running, maybe neither Lawrence or the library'll be there when we get there."

But those guides Lawrence had dispatched knew their job. They led us through alleys always a street away from the worst of the fighting, and never did we have to double back or duck a flying missile.

Welch and Nichols spoke of "Turks and Arabs, and Brits and Germans," but I could not tell one faction from another. Men in mortal combat are, each soul, alone, and I saw Confucius wipe his eyes as we cantered through streets lit with self-combusting corpses as if some macabre festival were under way.

When we reached the library, Alexander was off his horse first, and helping the woman dismount, before Confucius and I had even halted our steeds.

"Hurry!" Welch shouted over the din, for blazing bodies were everywhere in the dark, and fighting groups of men and horses threatened to spill onto the very steps of the library itself.

We had all dismounted and were running, as Welch and Nichols urged us, into the library when I chanced to look back.

Then I called to Confucius, "Look!" and he looked back as well.

There, behind us, the streetfighters and the corpses—the very streets themselves—were fading. They shimmered; they were engulfed in mist; they blurred away. They disappeared.

This stopped us both in our tracks, despite the calls from Welch and Nichols to hurry.

It wasn't until Lawrence himself, striding out of the library's gloom in a white robe like some avenging wraith, called to me that I found the strength to move.

"My dear Homer," he said, coming toward us, arms outstretched, his wicked smile gleaming, "don't think about what's behind us. Think about what's ahead." And, as he reached us: "Ah, this must be the venerable Confucius. Sir, I'm honored beyond measure to meet you." He insinuated himself between us, put an arm around each of us and in that fashion, guided us gently into the library.

Confucius said, "My dreams of immortality never prepared me for such a sight as a great battle fading entirely away." He was visibly shaken. "Until we can make some tea, I cannot interpret these events. What do you think it means, Lawrence, that these men and their very battlefield should disappear, while joined in immoral combat?"

"Immorality I know. Immortality I cannot judge. Come with me, venerable Confucius and dearest Homer, and I'll show you the closest thing to immortality that I have ever seen."

Then Lawrence led us through the library and out the back, where a reed boat waited in a harbor called Alexandria that made our Alexander weaken at the knees, and demand, "Who are you, Lawrence? The angel of my salvation? A Judge in man's clothing? Or the vengeance of the gods?"

Chapter 10: Smile of the Nile

As we piled aboard the boat, it listed. As we cast off, the sky above began to change. The darkness of night was lifting as our sail caught the wind, I thought at first. Then I looked back, whence we'd come, and saw I was mistaken.

The library of Alexandria was in flames. A glow like dawn came from it, a glow against which the night was all the blacker, a glow which seemed to erase everything else within our view.

I shouted out a warning. Alexander rose in the little boat, demanding that we go back.

"No need," called Lawrence, from the tiller. "This happens all the time. It burned in life; it burns in Hell—repeatedly. And all those who died trying to save it die again."

I squinted into the glare and saw small figures, running, before Alexander brushed past me to argue with Lawrence face to face.

Confucius pulled on my sleeve. I turned to the sage and saw him pointing to the middle of the boat, where a low roof sheltered Nichols, Tanya, and Welch in a crude cabin. "Tea," Confucius yelled. "I'll make some," and he waddled off to join them.

Thus it was only I, Lawrence, and Alexander who saw the Devil when he came.

Alexander was still pleading for the library, and Lawrence, wind-whipped and leaning on his tiller, arguing for pressing on, when a great beast arose from the river's depths.

This beast had a mouth the size of a man, and flat-topped teeth which it showed us. It was as large as our boat, it seemed, and the river waters lapped its great back as it rose. It had a head like a dog, and round little ears like a horse's, and its eyes regarded us balefully as it yawned and showed its maw.

Alexander was struck dumb by the sight of it until Lawrence enlisted his aid with the sail, that we not run up on the monster's back.

But neither of them heard it speak, or they would not have worried.

It came right up to the side of the boat and said to me, "Where's my book, Homer? Where's my joy? My pride? My paean to all Hell's glories?"

The mouth of the beast spewed me with warm breath on which were all the smells of mucky river-bottom. The eyes it fixed me with were piercing and glowed red and blue.

I knew the Devil when I saw him. I hunkered down, my hands gripping the reeds tied into a railing, and said, "I am working on it, my lord. I am working on it."

"I am beginning not to trust you, Homer. These men you gather round you are no testament to your good intentions. I want a sample, and I want it by the time you reach Thebes—or you will never leave it."

"In Thebes, I promise," I said through unwieldly lips that could have belonged to another, so strange did using them to form words feel to me then. "I will satisfy you, Infernal Majesty."

"If you do not, then that is that: your safe-conducts, your privileges, even your freedom, I'll revoke. Remember what the New Dead say: publish or perish, Homer. It's beginning to be all the same to me."

"But what I have done to displease you?" I blurted.

"Oh, nothing," smiled the great mouth of the wide-snouted river dog. "You take up with disgraced agents of mine; with a one-time king who is a known Dissident; with a faggot who knows no difference between pain and pleasure, who cannot be disciplined by suffering because suffering is his preferred mode of pennance, and you dare ask me such a question? Perhaps I am merely tired of you, Homer. Tired of your sly Greek ways. Perhaps your style is not suited to my epic; perhaps your sort of book is, well, out of fashion. Maybe I don't want to risk a failure. Maybe I'll get Jacqueline Suzanne . . ."

"Who?" I did not know the name he mentioned, but I knew a threat when I heard one. As no violence upon my person, no denial, no tribulation, could have frightened me, the fear of losing this commission made me quake. If the Devil made good his awful threats, then where was I? Stuck in Thebes, wherever that was, in an alien culture, without a brief.

More to the point, where was my endeavor, my *Little Helliad* which by now obsessed me like a lover? Without the purport of the Devil's book, I'd never get it written. I had lost patrons before, and survived, but none so malevolent as the dog from the depths who wheezed on me with seaweed breath and a mouth that could swallow me whole.

I was barely aware of Lawrence and Alexander, shouting to one another as they tried to avoid colliding with the beast. But the beast found this amusing. He glided along beside us, telling me how little he cared what happened to me, or any soul who was with me.

"And you tell Welch for me, that the next time I appear to you, he will see me, also. And by then he'd better have something to show for his labors, or ill will come to him as well. I have better things to do than waste my time with incompetents," said those gaping jaws on a giant sigh that made waves froth against the current.

"Wait, lord!" I begged him. "I'll get Welch. You can talk to him yourself. And I'll sing you some of my first chapter, so you'll know I'm under way—"

Alas, by then all that could be seen of the giant river dog were his horse's ears and his snout. Then only ear-tips and nostrils. Then nothing.

"The Devil's gone away," I called to Lawrence, behind me, and to Alexander, by the mast.

"The Devil?" said the handsome boy-king, who was clearly aware of what a romantic figure he cut, posturing before Lawrence's liquid eyes. "What devil?"

"*The* Devil," I said, and tried to explain that "that was no sea monster we met, but a manifestation of Satan, bearing threats and warnings."

But Lawrence interrupted my discourse, saying, "That was just a hippo, Homer. H-i-p-p-o-p-o-t-a-m-u-s. Sacred to the natives here as 'Hapi'—a minor god of the river. If one doesn't ram your boat straightaway, or come up under it, you're generally safe."

Since Lawrence wouldn't listen, and Alexander was by now taken with the scenery on the riverbanks, I left the two together on deck. I heard Lawrence explaining about the "river Arabs without which the Nile wouldn't be the Nile, old man," to Alexander as I went below.

Down rickety stairs, the others huddled over a carefully banked cookfire in a cast-iron bowl. The woman looked up first, and said, "Homer, what's wrong? You look like you've seen a ghost."

Confucius was brewing tea and he did not look up, but merely moved over, making a place for me. I sat beside him and said, clearly but with a shaking voice: "The Devil just visited me, abovedecks. He appeared to me in the shape of the Nile's rivergod, and he threatened reprisals and repercussions on us all if we do not show him we are doing our respective jobs, when we get to Thebes."

The one called Welch looked up from the fire he was tending, and said, "What kind of reprisals?"

Nichols, crosslegged beside his leader, muttered, "Bet I can guess."

"I, at least," I replied, "will be cast adrift in Thebes, never allowed to return home, and worse. As for you, Welch . . . I doubt less than total success will satisfy His Infernal Majesty."

"Ain't that the way with H.I.M?" Nichols spoke again, before Welch could reply. "Give you an impossible mission, and expect it done yesterday."

Now Welch did speak. "In my time, a bureaucracy would give you three options: a) nuclear war, b) total surrender, or c) their preference. Hell's bureaucracy gives you only the Devil's preference." He shrugged and his clear eyes met mine. "Don't sweat it, Homer. What do you have to do—write something? So do I. So maybe our friends will clear out of here and you and I can draft a couple reports—whatever it takes to buy us a little more time." His face seemed reassuring. His manner was certainly so.

"As soon as the tea is drunk," Confucius said, "Nichols, Tanya and I will go see the sights of the river." He began handing out cups. "And when you both come on deck, we will tell you of all you've missed, whilst you labored to save our hides, if not our souls." His beatific smile tickled his plump cheeks. "Only tell us, Homer, the worst threat the Devil has made, so that we may know what is at risk."

"Freedom," I admitted very low. "Our freedom is at risk."

The woman reached out to touch Welch's arm in comfort. Nichols, balancing his tea carefully, rose into a crouch. "Come on, folks. You heard the man. Afterlife's tough enough without spending eternity in some filthy stockade."

When Confucius passed me, he handed me my writing kit, parchment and ink and quills, which I thought had been lost with his backpack.

By the time I had settled my implements on my knees, the clear-eyed Welch was already pecking away at a New Dead "lap-computer" from his duffle.

The sounds the two of us made, the scratch of my quills and the tap of his keys, were all I heard throughout that night, but for the slapping of the waves out of which the sea dog had come to harass me.

In the morning, when I unbended myself and climbed blinking into the dawn, before my eyes was a shore full of wonders.

Chapter 11: Lost City

We had come, Lawrence insisted, up the "Canopic Mouth" of the Nile, which was an evil omen to Alexander, who had been a conqueror of this river land in life. While Welch and I had worked through the night, Confucius assured me, many wonders had passed beneath our prow.

But I could not conceive of anything as wondrous as the city called Memphis that lay now before us, a place full of dead gods and animal-headed men.

In Memphis did we make port, and at Memphis did we go ashore. Here were monuments of antiquity, ruins of colossal statues, temples of Ba'al and Astarte as well as local gods, and peoples of all sorts.

"Beware the Thutmosids," Welch warned. "They used to rule this place."

"Beware the Nubians and their magicians," Alexander chimed in. "And priests of every denomination."

"Beware the Canaanite merchants," Lawrence added. "Do your business in the tongue of Syria."

By this the Brit meant haggle over whatever we might wish to buy, said the self-effacing Tanya with a pale smile. And: "This was . . . is . . . a special place. A religious capital doesn't come to Hell as a rule, Homer. I don't think any of us," her eyes flickered to Welch and Nichols, who flanked us with armaments as we went among the diverse peoples of Memphis, "really thought Memphis was here. It's a lost city, of sorts. It lost faith in its gods, and betrayed them. Its temples were overrun countless times; its allegiances changed . . . but there's power here." She rubbed her arms and shuddered on the hot and dusty street, as if she were cold.

"While you slept," Confucius told me, implacable in the keeping of his promise, "we passed many cities famous in later times—times after yours. And as we proceeded up the Nile, we found older settlements, intact, so Welch and Nichols are sure. It is as if, the New Dead say, the river leads back in time as it goes toward its headwaters. So perhaps this is the Memphis of your day, Homer . . . ?"

I shook my head. I had never traveled here. I had heard tales of the animal-headed ones, of course. "What cities did we pass, then?" I asked the sage, hoping to find a city, and a moment, if the New Dead were right, which made sense to me.

"We sailed by Naucratis and Heliopolis, and by Giza, whose stripped pyramids rent the sky. But both Alexander and Lawrence say Egypt really begins in Memphis—that all we passed was despoiled by Alexander's inheritors, and the Hyksos, and the Meriotes and the Romans." The strange names rolled off Confucius' tongue in a fashion that made me know they meant no more to him than me.

Still, I regretted not studying more history. I had

had time enough to learn all I wanted of these strange lands. But the New Dead knew little more than I, it seemed, for they kept muttering to themselves about the "lost" city through which we wandered.

What was lost about Memphis was her soul. Temples here were defaced; men had the heads of animals; women had haunted eyes above their veils.

We wandered through streets along which chariots of many styles would race without warning, scattering pedestrians as they came. We saw whitewashed huts with Christian fish scrawled upon them in blood; we saw monkeys fed better than children and bulls with gilded horns switching their tails on huge carts drawn by human slaves with curly hair.

All this time, Alexander grew quieter and quieter, and his pace slower and slower. Confucius took a hand from his sleeve and said, "Homer, the boy king loves you. Go comfort him. He will see this as his doing, all this decadence and destruction, all these lost souls."

I did not fully understand the sage, so I said, "What do you mean, Confucius?"

"This man, Alexander, conquered the world. He was made a god here in Egypt, at Siweh. But he knows that after he died, his lieutenant, Ptolemy, and all the sons and daughters of Ptolemy, brought this once-great nation to her knees. So speak with him. The fate of a land is no man's fault, even be that man a king."

Even for Confucius, this was too insightful. "Did the tea leaves speak to you of this? You never told me what last night's prognostication was."

"The leaves are angry with me, Homer. This land is lost, even to Hell's rulers, for a good reason. Gods and evil demons reigned here for thousands of years, and fought each other, and made the Underworld we now tread. It is a land without remorse, and Alexander must know this, before it takes a toll of him, and thusly of us all."

These words chilled me, and the look on the sage's face let me know I would learn no more from him, so I did as I was bid.

I dropped back, letting Lawrence, who was deep in conversation with Welch, pass by me, until I was walking by Alexander's side.

The woman, Tanya, looked at me, and said, "Well, I'm going up ahead. I've got to buy something to cover my hair; I don't like all these angry looks."

"Blonds," said the blond boy king, "mean foreigners with imported might. We did what we did here, and now the very inscriptions on the buildings cannot be read—once they were language, now they are mere decoration . . . or desecration, take your choice."

Tanya skipped ahead, slipping under Welch's arm, and for a moment I saw that there could be love and good fellowship even in Hell.

Then Alexander turned his tortured gaze on me and asked, "Homer, what would you say if I told you my armies did all this?"

"I would say you have forgotten that this is Hell. What is here, the Devil helped men make, and those who thrive among the ruins perpetuate. Lawrence said you created the city of Alexandria—the library, a feat in any age, the more when it survives even in Hell. No learning is evil, Alexander. And, also, if the river leads back in time, we are well before your reign, no?"

"Yes, I am beginning to think so. This is a Memphis under Nubian domination." The once-king pointed to a black man passing by, his head that of a great ass. "Perhaps during the reign of Piankhi, when the north was subjugated by the south, and the black men in turn fought the Assyrians of Shalmaneser. Whatever, it is this distress which brought Egypt low, so that when we came here, in life, there was so little of former times left to resist . . ." He shook his head. On his face was the distress of a man who had given his life to history, and liked not the way its sea rolled over each empire, each monarch in turn, undoing what life and blood had done.

"Do not be sad, Alexander. As Confucius would say, 'be like the sun at midday.'"

"I can hardly remember the sun," Alexander retorted bitterly. "It's been so long since I've seen it." He squinted up at Paradise, just visible atop the colossal temple buildings at the end of this dusty street we now trod. "Do you think this land is really lost? Is that why so many of the Hittites, the Assyrians, the Babylonians and such men wander in New Hell?"

"I am sure it is lost, but the Devil has given me leave to see the whole of Hell, and it is your lot to be with me when I do. And I, for one," I told the troubled king, "am grateful for your insight. Without you, to be distressed by all of this, I would merely gaze at these defiled temples and not understand their significance."

This was true enough, and the young king saw that in my face. He looked once more at the street around us, at the panthers on leashes and the men with beast's heads, and said, "The gods of Egypt have their revenge on these despoilers, giving them true heads of animals, for they have displeased the beast-headed gods." And he too shivered, as I had seen the woman do, though the day was still hot and Paradise blazed down with her unremitting eye.

Again a chariot raced by, and this time Alexander's eye judged the beasts pulling it. When they'd passed, we stepped back from the doorway into which we'd crowded and Alexander said to me, "You know, those were very fine horses. Perhaps this is where Piankhi himself has come to dwell—he was a horseman of passion, a man who loved the swift-footed steeds above all else. If we bought a good horse, and appeared at the palace . . ."

"As fellow monarchs, yes," I agreed, and we went to put this scheme before Welch and Nichols, who agreed to try.

Off we went to the horse bazaar, and there we haggled, with Welch's cache of gold coins, over a stallion as white as bone, with delicate pink skin around his deep brown eyes and pink lips that kissed Alexander's cheek immediately, though moments before the stallion had been rearing and screaming.

The horse-dealer had a black ram's head and his words, through his ram's mouth, were difficult to decipher.

"A horse-whisperer!" he said. And then again. "A horse-whisperer!" He strode up to Alexander and lowered his ram's head, twisting it first to the right, and then the left, to see the boy king clearly. "A man like you could make a fortune in Memphis, fellow. I myself will hire you! We have horses uncounted and unbroken who need your special touch."

Confucius, hands in his sleeves, was standing on the far side of the white stallion, who was now nickering and nuzzling Alexander's pockets for a treat. The treat came from Confucius' voluminous robes instead, and the sage nodded to me as if I had done something unutterably clever, instead of simply following the boy king's inclination to sleep in a palace and secure such lodging by buying its owner a gift.

Alexander, meanwhile, was saying slowly in careful Greek, "I have a small knack, but a busy schedule. Sell me this steed, and another of your finest, for I will present them to your lord and mighty ruler, the *turtan,* or the king."

"No turtan here, horse-whisperer," said the horse trader. "Piankhi himself rules in Memphis these days, and this horse is unparalleled outside of his own stables. Indeed, he would have had it, but for its murderous temperament."

"Then I will buy it alone for him, and if the price is fair, I will tame three more horses for you, after I've seen him and found your word good—if, that is, this horse pleases your lord."

They struck a bargain, determined a price, and the horse was ours.

He came with a silken blanket bound with gilt cord, and with a tassled halter on his head. Also, Alexander got directions to the palace, and off we went, to see Piankhi, the lord of Memphis.

Now, Lawrence knew of this Piankhi too, and vowed he was a black man, black as night.

But it was the woman, Tanya, who learned the most at the horse-market. She had talked to a groom while the men were haggling over the horse's price. "And the groom told me," she said, "that Piankhi has a human head. This is a big status symbol here, where many have the heads of animals." Her Greek was getting better. "But keep in mind," she said, sidling close to Welch, "that you'll see few women and women may be more prized by Piankhi than horses, since most women here were turned into cows by Hathor, an angry local goddess—or so the Memphites think."

"Explains why the Assyrians and the heavyweight

Egyptians don't hang out here," Nichols said with a chuckle. "Animal heads and a shortage of women . . . rough venue."

Only Lawrence disagreed. He was fascinated by the animal-headed men, who outnumbered the human-headed men greatly, and by the defaced architecture all around.

"This is a living slice of wisdom—the eighth pillar of wisdom, you might say," he told us as, following the horse vendor's directions, we came in sight of the palace of Piankhi. "All the vengeance of the gods is here in full array, as if the Devil were the one who carried out the judgments of antiquity. It used to be thought that, at the end of life, these souls were judged against a feather by Thoth, whose head was either an ibis's or an ape's, and that the Underworld got the ones found wanting. . . ."

Alexander turned upon Lawrence then and said, "Stop this! Are you so pure, are you so free of guilt, are you so learned that you can make fun of these poor, destroyed people—of their culture, of all that is frozen in a moment of loss here for us to see?"

Then Lawrence took the measure of the boy king, and said quietly, "Yes, I'd heard you were sentimental. These aren't my wogs, you know. I can't imagine you think they're yours. I know you adopted native dress, tried to adapt your armies to the customs of the conquered, but that doesn't make you better than the rest of us."

"I didn't say that. I said only, have some respect for these damned!"

"I took the part of my Arabs against the whole world, you fool! And where did it get me? It got me misery, and loneliness, and a death in despair. I lost myself, when I tried to become something I couldn't:

I wasn't an Arab, you see; I was an Englishman. Then I became neither one nor the other, and there was no place for me, not anywhere." He hunched his shoulders and stretched out his neck, looking like an angry tortoise or a striking snake as his chin jutted toward Alexander. "Surely, my good man, you've been in Hell long enough to have learned the simple truth that all that keeps us sane here is knowing, each one of us, who and what we are."

Alexander blinked rapidly, stuck out his hand, palm up, in a gesture that made Lawrence flush, and stalked away, leading his white stallion, so that Lawrence had to jump out of his path or be trampled.

So surfaced the enmity within our traveling party, which probably was born at the horse-dealer's, when Alexander showed such skill. Or so Confucius whispered to me.

Then I was busy listening, and learning. Welch thought that it might be true that there were only a handful of foreign women with human bodies in the city. Nichols was adamant that this place was among the most accursed in all the Underworld, and carried his modern weapon through the city unsheathed because of that.

The woman, Tanya, bought a veil and cowled herself, and in this fashion, leading the great white horse, we strode up to Piankhi's very gates.

"Ho," called Confucius, "I am the herald of venturing kings who have brought a gift to your lord!"

This opened the high and gilded gates, made of electrum pounded over cypress, and in we went, past sphinxes and archers with the heads of monkeys.

In the inner courtyard, our white horse danced and trumpeted, smelling mares on a breeze from the stables, and courtiers fussed around us—hare-headed, beetle-headed, and owl-headed over their ebony men's bodies.

Then a group of men with human heads and leopard uniforms came marching, and behind them thundered a mighty chariot with plumed and full-dressed horses whose blankets had bells and tassles.

This entourage stopped before us. The honor guard split into columns, and down from the chariot car dismounted the king.

It was him, no doubt. I have seen many kings, and this Piankhi was no exception: he went to great pains to make himself appear as what he was. He wore thick-soled boots to make him tall; he wore cloth of gold to make him rich; he wore weapons of ceremonial design with gods upon them to make him fierce.

But this was the first king I'd ever seen who wore the face of a rabbit upon his shoulders. He had great black rabbit ears and whiskers and even a quivery rabbit's nose. Apparently, Tanya's informant had been wrong.

From Piankhi's rabbit mouth came kingly words: "I am the king of this land, lord of Memphis, north and south. Doubtless you have read my edict, which is as follows: 'Every one of the princes, if he conceals his horses and hides his obligation to me, shall die a hideous death.' Thus you have brought to me the first and finest of your horses, and I shall offer you the hospitality of my house." As he was saying this, he was striding down the aisle of his bodyguard, toward the great white stallion, who arched its neck and snorted, then pawed the ground.

Nichols' eyes darted from the horse to Alexander and, as if Nichols had voiced his fear, Alexander scratched the white stallion underneath his jowls and said, "Have no fear. It is only the smell of hare and leopardskin that makes you nervous." Then, to us: "He is a kingly horse, and wants to go greet the mares in our host's stables."

When Piankhi, who was nearly twice Alexander's height in his stilt-like boots, reached the horse, Alexander handed over the silken tether and the horse let the king touch him, for Alexander was yet whispering in his ear.

The king stroked this pink-muzzled horse and a sigh of satisfaction escaped his rabbit's mouth. His bright teeth flashed as he said in his high voice, "I am your lord and host, Piankhi, at your service." He was looking pointedly at Alexander.

"Alexander the Great, king of Macedon."

Old habits die hard, I thought, awaiting a challenge as to where and what this Macedon was, since the Nile king could not know of it.

Piankhi only nodded, and said, "I am pleased beyond measure. I shall call this horse Macedon, after your country, and all of his sons shall bear that name as well. Now, you and your entourage must be tired, brother king. You and I will go to the stables while my servants make your servants comfortable. Later, we will have dinner and dancing, and magic tricks from our palace magician."

Thus did we come to the palace of Piankhi in lost and desecrated Memphis, where we were welcomed as retainers of the Macedonian, Alexander the Great.

That night, in the palace of Piankhi, which Tanya said had once been a Thutmoid temple, we were to dine with the king.

Fine clothing was given to us, linens and pectorals and sandals of red leather. Baths were given to us by monkeys in women's dresses, and by eunuchs who sang to us in sweet voices.

This toilette before the feast pleased Lawrence immensely. So did the fact that Alexander had not returned to us, but was still closeted with the king, so we were told, absorbed in matters of horseflesh.

Welch and Nichols were less than overjoyed by this communal bathing and oiling of the bodies. They kept their weapons close at hand and their eyes on Tanya. Nichols went so far as to say, "If good horses are rare here, a good woman's rarer than hen's teeth. I'm not lettin' you out of my sight, Tanya."

Even I had never seen a hen's tooth, so I understood just what warning Nichols was giving us all, and was not insulted when the three New Dead retired from the bath early, to "talk strategy and find a back door, in case we need to beat a hasty retreat," as Welch said.

Confucius loved the masseur and the fine oils, and soon he was snoring loudly.

"This is very good," I told Lawrence as my masseur relaxed my aching muscles and I listened to the snoring on the table at my right.

From the table on my left, Lawrence said, "Almost as good as Faisal's palace," dreamily.

"Faisal?" I asked. And then it occurred to me that I had been with this strange man long enough to get to know him, and yet I knew nothing more than Welch and Nichols had told me on our first encounter in an Arab street.

So when Lawrence replied, "A king I once knew," I said, "Tell me about him, or about some other thing that only you might know."

"Ah, your book. I had forgot," said Lawrence, between grunts as the masseur stroked him. "Not to be impolite, old son, but I've said all I had to say about my life, in life. And as for my afterlife, I don't know that I want stories of it bandied about."

I turned my head to look at him, not saying anything. His eyes met mine. He remembered what a man like that recalls when asked to tell a tale, and he remembered, too, I think, just who had asked him.

After a time, he said with a sigh, "I'll tell you a story, Homer, before the trip is done, I promise. But not until we're out of here safely. There's something about this place I don't like."

"The degree to which Alexander likes it?" I ventured, to keep the conversation going, so that no uncomfortable silence should follow his refusal.

"Partly that. Partly the fact that this Nile trip is an adventure into Hells unseen by outsiders for thousands of years. What lies ahead for us, if Welch is right and the farther up the Nile we head, the farther back in time we go?"

"Not in time," I corrected him; "only in cultures—in societies."

"You know that the best men of these ages aren't in this bottleneck—they're in New Hell. Maybe the Devil wants to get rid of you, Homer, and the rest of us will share your fate. Remember his threat on the river."

"It is Alexander you're worried about, is it not?" The conversation had slipped into English so smoothly I hadn't immediately noticed, yet I was glad when I did: such talk should not flow freely into the ears of slaves in a palace of a man whose temper is a mystery.

"For now, friend Homer. For now. We'll see how the dinner goes, and what kind of entertainment this Piankhi has in mind for us."

I did not know if Lawrence was cautious or merely spoiling the evening to come as best he could, but I was worried.

I soon left the bath and sought out Confucius in our quarters, where he was trying to wrap himself in Memphite festival garb with the help of a cobra-headed slave, and from there we went down to dinner with the king.

Chapter 12: Brother Kings

I had about me, that night as we were seated at Piankhi's festival board, a sense of foreboding, of ill-fatedness, of helplessly sliding headlong into danger, which I could neither banish nor justify.

Maybe it was my recent encounter with the Devil, I told myself. Maybe it was the threat to our freedom His Infernal Majesty had made. Maybe it was the palace itself, so ancient and so strange, whispering in my inner ear, but I did not believe that. Not then.

A man such as myself, with a muse well-trained over time, knows things such as danger intimately—by a feel in the air, by a feeling in the gut, by all means except the rational. And this very talent, this forewarning that has no basis in the phenomenal, often works against its own intent.

The mind cannot heed a baseless warning. The body's knowledge of danger is useless to a man of logic, until circumstances match the intuition.

So I was tortured by my muse exceedingly, sitting there with Confucius and the New Dead, waiting for

Alexander and Piankhi to arrive. Meanwhile, slaves came and went, bringing bounty of the sort my stomach, since I came to dwell in Hell, cannot abide: roast pig with honeyed skin; grapeleaves stuffed with meat and rice and boiled with raisins; three kinds of grain, including winter wheat, and breads of every sort, as well as dates, fresh figs and fruited, heavy wines.

The New Dead drank profusely—or Nichols did, at least, and then demanded of the servants where Piankhi and Alexander were.

Their answer was, "The stables." Their response, beyond that, was to bring forth dancing girls—three human women, plus three cows with jewels upon their necks and diaphanous skirts about their haunches.

This sight, of the three cows and the three women dancing, made Confucius bewail the lack of tea or fortune cookies. Even Tanya drank deeply then as pipers, drummers and harpists played.

Nichols put his short rifle right upon the table, his elbow beside it, and glared truculently around. Welch leaned across his lieutenant to Lawrence, who had never lowered his goblet from his lips, but sipped and sipped and sipped, as if the goblet and the wine could hide his surreptitious smile.

"Another few minutes," Welch told Lawrence, "and we go find Alexander. All of us. No matter what it takes." Then Welch unsheathed his weapon also and put the pistol on the table.

"Tsk, tsk, my good man, relax," said Lawrence, who had his left hand in his lap and never let it touch his food, as if he were in an Arab town. "They'll be along. They're brother kings, you'll recall. We're just retainers." And he shifted on his cushion as a cow danced by and fixed him with a sultry, big brown eye.

Then one of the three human women began shaking her nether parts before the New Dead men, shaking them so fast that her navel blurred.

Nichols started to rise up, saying, "Sure, honey, I'll dance with you," but Welch grabbed his arm and pulled him back.

At this, our woman, Tanya, slid her head more deeply in her cowl and hunched her shoulders, seeming on the verge of tears.

I asked her, "What troubles you, fair Tanya?" and she replied, "These poor women—turned to cows. Doesn't it bother you, Homer? Aren't you curious about how it happens—and why?"

"Don't waste your sympathy," Nichols told her, slurring his words. "You ain't seen the bulls!"

Welch then told Nichols to put down his goblet, that he'd had enough, and Nichols protested that he was fine, as ready to get Alexander out of whatever the king had gotten him into as he needed to be, and the two New Dead locked stares.

This made Confucius try to start up a casual conversation with Lawrence, and reminded me of the discord I'd seen earlier between Lawrence and Alexander. Or perhaps it was my muse which made me restless.

But just then, in came Piankhi and Alexander, smelling of horse, with sparkling excited eyes and their arms over each other's shoulders.

"Hi!" called Piankhi through his rabbit's mouth. "We are two hungry kings!" and the feast was served in earnest.

Alexander was full of tales of Piankhi's magnificent stables, and Piankhi was full of Alexander's praises.

"No better horsemaster have I ever met," Piankhi proclaimed to us, "than your great king. Would that he—and you of course—might stay here with me.

We could raise such horses as would make the gods cry!"

Tanya whispered to Welch then, and let her cowl fall back, for the dancing women and the cows had retired.

Piankhi stared through his pink rabbit's eyes at Tanya's golden hair and said nothing for a time. Finally he lifted his goblet high, and ate and drank, and praised the chef.

"Do as he does," Confucius advised us under his breath. "Praise the food, praise the hospitality of our host," and he did so, at length, to set us a good example.

When he had done, the king arose and bowed low, his rabbit ears wobbling. When he straightened, he pointed to his plate, on which only greens were strewn, and said, "With your indulgence, honorable guests, I shall call my magician, that I too can enjoy this feast."

Perhaps Confucius understood what was coming, but no one else did—unless my muse had an inkling, for she was restless in my head.

Piankhi clapped his hands and the sound resounded in the hall. From a shadowed corner, into the torchlit room came a man as tall as Welch, with a great chaplet on his human head and a uraeus on a velvet pillow in his hands. He strode to the board and stood opposite the king, where we could see him very well.

This magician wore an embroidered robe on which were all manner of animals, and in his eyes were sparks of silver. He said, "Long live the Son of the Sun, King of the North and South, Piankhi, the Valiant, Protector of Memphis. Life! Health! Prosperity!" Then from his robe he pulled a scepter and this he brandished, mincing forward.

Tanya scurried back from the table, horror in her eyes.

Nichols grabbed his little rifle from the linen beside his plate and pointed it at the magician.

Welch slid his own hand over his pistol and sat firm.

Confucius touched my arm and held me resolutely still with his wise old eyes.

Lawrence, meanwhile, had gotten up from his cushioned seat and was making his way toward Alexander, beside the king.

I felt as if everything were happening on a frieze, frozen for eternity; as if we were all depicted on a rhyton whose conclusive scene was turned away from me.

The magician minced toward the king as if we did not exist, muttering strange words and waving his scepter.

King Piankhi did nothing but bow his head. His rabbit's ears drooped wide. His shoulders slumped. He sat there until the magician reached him and, with a flourish, struck him with the scepter upon his rabbit's head.

There was a blaze of light; a sudden, choking odor. When I opened my eyes again, no rabbit-headed king was sitting there.

The head of Piankhi was now the head of the man. It was no parlor trick—no switching of men—for the robes of the king were the same; the hands of the king, with their rings of royalty, were the same. The body of the king and everything else were the same, only his head was now the ebony head of a proud Nubian man of middle years.

Piankhi raised this head and his white teeth gleamed widely. "Do not be alarmed, guests. Do not be concerned, brother king, Alexander the Horse-whisperer.

Though the magic of my magician is unparalleled, even he cannot give me the head of a man for all eternity. But tonight, I have got it. Tonight I will feast on fruited pig and stuffed grape leaves; I will drink wine like a man and engage in conversation like a man. Tonight, I am a man!" Piankhi reached into his robe and pulled out a jewel, a deep amethyst carved like a horse, which he gave into the magician's open palm.

"Thank you, sire," said the magician, and then turned to bow to us as if we too were expected to reward his feat of sorcery.

Confucius said, "Quick, Welch—a coin!" and dug in his own deep sleeves for something to offer.

I, alas, had nothing to give the magician. Neither, it seemed, did any of the New Dead. Lawrence was harassing Alexander in a voice too low for us to hear, but clearly enough: he was tugging on Alexander's arm, dragging him to the far end of the table.

While I watched, Lawrence pushed the Macedonian into a seat and then said very loudly, "Come to your senses, boy, before you get in too deep! Horses be damned, this place stinks of treachery!"

Piankhi, I hoped, did not hear this last, for he was telling his magician to perform ". . . feats to entertain my guests." The magician, having taken a tiny jade Buddha from Confucius, was abasing himself with deep bows as he stepped back to the center of the room.

Piankhi was now telling the magician of Alexander's prowess with horses, saying that a horse-whisperer such as he was priceless in Memphis, and that such a talent, if it could be Piankhi's, would satisfy the Memphite king for all eternity.

I thought the king was asking to be taught the

horse-whispering ways of Alexander, but the magician thought differently.

He minced down the length of the table, to where Alexander sat, and his approach drove Lawrence back.

Before Alexander the magician stopped, then began droning in a flat voice, invoking the "spirit of the horse and the wisdom of the horse and the very nature of the horse." The magician paused dramatically and waved his scepter at Alexander. Then he continued his invocation.

When the magician spoke the words, "the visage of the horse," it was almost too late.

A nimbus was coming to be around Alexander's head, and through it we could see a velvet muzzle and flowing forelock forming.

I cannot determine whether it was Welch who started shooting first, or Nichols. I have asked Confucius and he does not recall the truth of it either. Suddenly the hall erupted with the violence of the New Dead.

The magician's embroidered robe was rent. It spouted blood. His body danced across the flags, swaying and jerking each time a slingshotted bullet struck it with the New Dead's awful force.

I was horrified, frozen, watching the magician's dance of death, so that I did not realize that Piankhi, too, was being riddled with bullets.

Confucius jerked me up by the collar, and the next thing I knew we were running. Lawrence had Alexander, whose head was still swathed in clouds, by the arm and was dragging him toward us.

Welch, Tanya in one hand and his pistol in the other, was yelling to Nichols: "Make sure they're dead, make damned sure they're both dead! For Alexander's sake!"

Nichols was yelling back, "This way, everybody! Follow me!"

Then I recalled that the New Dead had gone in search of an escape route earlier, while Confucius, Lawrence and I languished in the baths.

We followed them, running blindly in their wake, as servants of the king came clattering into the dining chamber. Screaming began. Bellowing from the bebaubled cows shook the rafters. Pandemonium raged behind us.

Down into a dusty passageway we went, and around three corners. All the while, behind us, we could hear the slap of feet, and the thunder of hooves in our wake.

It was dark in the passage, though the New Dead had their flameless lights. It was too dark to see Alexander's body, let alone his head.

So it was not until we came bursting out of the corridor into the kitchen scullery that I saw what rested on Alexander's shoulders.

It was his own head, and I nearly fell to the floor there and then in my relief. It was his own head, though there could still be seen a residue, like a ghost, of a great white horse's head hovering about his shoulders.

Lawrence still had Alexander by the scruff of his neck, and now pushed him to the fore. "The stables! Quick, Alexander, we need horses!"

And Alexander spoke then, for the first time since the magician had approached him. Hesitant and careful were his few words, as if his tongue were a stranger to his mouth: "The stables. Horses. Yes, come with me!"

We let the dazed Macedonian guide us to the stables, using the New Dead's lights. Around us, the palace was reechoing with the wails of servants. Someone shouted that King Piankhi was dead. Another raised alarms meant to apprehend us.

But Alexander got us to the stables, and the horses there all whickered joyously to see him. With skill beyond my dreams, he and Lawrence bridled us seven horses, including the great white stallion, and boosted us all aboard.

Then we raced for the gates in the dark, while all the servants of the king raced the other way. When we got there, the gates were opening for other riders, and before they could be closed, we dashed through them, unrecognized in the confusion.

Now this may seem simple to you, but I am a poet, not a horseman. I hugged my horse's neck and twisted my fingers in his mane and prayed no spear would skewer me from the battlements as we fled into the dark.

The horses ran and ran. My eyes teared, whipped by wind and dust and mane. My horse stumbled; his hide frothed up so that I slid about on his back. I called out repeatedly that we must stop, but no one heeded me.

Perhaps no one heard. Confucius thinks that the horses were running out of control then, but whatever the case, they did not stop for what seemed like hours.

And when they did, blowing and stamping and shivering, Alexander refused to let us dismount "until each horse is cool and has his breath. These noble steeds saved us."

"Saved you, you mean," said Lawrence, and added: "But he's right. We needn't founder them. And there may be pursuit."

If there was pursuit, we never saw it. As a matter of fact, the horses had run so far and fast that we couldn't see the lights of Memphis. Around us was only the river, the wise and ancient river, running silent and deep like a snake in the night.

When we finally dared make camp and light a fire, Tanya was the first to go up to Alexander and demand to feel his head.

"He's fine," she announced with relief.

Then we all went up and felt him all over, and the New Dead congratulated each other for their murder in that rough and calloused way of theirs. Only Confucius and I, it seemed, were shaken by what we had escaped and what we had seen.

But later I asked Alexander what it had been like to be in the magician's thrall, and he said, very low, his eyes downcast, "Better than being a man, Homer. Better than being a man—to view the extent of Hell as a noble stallion, without any thought but mares and clover."

To this day, I am sure he did not mean that. He only said it because Lawrence was close enough to overhear.

Chapter 13: Tales of Times to Come

On the subject of tales from times to come, I am not
so sure of myself as in the matter of relating tales of
my own epoch, or of Confucius', or of tales told to
me in Greek.

But on this remarkable journey up the Nile, which
Confucius was sure was a backward venture through
the epochs, I was witness to the New Dead telling
their tales. And if any tales belong in the *Little
Helliad*, these do.

These tales were told to me in English, one night
as we sat by the fire during our horseback trek
toward Thebes. We had passed by Dashur and had
not yet reached Lisht, and it was clear to all that
going to Thebes by horse would take many days, and
that during each of those days we would be exposed
to fresh and unknowable dangers.

Everyone was cranky and despondent. An argument had broken out between Welch and Lawrence,
who wanted to head for Crocodilopolis. Alexander
had taken Welch's part, agreeing that such a side

trip, away from the Nile, was not only senseless, but risky—once we had left it, we might never find the Nile again.

Both Alexander and Confucius had retired early, and the remainder of our party drank too much beer and tended the fire.

It might have been a flying spark that made the woman Tanya cry, I thought at first, until Welch put an arm around her and they walked away into the unending night. Hell's days and nights can last far longer than days and nights did in life, and this night was a long one.

"If we had a boat," Nichols grumbled, "it wouldn't matter about the darkness—we could be makin' time." He craned his neck to see where Welch and the woman had gone.

"What troubles Tanya?" I asked the New Dead lieutenant.

"You're askin' me? Maybe the Devil's threat—who knows? She's worried about Welch, that's for sure. She's not the crying type."

These were the most words I'd ever heard Nichols speak in series, and I was fascinated. "Worried about Welch?" I asked innocently. "Whatever for? Are you not all the Devil's Children, agents of the lord of Hell?"

"We're all human, buddy," said the unfriendly Nichols. "And H.I.M. threatened Welch as well as you."

Lawrence, still sulky from his argument with Alexander, stretched out on his side. "You don't understand our modern friends, Homer. Neither does Alexander. Their places in the power structure of Hell are at stake. That's the New Dead way—dig into the bureaucracy and claw your way to the top,

no matter how foul a bureaucracy it happens to be."
He cast a defiant look at Nichols.

"A lot you know, faggot."

This discussion took place in English, and Nichols'
response was in that American derivative which dis-
penses with grammar whenever the context will convey the meaning. However, I found it difficult to
follow.

So when Lawrence took exception to Nichols' re-
mark, I did not at first comprehend his reasons.

Lawrence said, with cold danger in his voice, "I
know more of New Hell than you might guess—and
more of dealing with underlings such as you than
a man of your sort ever can. As for my . . . choices in
life, who are you to judge them?"

"I'm a guy who got his ass greased honestly, not
somebody who committed suicide," Nichols rejoined.
"Not somebody who flogged himself and got other
guys to whip his butt for kicks."

"I heard you raped a woman," Lawrence said.

"I know you used to beg guys to switch you till
you couldn't sit down—in your RAF days, wasn't it?"

"Wait, you two," I pleaded. "There must be some
misunderstanding here, between you. Why don't each
of you say the truth about your deaths, that I, at
least, may hear the truth from the mouth of the only
man who knows it. One thing no one else can ever
know is the circumstances of a man's passing."

"What is this, some kind of contest?" Nichols said,
swigging the local beer we'd bought. "I died after I
should have, Homer, if that makes sense to you. I
should have died with my unit, in the fighting. That
was a war . . ." His eyes seemed to lose their focus.
"You Old Dead don't know how good Hell is. You've
never been in a nuclear exchange. You haven't seen
guys' flesh melted off their bones. You don't have a

clue what pain is, if you haven't seen the casualties of
modern warfare—skin burned away, eyes blind, bleeding from every pore. . . . Coming here was a damned
reprieve. And yeah, I raped a woman. Sort of. She
was willing, her daddy wasn't. I made it all the way
back to America, after the Middle East started to
glow, and got my ass blown away by a local poppa
who didn't like vets. Second war in a row that America blamed on American vets who fought and died for
her. . . ." He shook his head. "Hell ain't bad. It's an
equal opportunity destroyer. Equal's good enough
for me."

"You are a Quisling," Lawrence sniffed. "You labor for our oppressor, the very Devil. You are a tool
of Hell, a torturer, a damning spy who makes Hell
worse for all of us who still hold on to our souls."

"You sayin' I ain't got no soul, man?" Nichols sat
up straight. His eyes glittered in the firelight. "You
think you're better'n me? How many wogs did you
get killed, for Brit reasons none of them could understand? Didya ever think that if you and your kind
hadn'ta done what you did, there never woulda been
the war that killed me and half the goddamned planet?
You and your noble nomads, your Middle East romantic notions . . ." Nichols was on his feet, fists
balled. "America went to her knees protecting the
Persian Gulf and the Khyber Pass . . ."

"Nichols," said Welch's quiet voice from the dark.
"Cool it."

Lawrence did not look away from Nichols, even
after the man sat down, swigged more beer, and
Tanya and Welch rejoined us.

"Colonists," Lawrence indicted them all. "Riffraff.
Malcontents. Those who rule in Hell . . ." He looked
then at me. "Once before, Homer, you asked for my
story and I declined. But I'll tell you this—we

restored Palestine, took her from the Turks, and
began all modern times with that morning we declared the Arabs as 'belligerents.' Don't worry if you
don't understand that phrase—none of us did. But
let me tell you," and it was his turn to swig on his
beer, "what my grateful nation did to me for a lifetime of service . . ."

LAWRENCE'S GIFT

I was summoned to Damascus, after all was said and
done—after endless warring; after Faisal and I had
made the world match the balance of our dreams.

I always remember a night like this, on which tales
were told. The prizewinning tale of one such previous night reoccurred to me that day in Damascus,
when I turned a corner, saw a Rolls Royce waiting,
and knew who was within.

The tale I remembered was one of Enver Pasha.
This was right after the Turks recaptured Sharkeui
and Enver went there to take a look, with his whole
full-dressed retinue. Bulgars had overrun the place
and massacred the Turks; when they left, the peas-
ants went along with them. So when the Turks arrived, there was hardly anyone left to kill. This
frustrated the hell out of Enver, who wanted to
wreak some ceremonial havoc. Finally they found a
gray-bearded unfortunate and brought the old man
aboard the entourage's penny-steamer. Enver railed
at the man, and gloated, but the old gray-beard was
too beat to even retort. So Enver strode over to the
furnace of the steamer, threw open its door, and told
two of his aides to stuff the old man in, as if one
man's agony would suffice for all the revenge due the
Bulgars.

The old man screamed, but Enver's aides jammed
him into the furnace and slammed the door shut on
him. And Enver wouldn't leave, even though the
smell was sickening. He stayed right there until,
from the furnace, there came a thump. Then he
nodded, smiled, and said, "Their heads always pop
like that."

I was reminded of that tale, in Damascus when all
the politicians swarmed around like fire-ants, now
that the stores were open, the street bazaars busy,
the electric trams coming and going.

Because it was an end, you see. I could feel it in
my gut. Seeing the Rolls only clinched it for me. I
put off meeting its owner for as long as I could, being
concerned with setting the Damascene hospital to
rights. We had a Tower of Babel on our hands but
we were managing, what with slave gangs and Turkish
orderlies, to feed everyone but the most critical cases,
who would have died at any rate.

And we got the place clean enough, I thought,
until a medical major strode up to me and cursed me
for a blaggart, saying I ought to be shot.

This, when I was just getting things straightened
away. If he had seen the charnal house of the hospital the day before, he'd have shot me himself. He
looked at me, said to my face, "Bloody brute," and
smacked me hard. Then he stalked off.

And that was when I came to Hell, not afterwards,
gentlemen. For the man was right. I said of this, in
my memoirs, that 'anyone who pushed through to
success a rebellion of the weak against their masters
must come out of it so stained in estimation that
afterward nothing in the world would make him feel
clean.' I said that in the *Seven Pillars*, word for
word. What I didn't say was that I entered Hell upon

that moment. My body only had to be convinced to leave the scene of the crime.

So, back to the Rolls and its occupant: The Rolls was Allenby's. He backed my imposition of Arab governments in Damascus and elsewhere, took the hospital off my hands, and looked at me kindly.

Then he gave me a telegram for Faisal from Higher Ups, I introduced Faisal and Allenby, and Allenby gave me leave to go.

Oh, I asked for it, but it was leave to die, you see. I won a world for people who were not my people, and the world my people had was a living Hell for me. It wasn't suicide, though, on that bike. It was only impatience. I'd spent so long being sorry; I couldn't find peace anywhere, not even in my writing. And I thought peace was what I wanted, until I came to Hell and realized that the battle wasn't over. That's what Hell holds for a man like me: punishment to rest the soul. Torments I fully deserve, and want . . . expiation for eternity. In short, war, in which a man's evil has a rightful place. War is Hell's gift, to a man like me who saw the kindness in Allenby's eyes and knew his own soul bereft of it.

At this last, Lawrence stood up, murmuring to Tanya that a gentleman always stands when a lady joins him, and bowed a low and sweeping bow.

Once she and Welch had seated themselves, Lawrence did not sit, however, but retreated from the firelight, saying: "I don't think any of you know where you are, or what you are, but Hell has taught me to know myself. I'm off to Crocodilopolis in the morning. You and your Macedonian king, Homer, and your agents of the Devil, will have to go your own way without me."

No one tried to stop him. There was too much

about him that was divisive. But his story, although I'm unclear on the war he fought, or even what a penny-steamer is, has stayed with me more clearly than the other one I heard that night—perhaps because of his very inability to tell it, which collided with his need to tell it, and thus told me more about T. E. Lawrence than could any well-spoken tale.

This other story came out of the woman, when Welch lay snoring softly in her lap and Nichols was curled around his beer jar. She said, "Homer, you mustn't listen to Lawrence—not about Welch, or Nichols. They're doing the best they can, that's all."

"Do you mean," I said in my halting English, "that they are not agents of the Devil?" I well recalled what the angel had told me. I didn't need Lawrence's cautions to beware these men, creatures of destruction who were in truth what Lawrence only thought himself to be.

"Welch," she said, stroking the man's short hair as he slept with his head on her knee, "is in more danger from the Devil than even you. He's the best of all of us—all the ones who work for His Satanic Majesty's Secret Service. He's the best because he meets his own standards. He'll get us through to Thebes, or die trying. You can always count on him to do exactly what he says."

"Is that so?" Lawrence had given me a gift of perspective with his story. My mind's eye made up battles in towns where steam-belching chimeras and sea-going dragons of war did men's bidding; where Turks and Arabs and Englishmen lay screaming in hospitals—where war was more horrid even than in Hell, for Lawrence, obviously, did not believe in anything but the evil of mankind—not in a single god had he ever put his faith.

And this, I realized then, was the New Dead's

curse. This was why so many of them were here, and why those worked for the Devil, seeking something to believe in now that there was nothing of the kind to be had. All my heroes, and Heraclitus, who knew that change was all things, yet profoundly believed in godhead—in a god of many faces, of many persons, but in the reality of righteousness. These New Dead, Lawrence, who saw war only in terms of his personal fate, and the men and women with me by that fire, believed in nothing at all but themselves.

This had brought them to Hell, and it would sustain them here eternally. Watching the woman watch her men, I knew that she too knew this truth. Although Alexander might have a Judge in the guise of Bucephalus; although Achilles might be the most obstreperous of men, and a long way from salvation—for them and everyone we'd met, Hell offered out eternal chances of salvation. For everyone, that is, but these.

Without faith, where was honor? Without honor, where was the joy of serving god? Without the gods, where was acceptance of ill fortune? Without all of these, where was the eternal spark that made the human soul worth saving?

"This is the night for telling of how one came to Hell, sweet Tanya," I said gently, not prodding, only suggesting.

She looked me right in the eye and said, "I worked for a government, which wanted to kill a rebel chief. I lured him to his death. I entrapped him by pretending to love him. I think a woman who uses a man's love to bring him to his death deserves to be here, don't you?"

Though she did not say it, I knew from my time among the Dissidents that the rebel chief she spoke of was Che Guevara. And though she spoke no more, only sat with her fellow agents of Demonic Order, her story is among the saddest I learned on my trek through Hell. What made it so was the look she gave me, of tortured resignation, for this woman was hopelessly in love with Welch, the man snoring on her thigh. And a woman who has used her love to kill feels herself unfit to love, and fears the Devil's just retribution.

So I learned, that night, too much about the Devil's Children, the agents of this fallen god, who were not so fearsome after that, since their punishments were eternal loneliness and unmitigated mistrust, even of their own emotions. And I learned more of the future of mankind than any man should know.

When I got up to leave the cookfire, I found Confucius, not asleep, as I had thought, but ensconced among the shadows.

"Did you listen?" I asked my friend.

"Yes," he replied.

"Shall we scuttle away like Lawrence, depart like thieves in the night from these benighted creatures?"

"No," said Confucius, so certain that I wondered if he had found a new source of fortune cookies. "If the Devil has his men with us, he knows our every move."

"That is what I mean," I said.

"It is what I mean, also," Confucius rejoined, and stepped out from the shadows. "Come, Homer, let us make some tea. Clouds come and go, but man's nature remains constant. You have seen and heard from the New Dead of a world more cruel than even Hell. And if we do not want to find ourselves in a Hell of their making, then we should continue on this path. Rejoice, for what lies before us is a land full of antiquities. And where there are antiquities, there are the memories of mankind. If a man does not forget his true nature, there is nothing that can harm him. For in all men there is good, even in those around your fire. Even in Lawrence, whose purported evil stems from his unmeasurable remorse."

So I went with the sage, though my heart was aching for the woman who was afraid to love, and for the man she loved, and for the unfriendly Nichols who had looked upon a war worse than Hell, and for Lawrence, who found it necessary to leave us, so that his loneliness could match his crimes.

And Confucius made me tea, in the leaves of which we saw like sybils. In my mind, which on that night was as clear as the mind of a Pythia, I saw the battle engines of destruction that Nichols had spoken of, and a land charred to cinders under a glowing sky. But I also saw what Confucius saw—a prognosticator of our journey, a place where the streets glittered with gold and a beautiful woman reigned beside a king who had a vision worth damnation. And I took heart from our future, as a man always must when he cannot get comfort from his past.

Chapter 14: A Ray of Light

We trekked on horseback only until we could find a man who'd take our horses in trade for his raft. This raft had a makeshift sail, and yet it suited our shrunken party.

Alexander stood on the shore of the river, which was green for only half so far as the eye could see, and said, "This time, we do the proper thing." He stripped off the belt he wore. He took his dagger from its sheath. He took his slingshotting rifle from its holster.

Then, while Welch frowned and Nichols watched, arms akimbo, and Tanya held her hair in the whipping breeze, Alexander strode knee-deep into the river.

There he beat the river with his belt, repeatedly. He struck its surface as if he were whipping an untrustworthy slave. And as he did, he adjured it. He told the river not to obstruct our progress. He told it that it was his slave, bound to his will, and that it dared not defy him. Then, when he had

176

finished whipping it, he tied his belt into manacles, as if the river had wrists to bind.

Then at last he threw the belt, with its loops for binding wrists, into the river, and proclaimed: "You are my slave, O Nile. You will obey me and carry me swiftly to my destination. You will honor me and never strike at me in anger, for you are bound to me with restraints I myself have made."

Then he stepped slowly back from the river, which seemed unconcerned at what he had done.

Grinning, he came aboard the raft, saying, "There. I learned that from Darius. Keeps the river in line." And he looked boldly at me. "If the Devil comes again, Homer, he cannot now use the river against us—no beast in it will threaten us. Nor will the waves themselves rise up against us."

He was beautiful there, that boy king, in the bright light of Paradise with canny triumph upon his face.

Only Nichols made any comment, and that was quickly silenced by Welch, who said, "Who knows what works, Nichols? I sure don't." He turned to Alexander and gravely thanked the king, and we cast off with our poles.

Poling down the Nile was hard work, but honest work. The river had been truly chastened by Alexander, or else it had had no intention of defying us. And everyone wanted to be busy: no one wanted to talk about Lawrence's leavetaking, or the words exchanged the night before.

If I thought these New Dead agents of the Devil had real souls, I would say those souls were embarassed, ashamed of telling their innermost thoughts and fears.

Confucius had regaled us with favorable omens over the morning's tea, and I, for one, believed those, rather than the dark clouds in the New Dead's eyes.

We proceeded that way for three days, pulling into the reeds at night to make camp on solid ground. On the third night, Confucius came to me and said, "Beware, Homer. The angel appeared to me. The angel you call Altos came to me and said, 'Beware the city of the solar disk.' What do you think it means?"

"The angel? Why did he not show himself to me?" My feelings were hurt. My soul shrivelled. The angel was my true talisman, proof that hope exists in Hell for good reason.

"The angel said the time was not right for him to approach you. He will come to you, he says, when you call out for him in direst need. He was crying, Homer. He was crying."

I had never seen Confucius so upset. I, too, was deeply troubled. "Shall we tell the others?"

"Not unless we can determine what this warning means," said Confucius, all his chins aquiver.

So we kept our own counsel on the dangers of the city of the solar disk, until we came in sight of a great metropolis.

"What is the name of this city?" Confucius asked.

No one among us knew its name.

"Perhaps we should not make another side trip," I suggested, "but go by this place, since it is nothing like the fabled Thebes. Who knows how much time we might waste here?"

"Waste?" said Alexander to me. "Waste?" He wanted to see this city. His whole countenance was curious. His eyes shined. "You are the one who's collecting stories. Do not be afraid, Homer. I will protect you."

"Remember what happened in Memphis," Confucius said softly, and Alexander scowled at him.

"Welch," Alexander demanded imperiously, "what do you say? Shall we lose this chance to explore such a wondrous place? Sail by at night like skulking thieves? Or stride forth like men."

"We're not men, we're damned souls," Nichols said. Nichols had been even more unfriendly since the night he'd argued with Lawrence by the fire. He looked at us now like burdens, like senile charges who did not know their own minds.

"I've got to give the Devil my report in Thebes, Nichols," Welch reminded his lieutenant. "And I'm nowhere near finished with it yet. Maybe a night or two here, if Alexander feels so strongly, won't hurt. I could get some work done." He flexed his blistered palms, for we had been poling all day through windless air.

"I will not go forth into that city," I said, folding my arms.

"I will stay with Homer," Confucius seconded my motion. "The omens are bad for this city."

"How can that be, if you don't even know what city it is?" demanded Alexander. And the look he gave me made me sad. I did not want Alexander to be angry, and his eyes were smoky with ire.

"Come with me, Homer. You are my luck on this journey. We will enter the city, look it over, and find out its name. If, inside its walls, the omens are bad, then we will leave straightaway."

I should not have listened to the wheedling of the king, who got to Hell when he did by ignoring omens. But Alexander can charm the strongest soul, and I am no exception.

Confucius, all the way to the riverbank, complained

beneath his breath, urging me to tell the others of the angel's visitation. But we had waited too long to do that. To tell it now would be to admit a treachery, to show ourselves untrustworthy.

In the eyes of the New Dead, I did not want to appear to be a traitor. Not when they trusted nothing. I wanted to show them that their fellow man—or fellow soul—was better than they expected, not worse.

This city was white and gold and gleaming, exotic and full of riotous colors and oddly dressed folk. There were people from what must have been a dozen lost nations; there were men with braids and men with shaven heads and men with long noses and short, wearing every conceivable kind of dress.

At its gates, no one challenged us. When we passed through the gates, no one remarked us. There were crowds everywhere, and flowers strewn about. Soon we heard music and singing, and Welch said, "There's some kind of religious festival under way here."

He was right. Soon we saw the processional coming down the broad street, and it was so magnificent and full of splendorous floats that I thought perhaps I'd find one of my own heroes in this place. For it was just the sort of place for heroes. It was magical. It was cyclopean. It was grand.

In the crowd gathered to watch the parade, people greeted us. "Peace!" said a woman, smiling as she threw a garland to Confucius.

"Life!" said a child, as if it did not know it was dead, a child who handed prodigious Nichols a piece of candy.

"Re-Harakhty-Aten!" said a grave young man who blessed us with perfumed water.

"The sun disk?" said Welch in a voice quieted with awe, and looked up at Paradise, glorious and solitary, in the cloudy sky of Hell.

For the first time I noticed that the sky here was pink as a baby's smile, and then someone blessed me, and I looked up.

This was not a simple celebrant, I realized immediately. The first sign of this was how the crowd had given way for him. Around him was an aisle of respectful emptiness.

He was an old man, one of the oldest I have ever seen. His head was bare and his robes were simple, as if he knew his carriage and his personage were sufficient to announce his dignity. He was tall, this ancient man; he might have been as tall as the New Dead were he straight, but he was bent with age. And on his right hand was a single glove, and this glove was red.

To this man I said, before he could pass by, just as I spied others dressed similarly, filing singly in his wake, "Where am I, kind sir? What city is this and whose procession is this?"

"This is the city of Akhetaten," said the sepulchral giant, as if he could not believe his ears. "And this is the procession of the Sun, Neferkheprure Wanre Akhenaten, Blessed Be He Who Rises In Aten, Child of the Living Disk." The old man lifted rheumy eyes toward Paradise, then continued: ". . . and of his Great Wife, Nefertiti, the Beautiful One, may she live in Aten!" And with that, the old man swept by me, and so did the men behind him.

I realized then that this man was some sort of priest, only moments before Confucius whispered the same supposition to me.

Welch, however, did us both one better. He was telling Tanya, "That old man's got to be Aye, the high priest. The glove clinches it." In Welch's voice, as I had not often heard it, I heard caution.

And this most knowledgeable of the New Dead turned out to be right about the priest's name. As we watched the crowd close around him, I spied a story-teller in the throng.

I know the fellows of my profession when I see them, and this man had just finished telling a tale to three children, who were laughing.

So I walked right up to him, put a hand on the closest child's head, and said, "Come and tell us what is going on here, friend, for I and my comrades are strangers."

This man was a fellow of square-cut hair, who wore a wide pectoral, a linen skirt, and sandals, all of which were slightly worn. I held out a coin of gold and it glittered in the rays of Paradise. As the man reached out to take it, greeting me in hesitant Greek, he seemed slightly familiar, but I paid no attention to this. His Greek was good enough, and I was luring him back toward my travelling party.

He followed me, and when I was within earshot of Confucius I said, "Good. Here is your coin, and for it you must tell me about the king of this land, and a very short tale of the nature of this place. Whatever it is best for a stranger to know."

Still I did not recognize him, although there was something very Greek about his face under its weath-ering and that black hair cut so straight.

His piercing eyes met mine and I felt something like a shock of recognition, but this I attributed to the meeting of two storytellers, nothing more.

The man's hand reached for my coin and I noticed his swollen joints. So I let him take his payment then, instead of waiting for the story's end.

He bit upon the coin to prove it good, nodded, and began to speak.

All my friends crowded around me, ignoring the beginnings of the procession at our backs.

"Strangers, you are in the city called Horizon of the Disc. Here there is but one God, and he lives in the body of Pharaoh, its king, so these folk think.

"The king here is named Akhenaten, and his father was Amenophis the Third. Now, when Amenophis, a statesman and a hunter, died of an abcessed tooth, this son who would be king still bore his father's name. His older brother had died in mysterious circumstances, and he took over the throne, changed his name from the name of his father, and began to change the world.

"He married the most beautiful woman he could find, because he was very ugly. He turned his back upon all the gods who had made him ugly, raising up the one God, Aten the Solar Disk, in their place. And in doing so, he made enemies of the priests of all the other gods, especially the priests of Amun, who had been his father's favorite. He forced the worship of this single god, whose representative on Earth he was, upon the people and began building this city to honor the Living God—himself.

"And here he came to dwell, with his beautiful wife and his treacherous younger brother, Smenkhare, and all the girl children his wife had borne him. And here do they all dwell, in Akhetaten which he has made. Sometimes, he rides through the streets with his wife beside him, and all the monuments of Akhetaten bear her name. Sometimes the pair are naked in the streets, naked before the Solar Disk. Sometimes, too, he rides through the streets with his brother, Smenkhare, beside him, in intimate embrace. And when this happens, his wife's name disappears from all the monuments, and his brother's name takes her place."

"Which is it now?" said Welch, who didn't have enough sense not to interrupt the storyteller.

"Today it is Nefertiti who rides with him, in naked glory. Soon the upheaval will occur again, and she will be outcast, as she often is. But then it starts all over again." The storyteller smiled a very Greek smile, and there was no pleasure in it. "I have been trapped here for a long time, and always, they repeat the cycle. Brother loves wife, then he loves brother; priests come and go, and plots are hatched and played out, but nothing stops the circle that the king and his lovers make."

"Trapped?" I said. "You are trapped here? How did this happen, and why? We are only visiting, perhaps we can be of some small service . . . ?" I let the question dangle, let my inference resound in the storyteller's ears.

But the procession was becoming louder as the king's chariot approached. The storyteller looked piercingly at me, and then the crowd separated us.

Confucius was tugging on my arm, and thus I turned around in time to see the "ugly" king.

Ugly this man was: his ears were huge, his skull misshapen so that his jaw was slung back. His lips were large and loose and his eyes slanted around to the sides of his head. He was naked as a babe and his belly was like the belly of a woman, heavy with child. His hips were like the hips of a woman; his arms were long and spindly.

His wife, the queen, was naked too, and hers was the body of a goddess. Her face was as beautiful as the face of Helen, though her hair was shaved from her head. These two rode, arm in arm, on a chariot of electrum pulled by snow white horses whose hooves had been painted gold.

And when they passed, people threw flowers before them, and after them came the tall sepulchral man I had dared to speak to, with his red-gloved hand raised in benediction before the people. And behind him were all the priests of the cult, with their sun-disk standards and their bells. And then came men of the armies, with their accouterments jingling and gleaming. Behind these were jugglers and musicians and acrobats, followed by lions in cages and leopards on leashes and great monstrous elephants with bells on their feet.

All the while the procession was in view and the army was with it, the people cheered and threw more flowers, and there was celebration in the streets.

But once the parade had passed, gloom overcame the people. Women moved desultorily along the street with its carpet of blossoms. Men muttered to themselves about whether they would go to the "window of appearances" or not. Mothers grabbed up their children and scurried off, looking over their shoulders. As the crowd began to thin, I noticed how many soldiers were there, watching the people, as if the whole celebration had been decreed, and policed, and was not spontaneous at all.

Welch said to us, where we were standing together, "We ought to get out of there. I've heard of this place, and it's not a city of the sort you're used to, Homer. I, for one, have seen enough."

Because of the look in Welch's eye, I agreed. And so we made our way back, hoping to leave before Paradise set, but we were stopped at the gates by guards.

"Where do you go?" said the guard who wore a cloth upon his head. "There is no life outside the City of the Disk. The gates here are closed until the king returns from visiting the steles, and even then, what is beyond but the barbarians?"

This was a warning. It was in the guard's eyes and on his lips. And about us were many other guards. Nichols was the one who stepped forward, took my arm, and said, "We'll find another way," very softly.

But this guard's interest was aroused. He proceeded to ask us where we were going again, and then it came out that we were strangers.

"Strangers? That's different, then," said the guard, and called two others. "Take these strangers to the House of the Barbarians, for they need lodging."

Then more guards appeared—soldiers on small, fierce horses—and these rode along beside us until we reached the House of the Barbarians.

"I don't like it," said Nichols.

Neither did I. The House of the Barbarians was amid a necroplis, north of the city, a place of tombs and altars. The Nile was to our left, however, and Welch pointed this out in short, clipped English phrases, finishing with: "If we don't get thrown in prison, we'll be out of here by dawn."

And this was possible, so we all went meekly into the House of the Barbarians, our guards right behind us to see that we did as we were told.

There we had to register, and give our places of origin. I gave mine as Achaea, because I was flustered, and the man who ran the lodging house said, "We have another guest from there. Perhaps you know him? One citizen Hesiod?"

Then I realized why the storyteller I had met in the crowd had looked familiar, and my heart rent. Hesiod. An old enemy. An old friend. Trapped, he'd said, in this strange and unfriendly place.

Nichols was a man for unfriendly places, and it was he who took over then, getting us rooms that adjoined and telling the innkeeper all he needed to know, so that the guards went on their way.

"We're not out of the woods yet," said Nichols to Welch as we surveyed our rooms on the second floor. "This is as much a prison as an inn."

"You don't need to tell me that," Welch said shortly. Tanya looked meaningfully at me, as if I should understand why the New Dead were so nervous.

I understand only that Welch felt responsible for leading us into peril, as did I, for holding back the angel's warning.

Only Alexander seemed content to be here, among the linen and the lovers of the Sun-Disk. He was full of admiration for the ugly king, who had made such a beautiful city and married such a beautiful wife.

"I want to see it all," said the boy-king with great enthusiasm. "The Mansion of the Sun-Disk; the Sun-shade of the Queen; the House of Rejoicing . . . everything. Don't you realize that this place is a living legend?"

Welch said, "Remember Troy, Alex?" Only when Welch was very tense did he call Alexander by that diminutive. "That was a legend too. We're messing with things we don't understand. If the Devil let this deluded bastard keep his godhead in this city, then there's a reason. We don't want to get caught up in any of this."

"Legend says that Akhenaten was poisoned," Alexander shrugged. "And the old storyteller we met said that the royalty here is caught in a cycle of love and hate. What more do we need to know? They're too busy to bother with us. I don't want to go to the palace, not as a king. I just want to look around. You said you wished to write your reportage, Welch. Here you have a roof above your head, a solid surface on which to work. So write, man; write! And tomorrow, I'll be ready to leave with you."

"You didn't hear a goddamned thing that gate-guard was telling us, Alexander, did you?" Nichols demanded. "Nobody gets out, savvy? A regular roach motel—you walk in, you don't leave. I bet this town didn't have walls like the ones we saw, when it was a living city, not a tailored Hell built by and for the dead."

"There's still the Nile side, Nichols, take it easy," Welch said. But Nichols paced like a caged animal, cursing everything and all of us, and lamenting that we had not kept the dragon we had once had, but left her anchored in the sea.

"You're gonna wish we had some firepower, boss, before this is over," he told Welch. "You think that was a spontaneous demonstration back there, you're crazy. This place is a damned police state."

I left them at it, and walked out onto the little balcony we shared. Confucius was there, staring out at the Nile in the distance, sitting crosslegged on a mat of woven grass.

"We have erred," I said unnecessarily. "All that comes of this is our fault, not theirs."

"I know," said Confucius. "We must sit together and try to comprehend the nature of this place, if we are to find a way out of it."

Not one of us was comfortable in these quarters, under house arrest. There were guards below, not just for us, we assumed, but to keep all strangers from roaming the city at will. And there were fires in the distance, where the monuments to the dead sparkled in the bloody rays of Paradise as it set. At length Confucius asked, "How do you think this king manages to fool himself that this is the sun, above, and that these people here are full of life, not death?"

"He is mad, according to the storyteller." I had been avoiding considering that implication. Now I had to. "According to Hesiod. Do you know who he was?"

"Was?" asked Confucius, looking at me as if I were daft.

"Was . . . in life. He and I were rivals. Now we meet again, in a city that makes an angel weep. It must mean something."

"It means that you, on your search for compatriots in Hell, occasionally find some. You have not yet found all your heroes of the Iliad, Homer. Therefore, the Devil has his part of the bargain yet to keep. Do not fear for yourself, or myself, or these men with us. The worst that can befall us is death, and death is not something for the dead to fear."

"Death . . . can lose a man his health, his memory, his friends and his sense of place," I said bitterly, staring out over the necropolis. "Death is helplessness in the hands of the Devil's minions. If I die here, I might awake and remember nothing of the *Little Helliad*, and have to start all over again. There is a book, you should understand by now, that I will write which is not the book the Devil wants. But I need the Devil's leave to write it . . ." I was whispering, and leaning forward.

Confucius touched my arm. "I know, beloved Homer. I know. But fear breeds only incompetence. Fear will get us nowhere. Bold actions, caution and clear thinking—these are what we need."

"You are right," I sighed. "Let us reason together."

"And when we are done, we must convince our friends, who are of divergent minds, to follow the plan we make. For this I will need your help, at least with Alexander."

"I know." The boy-king would heed me sooner than Welch, or Nichols, or the others. We sat long, devising. Then we made tea, for scrying. When we were done and ready to present our plan, Paradise had set.

All about us was a night older than any I had ever known, and full of a death that was like another sort of life. There was the dust of thousands of years upon a sultry breeze from the river, and there was another wind that blew crosswise from the desert, bringing an odor like a tomb. I smelled natron and eucalyptus, and cats.

And I heard cats. There were cats in heat and cats at war. There were cats yowling in the dark and cats' eyes glowing like a hundred men with candles in the distance.

In fact, there were cats at large, under our windowsills, eating fish the innkeeper had put out on platters.

One of the cats jumped up to our balcony. It had a golden collar and an earring in its ear, and it looked at us regally, as if we were its subjects, and began licking a paw with a tongue that smelled of fish.

This made Confucius hungry, and he said, "Let us go down and find our dinner. Alexander must be tended to; we cannot have him wandering off, or we will be trapped here, trying to find him again."

Trapped. I did not want to hear that word again. I thought of Hesiod once more, and almost broached to Confucius my desire to find this old raconteur straightaway.

But I did not have time. As soon as we had reentered our quarters and suggested dinner, our plans were changed.

Welch was saying, "You go ahead. Bring me something." Hunched before his writing machine, he was deep in thought, unmovable even by Tanya, as a knock came upon our door.

It came again: a loud knock, an impatient knock, and when no one answered it, an imperious knock.

Finally, Alexander arose and answered it, saying, "I, for one, am not afraid."

"That's your problem, kid," Nichols told his turned back.

Outside the door were four guards, dressed in stripes and armed. "Come with us, gentlepersons. You are summoned by the Servant of the Sun-disc, Aten, to attend a feast."

The crossed arms of the guards and the flinty eyes that regarded us made it clear that we could not refuse.

Even Welch saw that, and came along without a fuss, though none of us had any idea who the "Servant" that summoned us might be.

So we were taken through the fragrant streets, through clouds of incense and myrrh, through gardens and gates, and past a great reflecting pool into a palace full of light and great columns styled like papyrus stalks.

There, in an empty chamber, we were told to wait.

Wait we did, while Nichols paced and Welch spoke earnest words of comfort to Tanya, and Alexander exulted in all the pomp around him.

We waited behind doors locked from without, facing an open window too high above the ground to provide an escape route. We waited and waited, until the door opened.

And there, to my surprise, was no mighty Egyptian potentate, but only Hesiod, dressed in fine robes, who said, "Glad you could make it, Homer," and smiled a wicked smile. "Hope you're ready. Come, come, let us not dawdle." And he motioned us to follow.

"Ready for what?" Confucius and I demanded at the same time.

"For what?" Turning on his heel, Hesiod regarded me from beneath what I now realized was a wig. "For the contest, of course. For the contest, wherein we shall vie for the favor of Akhenaten before the whole court of the king."

Chapter 15: The Contest

Hesiod the Heliconian was really from the little village of Ascra, a place muddy in winter, humid in summer, and generally unpleasant at any season. How far he had come, this poet who had the ear of Akhenaten and the favor of Pharaoh's court.

With Hesiod leading us, the guards of the streets of Akhetaten; of the pharaoh; and of the very royal household bowed and scraped before us. If this was the trap of which Hesiod had spoken previously, Confucius confided to me, it was a trap of silk and velvet.

But Confucius did not know Hesiod as I did. The man I had met in the street was frayed and tattered, a creature freed of responsibilities who spoke his true mind.

This bejeweled Hesiod had sorrow in his eyes, and on his tongue was all the inventiveness that had allowed him to defeat me the last time we contested.

Let me be most plain about my feelings, and about the nature of Hesiod. This man was—and is—a liar and a cozener, a dissembler of extraordinary ability. A king-pleaser. A palm-greaser. A speech-maker in whose compositions truth and its protection has no part.

But he is good. Oh, he is very, very good, and simply because he spins his webs in Hell was no reason to discount this spider's sting. Yet I saw through the facade of the arch enemy—a man flaunting his station and displaying his privilege—to the anguished soul within.

No Greek, no man who wrote what Hesiod did, could be less than entrapped in accursed Akhetaten. No man of honor, who loves the gods, could bow before a disfigured mortal and call him divine. No man could, unless terrible punishment awaited his refusal.

So as I watched Hesiod bow before the king upon his gilded throne with all the flourish of a free man, I regarded a slave. And as I watched him kiss the crook and flail of the king, I knew he kissed Pharaoh's wrinkled backside. And as I watched him smile at the Chief Wife, Nefertiti, I knew he wept. And as I watched him abase himself before the lesser wives and all the princesses and the brothers of the freakish pharaoh, I knew he shriveled with shame.

I whispered to Confucius, "We must execute our plan, whatever the consequences. Tell Tanya."

This, Confucius contrived to do, in the inscrutable manner of his kind, as Alexander was being presented to Akhenaten in the great audience hall of Akhetaten.

An audience such as this, I had never had before. I was too absorbed with the coming contest to pay much heed to Alexander, who now was claiming all the rights of fellow kingship: he would not bow before Pharaoh, but demanded a throne be brought for him, a throne no lower than Akhenaten's.

Nichols worried over this, and Welch told him, "Ssh. Wait and see," in that bemused voice of a man swimming in history's dark and laden sea.

Welch's calm ran through our group, even to Nichols, who still had his weapon because here in Akhetaten, no one had ever seen a slingshotting rifle before, and thus no guard thought to take it from him.

Only Hesiod knew what the modern weapons of Welch and Nichols could do, and he refrained from mentioning this to his patron—clear proof, I thought, that the Hesiod I'd met on the processional route was the true man, and this maven of the court only a guise.

When the woman, Tanya, was presented to the king, Pharaoh looked her over critically and said, "Come here, fair lady, that I may feel your hair of gold. Gold, you know, is sacred to the Solar Disk. It belongs to Aten, and to myself, His living representative."

Welch muttered then, "If he pulls anything with her, Nichols, he's yours."

Nichols' finger made his weapon click, a sound I had come to associate with imminent carnage. Welch had one hand on his hip as Tanya ascended the dais.

There, Akhenaten reached out and touched a lock of her golden hair, rubbing it between his fingers. "Amazing," said Pharaoh. "You are the very expression of the living Aten, a creature sacred to the gods, like your King Alexander beside me." And he called for another throne for Tanya—one fit for a queen, to be placed by Alexander's.

This assumption that Tanya was Alexander's consort was natural to make, if you had never seen fair-haired people. But Welch could not excuse it, and began redefining the plan with Nichols in earnest, then, under Confucius' watchful eye.

"Let Hesiod and Homer play out their contest," Confucius advised; "let Tanya do what she wills. Then, if all else fails, there is still time for bloodshed."

This was the last advice I heard from Confucius before he, with Welch and Nichols, was seated among the audience.

Then there was a silence, broken at last by the king's flail cracking against his chair. "On the night of my Four Thousandth Jubilee, let the contest begin," he intoned, and a scribe took down his words. As that same scribe would take down ours.

Confucius smiled at me as I stepped forward to meet Hesiod in the middle of that hypostyle hall, where draped lengths of linen drooped over our heads like sagging tents and curtains stirred like ghosts in the open doors which overlooked the Nile.

"Homer, whose father was Meles, we here contest for the prize of freedom—yours, or mine, to leave this place or stay. One of us will go abroad, unencumbered, with his household and his friends, when this is over. One will stay here, to tell stories to the household of the Aten, to make the children wise and make their parents gay."

I had not realized what the prize would be, but I should have. I should have. My throat tightened up. Then I remembered the plan that Confucius and I had made, and how the angel's warning had led us to conspire to save ourselves. And I also remembered the Devil's threat, and considered what I risked: my freedom; all of ours.

So I said, "Hesiod, son of Calliope, the Muse: a man's freedom can be neither won nor lost; it is within him, or it is not."

Thus the contest had already begun, with my refutation of Hesiod's first statement.

He frowned and took another step toward me, looking somehow ludicrous in his Egyptian court garb as he spoke to our audience: "The method of this contest, noble House of the Solar Disk, is one of declaration and response. Whoever is judged the best by you, will be the winner; the prize to be eternal fame and whatever gifts this house decrees."

He smiled at me, having changed the terms.

I only bowed, and as I straightened up, cast a glance at the dais where Akhenaten was, as I hoped, leaning toward golden-haired Tanya and whispering in her ear.

"For old times' sake, and in respect of long tradition, the first question I pose to you, Homer, is one I have posed before. Your answer, should the truth seem different to you now, does not have to be the same as it was when we contested in long-lost Chalcis."

He paused and I knew, before he uttered them, what words he would speak to start the competition in earnest: "Melian Homer, inspired by wisdom, come—tell me what is best for mortal man?"

And I replied, as I had replied in life, "For men on earth it is best never to get born; or, once born, to pass through Hades' gates as quickly as possible."

At this, Akhenaten clapped his hand against his breast and chuckled loudly. Whereupon, his household broke into an appreciative clamor like chickens in a coop.

But what Akhenaten thought was a clever play on current circumstance, a compliment to his household and his hospitality, was but the simple truth. As I had said it long ago in life, I cling to it in death.

Then Hesiod asked me, "Come and speak, magnificent Homer: What is the finest thing you know, that most delights men?"

This was not an easy question; not when put to me in Hell before its mad, disfigured ruler.

"The sound of joy, and music, and pleasant company at a laden table where freedom reigns," I said.

This made Akhenaten scowl, and Hesiod's back grow straight and stiff.

So he said to me, "Come, Homer, consult your Muse and tell me of those things which neither happened before nor shall be hereafter."

I had never suspected Hesiod to be a plagiarizer. My own words he used against me there, before a royal family caught in a cycle of its own devising, in which nothing at all that happened to them—nothing that mattered, at least—could be unique.

Confucius caught my eye and nodded gravely, as if the plan were under way. So I said then, to buy us time and see if I could win my own contest in any case: "Never shall the like of contesting bards in the palace of the king be seen again, as heretofore it never happened; nor shall the results of this night be spoken of hereafter by the Solar Disk."

This met Hesiod's rascally conditions fairly, and the clever tongue-waggler took another tack. "Now, for the second part of the contest. In this, I shall begin the verse and Homer must finish it appropriately." He smiled at the audience and bowed, then turned back to me.

"In Akhetaten they dine on the flesh of dates and cats . . ."

And this was a dangerous trap, for cats were sacred here. But I finished the verse calmly, knowing now that Hesiod's strategy was the same he'd used in life at Chalcis: ". . . they comb with ivory combs, and feed the daintiest fish."

Undaunted, Hesiod posed another conundrum: "And the daughters of the king, who of all women are the handiest at intrigue . . ."

". . . bring forth the future with their virtue, and the past with their divine blood." Here too I was on dangerous ground, for I did not know the history of this family, beyond what Welch had told me—that Akhenaten had, in life, married at least one of his daughters. I scanned these children of the pharaoh and saw one blush; another lowered her eyes.

Hesiod, gesturing toward Pharaoh, was yet undaunted: "This man is the son of a bold father and a weakling . . ."

". . . God, who could not raise him up to heaven."

That brought a murmur from the crowd. But not from Akhenaten, who had his head together with Tanya, and was sharing sugared grapes with her, and offering her wine.

"Hesiod," I said under my breath, "to make it fair, do better than paraphrase your living words." And, still quieter: "Old rival, be on your guard. A moment comes when freedom could be both of ours."

But Hesiod either would not or could not think of new riddles for me. Or perhaps it was to show that he understood, that he chose this next and ancient line: "Eat, fine guests; drink deeply, and may none of you return to your dear homeland . . ."

". . . unhappy, but may you all reach home unfettered and unscathed."

At this, Hesiod shook his head and said, "Home in Hell is where the pain is . . ."

". . . gone, and all true friends abide in acceptance of their lot," I replied, hardly able to keep my eyes from Akhenaten, to see how the plan was working.

By now, Hesiod's heart was pricked sore, for I had met him or bested him on every point, and he changed the rules once more: "Homer, son of Meles, if your Muse truly abides with you, though you are among the living dead, then tell me a standard that is both best and worst for once-mortal men, for I long to learn of it."

I replied, moving as I spoke so that I could see the audience, and especially Akhenaten, better: "Hesiod, son of Dius, my answer to you is the same as it was when last you asked me: 'For any man to be his own standard is most excellent for whomever is good; but for whomever is evil, it is the worst of all things.' "

"Then," Hesiod said, following my gaze, "what is the best thing for a damned soul to ask of the gods in prayer?" And this signified that Hesiod had at last realized what was afoot, for he would not have dared use the plural 'gods' before Akhenaten, if he still feared the Living God's wrath.

"The best thing for the damned is still the same thing as it was for those only in danger of damnation: ask to be always at peace with oneself."

"Tell me succinctly now," Hesiod said, and his voice was atremble as he looked upon the misshapen Akhenaten slouched in his chair, "what is the mark of wisdom among mankind's teeming souls?"

And I replied, with some thought, for Akhenaten might not yet be dead, or might not die at all from Tanya's poison, but only awaken with wrath within his narrow chest and revenge upon his lax and fleshy lips, "To rightly read the present, and to go forth as the occasion demands."

I saw Confucius nod. I saw Welch finger his weapon. I saw Nichols' tap his wrist, a signal I did not mistake. So I added, "Now I ask you, damned and recalcitrant Hesiod, to look upon your ruler here, who has made you a slave in his house, and renounce his service. For the only pleasure after death is the

least pain and the greatest honor, as all souls some-
day learn."

I bowed my head. Hesiod, after a moment, followed suit. Confucius, as we had devised, started
clapping, and Alexander murmured that, since the
king was asleep, the judging of the contest could wait
until another evening.

None of us had thought of Nefertiti, that the queen
might take a hand. We were gathering ourselves
together, amid the protestations of the children, ready
to leave in a group, even if by force, when Nefertiti
descended from her throne.

Even I was not sure of Hesiod at that moment—
whether he would help us, or give us away. If he
did, shooting would commence from the slingshotting
rifle, although Nichols had few missles left. Still, we
were prepared to try it, if Hesiod would not escort
us from the palace.

Thus when the beautiful woman came down off
her dais and approached me with shining eyes, I did
not know whether it was to grab me by the scruff
and sic guards upon me, or to work some other
treachery.

She had hardly looked at her husband. She did not
look at him now. Later, Confucius remarked that she
did not have to. That she must have known from the
outset, being a sybil of some repute.

Whatever her talents, she came right up to me,
and I realized what a tiny woman she was. Her hand,
which she held out to me, was no bigger than a
child's. Her voice, though, was a monarch's.

She said, "Homer, you have shown great bravery
and wit, and brilliance such as is seldom seen in
Akhetaten anymore. For the freedom you give me, I
give you freedom." She pulled a ring from her finger.
"For the curse you lift, I give you blessings. Know

that whatever happens, though the future cannot be changed and the past cannot be changed, the present *can* be changed. If, in New Hell, you see my sister queens of Egypt, tell them there will be an open city here, if ever I shall reign!" And she smiled a smile like Helen's smile, that sort of woman's smile that makes a man feel as bold as a god, as full of blood as Herakles, as indomitable as the wine-dark sea.

I took the ring, which barely fit my pinky, and bowed as low as I might. When I straightened up, Nichols was urging me silently to hurry, and he and Welch had Hesiod between them.

The children were being hustled off to bed and Nefertiti was climbing slowly up the dais.

As we left there, I glanced back to see her, calmly sitting beside her poisoned husband. Though he slumped in death, she sat tall. Though the crook and flail had fallen from his fingers, she held them firmly crossed over her breasts. Her head was high and the serpent crown was upon her brow, and I knew that she would sit there, giving no alarms, until we were out of the palace.

She might sit there longer. For the death of Akhenaten had broken the cycle of the lovers, and the queen had many plans to make. She was now sole regent, Hesiod explained to me in a hushed voice that quaked with fear. Since Akhenaten had died while she was in favor, Akhetaten was hers, if she could hold it.

It was enough of a gift that I was not surprised when no guards came to wrestle us to our knees, or manacle us, or spear us or overrun us with chariots and horses, as Hesiod feared. No, I was not surprised when the ring of Nefertiti got us through the gates, to where our raft was waiting.

Even in Hell, there is better and worse. And we

all congratulated ourselves, those who had devised
the plan and executed it, once the raft was safely
launched upon the river.

Only Alexander, who'd had no part in the murder
of the king, was unhappy. Welch, who'd known that
poisoning would break the cycle, said this to Alexander: "Look, Alex, you want to go back there and be
the next fool on that throne, we'll drop you off.
Otherwise, don't start this 'brother king' crap with
us."

Then Confucius crawled carefully over the raft's
reeds to Alexander, and sat with him, and talked to
him about the New Dead Americans, who had no
king, who wanted every man to be a king, and who
rebelled even against Satan himself, the Lord of
Hell.

Chapter 16: Hesiod's Tale

The First Cataract was still far ahead of us when the banks of the Nile began to grow strange before our eyes. At night they would shimmer with cities and settlements that were not there in the morning.

When we would go ashore, crocodiles would arise from the river like a living footbridge and stare at us, smiling and yawning and snapping their jaws. And birds would come to rest upon these crocodiles' heads, an omen Confucius read as daunting.

There is no tea for sale along the Nile, not so far into antiquity as we had traveled and this too distressed the sage. Nor was he the only one who grew restless upon our crowded raft. The hardship of the journey preyed upon Alexander most of all, I thought then, for he spoke of seeing mainland towns like phantoms in the night, towns that had no place or right upon the Nile—towns he hadn't seen since his former life as a once-born man.

But it was Tanya who suffered most of all, I learned one night when we were tied up amid head-high reeds and Welch took her off among them. From their shelter I heard sobbing. So did we all, and every man felt shame. This ability of a woman's weeping to make a man feel wanting is a thing of nature, I told the others.

To this Nichols replied, "My ass. She's the one had to slip that faggot cripple the poison, not you or me. So don't make no remarks, hear?" He glared around. "None of you. Without Tanya, we'd probably still be stuck in Akhetaten, sucking on our toes."

Alexander glared back at the American and said, "Would that I had stayed there, to rule that place wisely in its monarch's stead. It was not right, to murder a king through stealth and poison. If Tanya weeps, she has good reason."

"Right?" Hesiod scoffed. "What right or wrong is there in Hell? Is kingship sacred to any man other than a king? You know too little of what the Heretic made his people suffer—as all kings make their people suffer."

Alexander uttered an ancient formula that damned Hesiod.

Hesiod laughed at that: "What can you do to me with those words that Hell has not done already? That time has not done better? You know nothing of suffering, boy king of some hillside huts called Macedonia. Nothing."

"I know enough not to get trapped in Akhetaten," Alexander retorted. "Where no one but its own sinners belongs."

By this time, Confucius was gathering smooth stones from the riverbank, to throw at the river birds in hope of killing one. A bird omen may not be the best, but we were reduced to whatever oracles we could muster. I went to help him, content that Nichols could keep peace between Hesiod and Alexander.

When we returned, Welch and Tanya were back upon the raft. In the flickery glow of our cookfire, their faces seemed like masks as Welch bid us a restful night and pulled a blanket over them both.

"Good idea," Alexander said, and he too retired to the raft's far end, leaving us to examine our bird without him.

This bird died cleanly, peacefully, and we had no trouble finding its liver, which was not deformed in any way . . . except its color. It was veined with yellow, and the fat lay on it in a manner which told Confucius that "Things are about to change. The small departs. The great approaches. We must put our souls in order."

"I coulda told you that," Nichols said with strained jocularity. "Next stop, Thebes and that's where the Devil rates our records. Yours too, Homer. So what's it prove, except Confucius knows what's happening?"

"Before Thebes," Hesiod said in a low and angry voice, "there is still Abydos and Dendera—we must pass the temples of all the angry gods."

Then I voiced what was still only a suspicion, but I too had seen a strangeness in the liver of the river bird: "Are you so sure? Alexander, on nights like this, has seen strange towns upon the shore. Some, he thinks he recognizes. Have you been this far upriver, Hesiod? Or are you only telling tales?"

"Tales? *Tales?*" Hesiod's voice reechoed in a sudden pall bereft of even frogs' love calls. It seemed that the entire riverside held its breath. "You accuse me of fabrication, Homer? You? I'll tell you a tale that will teach you humility, you who have stayed by your comfy Achaean hearth, and ventured so seldom out among the damned that this place daunts you."

Nichols came to my defense while I still was dumbfounded, saying, "You been to New Hell, pal? You been out among the Dissidents? You risked your butt any time lately? Or spent your time 'captive' in ol' Akhetaten, where the heaviest thing that's gone down for thousands of years was who's ridin' the king's coattails this week?"

I said in a low voice, "Confucius, we must stop this, before trouble comes of it."

Confucius counselled, "Pay heed to what a man fills his mouth with."

Consequently, instead of conciliatory phrases, I spoke these words to Hesiod: "Tell us this tale, Hesiod, which you think will humble us with your wisdom. For wisdom is what we seek here, and we are all students."

Out of the corner of my eye, I saw Confucius' knee bang Nichols', looks exchanged; the tension in Nichols began to subside.

Meanwhile, Hesiod was drawing himself up and reaching for a jar of beer. "To whet the teller's tongue," he said. Then he drank and smacked his lips and peered at me. "Are you ready for a long tale, Homer? You will not interrupt? Nor question the truth of what I say, for it is a story none have ever heard in all of Hell before."

I agreed to these terms immediately. My curiosity was whetted. Hesiod, then, had not spent his time in eternity in vain, if he could boast of such a tale. For between us was the keenest of rivalries: whatever tale he told, would meet his specifications.

And this is the story Hesiod told that night, the most fabulous of all I'd heard in Hell, as the renowned bard promised. I leave it to you to judge the truth of it, keeping in mind that Hesiod claimed for it total veracity:

THE FURLOUGH

I, Hesiod, son of Dius, tell this tale as a warning to men who love the Muses and renown better than women, and to men who love women better than honor, and to men who love victory best of all.

In life, I conquered divinely-inspired Homer in a contest of song before all the Hellenes—not because my verse was better, but because the king declared that I, who called upon men to follow peace and husbandry, rather than Homer, who incited men to war and slaughter, should have the prize.

This made me bold and full of myself, and I gave my prize, a brazen tripod, to the Heliconian Muses, inscribing it with a description of my victory, but leaving out the part where the Hellenes declared Homer the winner but the king overruled them, because of his feelings regarding peace and war.

Then I went to Delphi to consult the oracle, who was inspired as I approached her temple and gave this prophecy: "Blessed is Hesiod who serves my house, honored by the deathless Muses: certainly his renown shall go as far as the light of dawn spreads. But beware, Hesiod, the sylvan grove of Nemean Zeus; there death's end is destined to befall you."

Upon hearing this, I kept away from the Peloponnesus, sure that the god meant the Nemea of that country. I went instead to Oenoe, forgetting that the whole region was sacred to Nemean Zeus, and there some young men, suspecting me of seducing their sister, murdered me and cast me into the sea between Achaea and Locris.

These boys in turn were sacrificed to the gods of hospitality for killing me; and the sister hanged herself, after declaring it was not I who raped her, but another. So, my name cleared, my body was moved, upon the oracle's direction, from its shameful grave of a seducer, and put into a tomb in Locris.

And this was the inscription they made for me: "Ascra of the many cornfields was his native home, but in death the land of the horse-driving Minyans hold the bones of Hesiod, greatly renowned among all men judged by the test of wit."

So all men know I am not a liar, not a seducer or a man who abuses hospitality. Yet this tale I now tell is a tale I have told no soul, because the Devil cannot have such stories widely known. And I charge you, who hear it, to tell it sparingly and tell it well, for truth is a weapon against which no might can stand, not even the might of the Lord of Hell.

The Devil came to me, where I dwelled, a damned soul tending the Mourning Fields, and offered me this bargain: "Make me a great story, Hesiod. Make my Majesty shine like the Shield of Herakles, down through the ages. Make me a mythic hero; make my land proud and my laws like the laws that came down from Olympus in your day. Make a *Works and Days* for Hell, Hesiod, that will teach the damned souls how to behave and how to suffer, time unending. Teach them humility and patience, and bend them to my will. You who are the greatest teacher of homely values, bring your light to my darkness, and I will grant you any boon you ask that is within my power."

So I thought and thought, and I said to the Devil, "Come back another day, when I have had time to consider the problem you set me, and fair recompense. For I will not undertake a project I cannot complete, and I will not work for nothing."

You see, I did not trust the Devil, even then. He

is Hephaestus, when he appears to me, and this omen told me there was a trick in the deal, somewhere.

So the Devil went his way, and came back in seven days. Now, seven days in the Mourning Fields are like seven lifetimes. I had no knowledge, then, of other places in Hell. I had just found my way through Hades, where I had seen many blind men and deaf men and men looking for lopped off limbs—ghosts of men who could not give up their earthly concerns but hovered, ousted from life and unfit even for death, waiting for resignation to come upon them.

So when I found the Mourning Fields, and the Tree of the Unborn, I thought that the horrid plain would forever be my lot, that my ears would hear eternally the wailing, and that my eyes would never see another thing fit for poetry.

The Devil never plays a single soul fair. This I knew, for near the Mourning Fields is accursed Troy, and though I could not reach its battle plain, often I could hear the warring and the dying, the clashes of bronze and the screaming of men and horses, and the roar of the Minotaur disturbed my rest exceedingly all the time I wandered there.

When the Devil came again, he was Hephaestus in the flesh, all glowing eyes and blistered skin and majesty. On his chest was a cuirass depicting all the tortures of Hell, and these were myriad. The serpent was there, and the great bulls of Hades, and there also were the Fates and the cities of the Damned. I looked upon this cuirass and saw many awful wonders that theretofore I had not dreamed existed.

So I said to the Devil, "There is more to Hell than these fields of mine. I must be freed from here, if I am to even think about enfaming you in noble poetry. Let me wander Hell for just one year, and come back to me. If there is a way to satisfy your requirements, and make a *Works and Days* to guide the citizens of Hell through their seasons, then in a year I will know it."

The Devil agreed to this, though smoke issued from his mouth and he pounded on his great long sword in frustration.

So for a year I wandered, up and down the country, and visited many cities of the damned. At the end of that year, I was in Athens, when the Devil came back to me. And in Athens, I had learned that there was much more of Hell than I had yet seen.

So I said to the Devil, "I have made a terrible mistake. A year is not long enough to view the manifold nature of Hell in all its horrid glory. I have not seen the teeming cities of the West; I have not been among the cosmopolitan dead of New Hell, of whom everyone here speaks. I have not seen the Celestial Kingdom of the slant-eyed people, or the jungle temples of the brown people, or the pyramids of the ancient people. Nor have I seen the face of the Moon, which is rumored to be part of Your domain, nor the Underworlds which lie below our feet, or even the great monuments of neverending sand. Until I have seen every way that souls live in Hell, I cannot in good conscience commit myself, lest I fail in giving them good guidance."

At this, the Devil became wroth. He turned into a great serpent with twelve legs and wings as wide as the Mourning Fields themselves. From his fanged jaws came out a bellow that shook some dead from the Tree of the Unborn, so loud it was. In one claw he picked me up, and into the air of Hell he sprang.

In the Devil's clutches, I did fly, over all the Hellish landscape, and the bellows of his dragon's mouth told me to "Look well, Hesiod, upon My Kingdom, down below."

But my eyes were tearing from the cold and the wind, and the Devil's claws had pierced my belly, so that soon I died there, impaled in his furious grasp.

When I awoke in New Hell, I was taken to him straightaway. Now he was no more a dragon, but Hephaestus pounding on his forge. The hammer in his hand could have crushed my skull, and this he pointed at me as he said, "A decision, Hesiod. I must have your decision."

But I had died in Hell, and every time a soul dies here, he learns. I knew what I had to fear, I thought, and fresh from the jaws of death's restless sleep, I was emboldened. So I said to the Devil, "I have learned a great deal, but not enough. I must find out more. Give me another year, here among the newcomers to damnation, to learn if I can satisfy your needs."

The Devil threw down his hammer and the whole world shook. He snarled and he raged, and he said at last to me, "There are things in Hell you do not want to see, Hesiod. There are great blocks of ice that can crush you, that can chase you across the landscape for eternity, with no death in sight to save you. There are dragons in whose stomach you will not die after you are eaten, but only boil in acid, never seeing another soul but those who are lunched upon. There are worse fates than that, even . . . there is New Hell itself, where time is not trustworthy and no soul finds a friend."

"Then, Lord, as you have just shown me, I must see all of this—and survive. Else no manual of comportment, no wise hints and noble philosophy, will touch the hearts of your subjects, for they will say, 'This is for men less damned than me.' "

At this the Devil laughed, and that laugh cracked three of my teeth, which have pained me ever since.

But he said, "Another year, overzealous Hesiod, and then your time of quandary is at an end—one way or the other."

Thus once more I saved myself from the Devil's scheme, and went abroad, a free soul still. This time, I walked among the wondrous artifacts and possessions of the New Dead, and learned that they suffered differently than we.

Among the denizens of New Hell I met men from thousands of years, men from godless times, men from times when every man was a god. I met men who thought to mold Hell itself, and to outwit the Devil forever. I met men who worshipped machines, and men who worshipped only their power over other men. And among the New Dead, I met no one who was kind, no one who was patient, no one who cared for anything outside his door.

So when the Devil came again, I was in my den, with my stereo videotape machine, watching war movies with Anwar Sadat and an American cowboy who smoked cigarettes incessantly. We had been expecting the Devil, so my friends, having given me good counsel and sage advice as to what I might say when the Lord of Hell arrived, left by the back door as Satan began materializing.

As was his wont, Satan garbed himself in the image of Hephaestus, and with a snap of his fingers, my apartment disappeared, to become his subterranean forge. This time, he was forging an effigy of me, smiting it repeatedly.

And every time he smote its head, my head felt the hammer strike.

"What excuse," said the Devil, "have you for me this time?" *Clang* went the hammer upon the iron head of my likeness; black went everything before my eyes. "Well, Hesiod, speak up!" *Clang!*

When my vision cleared, I was holding my temples, but I said bravely, "I am ready to concede that such a book can be written, ignoble Lord. But—"

Clang! "But *what*, foolish damned slave!"

"But such a book," I said slyly, "should not be written in Hell—certainly not published in Hell."

Clang! Clang! "Are you telling me *no?*" *Clang!* "If you are, I assure you, Hesiod, you will eternally regret it."

My head felt as though one more hammerstrike would split my very skull. "No, Sire, I am not saying that," I hurried to protest. And, shameful though it is to tell, I fell down on my knees before the Devil—a matter of the pain I was in, not any weakness of my spirit.

"Then," said the Devil, putting down his hammer to hunker over me, "what *are* you saying, Hesiod?"

"I am saying," I gasped through the pain, "that a *Works and Days* for the damned must be composed, and published, among the living and by the living, and for the living—otherwise, it cannot become mythology, part of the human record, truth without argument, or the true rules of Hell."

When the Devil did not immediately reach for his hammer to smite me, I rushed on. "All things in Hell, if those I have seen are not in error, are born on Earth—all the ways of men, all the hearts of men, all the knowledge of men and the behavior of men is minted while they live, not after they die. Therefore, for such a work to be taken seriously, to become a part of men like the other beliefs that drive them here, that work must be learned by them while they live. They must learn the fear of You, the respect of You, the rules of You . . . before they die. Hence, they will obey them, for it will not be a matter of their choice. Do men choose to do again in Hell what they have done in life? They do not. It is habit born of expectation. They must expect to bend their knee to you, to serve you forever, to be your humble citizens. They must find it the unbreakable bond that guides them, as my race finds its heritage, and every other race adheres to its own divergent lore."

Instead of punishing me, the Devil stroked his chin with black-clawed fingers. "Go on, Hesiod; go on."

"I propose to write the book, to get it published, to make it as much a part of man as Olympus in her glories, as Hephaestus himself, as Troy and the Russian Revolution, as Nagasaki and Pompeii . . . I propose to teach them, while they live, how they should die, and prepare themselves for Hell. Then, they will do it, as men always do what they have been taught. And when they come here, they will not be so troublesome as they are now, for they will know what they have learned, what they have earned, and what they must expect. After all, every soul here has chosen Hell, by his deeds—what they do not do is admit to it." It seemed simple, the way I put it.

"Let me see if I understand you," said the Devil, clacking his claws. "You wish a furlough. You wish to go back to life, to write my book, to make it spread upon the land among the living, and then *come back*? Freely, of your own accord?"

"Could you not bring me back forcibly, if I were so foolish as to try to trick you? Is there any way a mere mortal damned soul can confound the powers of eternity? Of course, I will come back. You will bring me back, when you decide, for as I do not know how to leave here, I do not know how to return."

Sadat had said the Devil might agree; the cowboy had been doubtful. But all of us thought this ploy was worth a try. If men were warned, would they not change their ways? If Hell was proved to lie at the end of evil, might evil be not so common among men?

We thought it so, fools that we were. And thus I struck this bargain with the Devil, who agreed to furlough me among the living, and even decided where and when:

"I will put you in twentieth-century New York, a part of America where much publishing is done. You will need to write in English, but that should be no problem. But I warn you Hesiod, I will not lift a hand to help you, and this is your final reprieve. One more year you get, a year among the living. At the end of that time, the book must be written. It must suit my purpose. If it does not, or you fail me in any other way, I will put you in a Hell so circumscribed that your soul will shrivel with boredom, and from it you will not escape until there are two of you, side by side."

And then, with no more preparation than that, the Devil spat me out of Hell.

I found myself on a busy streetcorner, cacaphonous and chaotic. The wind was foul and full of dirt; there was hardly any air to breathe, and around me no one else was wearing just a robe and sandals, though the day was hot.

I looked up, and buildings towered over me, scratching the sky. It was like New Hell, this city of New York, and in it I was a lost soul.

I wandered all those first days, and slept under a bridge in the woods in the center of the town, until I found a place that would take the gold coins of Hell. Then I settled into a garret and I wrote and wrote. I wrote for a month; I wrote for two months; I wrote for three months and the weather was getting cold.

I wrote until my money ran out, and then I wrote

some more. In the dead of winter, I finished my book *Labors and Pennance*, and began taking it around to the publishers in New York, for I could not find an agent to do this for me, although I joined the Pen Club, where writers meet, to help me find a friend.

In New York are mostly Amerikanoi and these do not know friendship. There is no guesting there, and people are afraid of one another. Most of the writers I met were terrified that I would steal their thoughts; the others were jealous of their positions, and no one helped anyone, whoever that man might be.

Worse, no one believed me when I said who I was. I might have given up, but I had an entire paperbox filled with cautions meant to keep mankind from Hell, an exposition of what awaited men if they failed to heed me.

So I went from publisher to publisher, and to a man they accused me of plagiarizing ancient texts—my own. One woman told me that there was no market for "this sort of stuff anymore," and suggested that I write a "romance, about ancient Greece if you like—you know the period. Just make sure there's plenty of sex and violence, that the p.o.v. character's a woman—and that the sentences are short. Your sentences are way too long."

I did not even ask this crone what a "p.o.v." was, and I still have not found out. But I'm sure I would not have liked the answer that this Madison Avenue woman would have given me, for by then I was very angry.

I went that day, in snow that gusted like a white curtain over the city, to the Metropolitan Museum, to be among the artifacts that reminded me of home. There I met, by chance, someone from the department that oversaw my century, for I was mumbling prayers before a votive tripod and he noticed me.

I tried to tell him who I was, but he became unfriendly. I tried to give him my book to read, but he called a guard. I was ousted ignominiously from the museum, which had been the single place in that horrid city I felt at home.

Then I went back to putting my work before publishers. From them I received the news that I had no talent whatsoever, that I should think of working in "academia," that there was no "market for this classical stuff unless you're dead or famous," and a suggestion to try an "occult" publisher.

So I went to such a place, where purported Devilworshippers were, and there I found no one who worshipped the Devil at all, but only men bilking other men.

By then, I was out of money entirely. I'd sold everything I had, even my warm coat, and I was eating in a soup kitchen. There, I found two men who read my book, but neither of them could stop drinking long enough to tell me what they thought of it.

One day, during the dirty depths of what seemed an endless winter, I fell into the snow, and an ague overtook me.

In the shelter of a mission, on a cot in a room with three hundred other homeless wanderers, I coughed myself to death, still holding my paperbox with the manuscript within.

And I woke up facing Hephaestus again, who was wroth with me beyond words for having failed.

Not only had my work remained unpublished by the living, but the paramedics who carted my dead husk away cast the manuscript aside, into some handy trashbin, so I had nothing at all to show the Devil.

Satan listened to my tale of woe without a spark of pity in his glowing eyes, and then he banished me to the outreach Hells, to the Nile Valley, to Akhetaten where I have dwelled ever since, where no new stories ever happened, where most things worth telling could not be told.

And I could have dealt with all the punishment, with the misery of telling bawdlerized tales to the children of the royal family, unto eternity, if only my book had not been lost. And I say to you, if you could only read it, that it would make a difference in your life. Without it, I am a rotted shell, a poured out rind, an empty man. For my punishment from the Devil was never to be able to record a single tale again, not on paper, not on clay, not even on stone.

So recall this story, you who hear it, and tell it in the old way, mouth to mouth, and I, Hesiod, who once was a great poet, will be eternally in your debt.

Hesiod dropped his head and his shoulders shook. In the silence, we could hear Nichols, who had fallen asleep during the tale's telling, snoring.

My own hands were shaking. It was Confucius who kicked Nichols, so that the affronting snores would stop. I could not think of a single thing to say to Hesiod. I certainly could not tell him of my mission, of my book in progress, or of my own deal with the Devil.

Confucius must have thought the same. He looked me straight in the eye and slowly shook his head. Then he told Hesiod, "That was a stirring tale, and I will always remember it. The truth of it is beyond doubt, and the wisdom of the man who told it is unparalleled. But tell me this: am I mistaken, or do you imperil yourself by telling us this story?"

Hesiod stood up on the raft then, a foolish thing to

do in any case, and stepped backward. "Imperil?" His voice was choked. "What difference does it make? What have I left to lose? You have freed me from stultifying Akhetaten, and for that I am grateful, but—" He took another step backward, and over-balanced as his questing foot went off the raft.

Behind him, up out of the water in a sudden and noisy burst, sprang a great crocodile with a wide open mouth. The jaws of this croc were so huge, at first I thought I dreamed it.

But Hesiod did not. His arms flailing, he screamed as he fell backward, into the waiting crocodile's maw.

Confucius lunged to save him, and that further unbalanced the raft, which brought everyone awake. Nichols tackled Confucius and brought him down, holding him to the raft and safety.

But I hardly noticed. My eyes were fixed upon the swirling water with its phosphorescent foam. A moment ago, Hesiod had been there, his trunk in the jaws of a crocodile, his limbs flailing.

And now he was not. There was nothing to be seen but the bubbly surface of the river as it settled.

Nichols came to me, soon after, and told me there was nothing I could do.

"I know that," I snapped. "Can't a man mourn a friend in peace?" But then I remembered that Americans had no true friends, only friends of convenience, and I apologized to Nichols, who had already turned his back on me.

No one slept that night. Nichols gave a report on what had befallen Hesiod to Welch, who was angry in his quiet way, and Tanya wept kindly tears for the departed poet.

This allowed me to thank her for mourning my friend, and thus began the mending of our tempers, although nothing on the journey was ever the same for me after that. Hesiod had sacrificed his current life, perhaps his freedom, to tell me that story, and I did not fail to understand the warning between its lines.

The Devil does not like to be tricked, nor to have his secrets told about, and I was planning to do all of that.

As for the caution invoked by Hesiod's tale, it was balanced by the fury roused in me by my friend's fate. The Devil might be the Devil, but to treat a poet so is to defile the very act of creation. My resolve hardened, on that night, to see my project through to the very end.

And Confucius knew my mind, for he said, "Anger blinds the heart. Slow, steady progress is the way." The sage took my hand that night, the first night we poled the raft despite the darkness.

I was grateful for his manly touch, for his sorrow, for his bravery. Only we two really knew what was at risk for us in Thebes. The others only knew they didn't want to spend the night where giant, hungry crocodiles chose to feed.

Chapter 17: Home Is Where The Heroes Are

The thing no one among our party recognized soon enough, was that the very Nile was becoming treacherous, as if the Devil caused the land and water of it to turn against us.

Alexander, who had disciplined the river previously, must have had some inkling. Not only was he the first to realize that the towns along the shore were changing, but the night before we reached Thebes he volunteered a camp story about the *other* Thebes— Boetian Thebes, where Alexander had been exiled six years in his youth.

"Then it joined Athens in a revolt against Macedonia," Alexander said in a voice with no boyishness about it, "and I tore the city stone from stone, for its punishment. The Sacred Band came from there and I destroyed them too, at Chaeronea, where they stood shoulder to shoulder against my cavalry."

"This ain't the same Thebes we're going to, right?" said Nichols impatiently.

And that was when Alexander looked bemused,

and lowered his long-lashed lids in the firelight, and said, "I hope beyond hope you're right. But this place looks increasingly like Boetia, and less and less like Egypt." He raised a defiant head. "Remember, I have been to Egypt before. Egyptian Thebes was still a city of repute when I was here. The Nile is too small now, she is not the river she was when I was alive—or when we started upriver with Lawrence."

"What do you mean, Alexander?" said Welch, coming up on an elbow.

Said Tanya, who seldom spoke freely around the fire: "He means just what he says, *sir*. It doesn't look right to him."

"It don't look right to me, neither," Nichols agreed under his breath, gnawing at the grouse we'd killed for dinner. "Remember Ilion, Welch—remember the way the topography played tricks."

"Easy, Nichols. Easy," said Welch, and then: "I still don't remember as much of Troy as I should." He looked at me, then at Confucius, and explained: "Somebody on that mission dosed me with Lethe water, or so we've gathered. Anyhow, what they're talking about, these veterans of the Second Trojan War, is the way the lay of the land went crazy— rivers moving in their courses, becoming the shores of the Aegean; Troy's citadel, and Greek mainland features, melding into Mycenae, and such."

"And such?" Confucius repeated. "And such?"

"Such wonders—or travesties," Alexander tried to reinterpret Welch's explanation, "were common on the battle plain, indeed in all of the Hellenic Hells. I can't warrant that the same thing is happening here, but it feels the same. There is a queasiness to my stomach, a feeling of great events to come. But by my soul, I hope it isn't Boetia—I have enemies aplenty in that Thebes. The Nile's city would suit me better."

"I do not understand how you can talk so cavalierly of cities exchanging places." Confucius was disturbed.

"Don't you smell the air, venerable sage?" said the boy king who'd campaigned in foreign lands for most of his life. "Does it smell like Nile air to you? Where is the fetid river smell? The marsh gas? The mix of animal feces and mulch? And where is the dry air blowing over from the deserts, the occasional parched gust full of ancient dust? And where is the very breadth of the Nile itself? It is a wellspring to its nation, and this place is but a trickle. Hardly more than a creek."

"Some creek," Nichols objected, shifting uncomfortably and reminding me that the Amerikanoi had seen the battle plain of Ilion as Hell had reconstructed it. So had Alexander, who had first met Achilles and Diomedes there.

"Confucius and I have no experience with lands that remake themselves or with palaces that turn into other places," I reminded the others, "or with anything such as you warriors saw at Troy together. Tell us of the dangers, that we may be ready, in case Alexander is right and we wake up tomorrow to face a different landscape."

"No way," Welch decreed. "That mission's classified." He crossed his arms.

"Classified as what?" Confucius asked. "A triumph or a failure?"

"Classified as in we ain't tellin' you squat because you got no need to know," Nichols responded savagely. Nichols was the most discomfitted of the party by the thought that the river under our raft and the land to which we were anchored might betray us.

In his face, as he struggled to control his feelings, I saw a hero of the sort few bards ever sing about:

Nichols wanted only not to show his misery, not to share his mystery, to *be* as he wished to appear: a man in whose hands your fate was safe if brawn and courage could win the day; a man you could give a task and consider it, as of that moment, done.

Tanya had her hand on Welch's arm and was soothing the American leader, who had been looking stolidly into the fire since he admitted he did not remember much of Troy. How must it be to lose an adventure you have paid dearly to endure?

I could not bear to think of that. It frightened me too much. I had crossed the Lethe with Heraclitus, who had lost so much to the waters. My heart went out to Welch, who seemed to be wrestling with his mind as if determination could part the Lethe's clouds and give him back what the waters had stolen.

Alexander whispered something into Tanya's ear. She smiled gratefully and nodded, then pulled Welch back into the shadows, where she could stroke his hair and kiss him.

At this, Alexander said, "It's true we shouldn't talk about Ilion, lest it be an omen and we call down a like fate upon us. But I will tell you the story of what happened after that, when I was still with Diomedes in the Achaean Hells, if Welch and Nichols do not mind."

"Will it clarify this quandary of moving rivers and mountains remaking their citadels and their summits?" Confucius wanted to know.

"I told you, revered sage, what I proposed to do. Give me a yes or a no, you and Homer. If yes, I'll give you my tale. If not, you'll give me one of yours. The night is yet deep and sleep far away."

Welch and Nichols gave their assent, and I said, "For Confucius' benefit, let me introduce the hero, Diomedes. His history in life was as follows: Son of

Tydeus and Diopyle, he was a bold counselor and fierce fighter during the first Trojan war, and left the war a hero. With Odysseus, at a later time, he murdered kings and restored other kings to their thrones. He came home from the war with Nestor, my mother's father, so I know this from tales told at my own hearth. He was one of sons of the Epigoni, and as a Son of the Seven, he took part in the second expedition against Thebes—Boetian Thebes—with Adrastus. With Odysseus, he stole the Palladium from Troy, it's said, but no one knows the truth of that. What is certain is that, on his return to Argos, he found that his wife, Aegialeia, was unfaithful, and roamed to Italy. There, his companions were turned into birds and this disheartened him, a fighting man who had led men all his life. Of his death and afterlife, Alexander may well know more than I." I bowed my head, inclining it to the youthful king, who blushed.

And Alexander said, quoting from my *Iliad:* " 'The sons of the Achaeans who held Argos and Tiryns, Hermoine and Asine of the deep bay, and Troezen, Eiones, and vine-clad Epidauris, and island Aegina, and Mases—all these followed strong-voiced Diomedes, son of Tydeus. With them were other leaders, but Diomedes was their chief of eighty dark ships wherein were men skilled in fighting, Argives with linen jerkins, the very goads of war.' "

Then he smiled at me, and with humility as only a king can muster, said, "Homer, you have asked for a tale, but to tell one to you, in these circumstances, is daunting. Like teaching mathematics to Aristotle, or making my own magic geometry. But I will try, if you'll bear with me, to give you some sense of what it was like in that Hell where we fought for Troy, once the battling was done. Just promise you will not

take it ill, or laugh at the poor quality of my story—I
am no poet, but merely a king who died too young."

The winning smile of Alexander could melt the
Devil's heart, if he'd just try it. It melted mine, and
both Confucius and I assured Alexander we wanted
nothing more than to hear his tale.

And it was more like an oracle of things to come
than a story, although none of us, except perhaps the
pragmatic Nichols with his superstitious soul, understood that then. Nichols said nothing, only sat drinking down his beer and worrying our fire with a stick
that wasn't reed, but cypress, as Alexander's story
haltingly began:

IN SEARCH OF THESEUS

Diomedes, the tall fair hero who had brought me to
Troy, stayed on there when the war was done, with
Helen, his cousin. Because they invited me to bide
with them, and no home was there for me in Hell, I
accepted their hospitality.

This I did because, in those days, Bucephalus was
with me and anything seemed possible. It even
seemed possible that I, Alexander, a modern man
next to the fabled citizens of myth, could make a
home among the very hills where my favorite saga
had raged.

I knew as much of Troy as any man who fought
there—and more than most who'd only heard of it,
having carried Homer's works with me throughout
my world and all my conquering. Though I knew so
much, I did not know that Helen and Diomedes
would fall out with one another, when the first flush
of lust had faded.

This happened, and Diomedes' wanderlust overtook him. He wanted to find his own home, he said, long-lamented Argos. He wanted to see if his wife was there. And he wanted, he confided one night before the echoing hearth of Troy's sacked citadel, to find his companions, who had been turned into birds while he lived.

There was guilt in the man as deep as Tartarus, over this ancient loss, and his eyes were pits of torture when he confided to me where his heart was leading him. "No one can hold this place, this Troy that is not Troy. I was foolish to try. It will find a way to shed more blood; that lust is in the very stones here. And Helen is a creature of this battle who can never leave, nor care for any man not fighting off an army for her. There are other suitors for her, other fools to fight here. I say to you, Alexander, you take your fleet-footed Bucephalus, and I'll take one of my bright-maned steeds, and we'll go venturing, to see how wide and broad this Hellenic Hell is."

"What can it hurt?" I encouraged him. "We will, at worst, come upon the borders of this land, or ride around until we find the Mourning Fields again, or tunnels leading to stranger Hells. I will go with you anywhere you say."

This was foolish, for I was not so restless as the Argive. I did not think then about all that befell Diomedes after the first war. No, I did not think of his bloody legends. I thought only of the honor, and the adventure. And anyway, Helen did not like me in her house, though Diomedes tried to hide this.

So we two men rode off one morning, provisioned and full of song, alone. It was not until we had crested the first round hill, and passed the first domed tomb of ancient Greece, that Diomedes said, "I hate to go forth without a destination. I have heard that somewhere hereabouts lies the very castle of Theseus.

He is to me as you once said I was to you—a legend, an image, a hero whose exploits are a goad to my labors. Shall we seek him and see if he is just a man?"

There was humor in Diomedes' eyes, for it had taken me a long time to accept that my heroes were simply men of prowess, and that I had a rightful place among them.

"If we cannot find Athene and get you to introduce me to her," I teased back, for Diomedes' relationship with that goddess was what had made him more than mortal in my mind's eye, all those years.

"We'll find a gate of Hell before we find My Lady in it," he said, laughing, and spurred his bright-maned steed so that Bucephalus squealed and lunged forward to catch up.

We rode until we tired, and slept and rode again, and all was well—normal land, a town here and there of no particular significance, where people plowed the land and made the seasonal sacrifices. Then when we were thinking we'd headed the wrong way, since there was no glint of the cerulean sea to our left or right, we began to come upon the signs.

First, we heard the unmistakable bellowing of the Minotaur—unmistakable to any man who'd ever heard it before, as we had. Then, the Marathonian bull of Herakles attacked us, and we had to kill him. Soon after, just as in legend, we found a woman dead in the barn where the bull belonged.

Now I was getting nervous, having been in the Labyrinth, as no man should have to be, so we decided to stop for a night and think over our decision. We stopped at a farmhouse and a woman offered us hospitality. Her name was Medea and we should have known, by that, that we were already in too deep. But in the morning, sick and poisoned, as we crawled out of her hut, we saw the sea.

There on the dunes were Amazons and Centaurs, playing. And these saw us and gave chase. If not for the speed of Bucephalus, I would not have escaped, to go back and rescue Diomedes from these women and their half-animal lovers. But I did, and as I cut his bonds, the very vault of Hell grew dark and low and quaked about us.

"The lower reaches—Gods, Alexander, I had forgotten about Persephone and her husband!"

We ran on foot across ground that opened up and tried to swallow us, with the Amazons and the Centaurs in hot pursuit.

If Bucephalus had not followed after us on his own, we would be imprisoned by the animal-men and their single-breasted women yet. But Bucephalus knew that the Amazons and Centaurs meant me harm; he jumped a wide, smoking chasm to bend his knee for me to mount.

Diomedes' horse was lost to the eye, perhaps swallowed by the bleeding, broken earth which spouted blazing blood. He clambered up behind me and Bucephalus jumped across the flaming rent in the fundament just as the whole world began to shake as though to burst apart.

Then out of the steam and the cracking of the earth came a growl like the Devil's belly. And before Bucephalus, screaming as he picked his way along the treacherous ground, a staircase opened up.

These were stairs like the gods might hew, only they opened out of the ground and led down, not up.

But there was no place else to go, only splitting land aflame and certain death all around.

So I urged Bucephalus, and he agreed to carry us down those stairs. Carefully, my mount picked his way, with both of us sitting hunched and very still, lest our balance make his job the harder. Horses don't like staircases, and Bucephalus was no different about that than any lesser steed.

We descended and descended, and around the staircase curved, until we couldn't see the sky at all, just stairs we had already trod. Farther we went, until it occurred to me that we did not have to ride him down this difficult descent. So I slipped off one side of him, and Diomedes slipped off the other, and, hands locked over his poll, we proceeded, side by side, down into darkness.

How long we walked, I cannot say. Long enough for Diomedes to regret involving me in danger; long enough for me to say I would not have let him get away without me.

"What can happen to us?" I said boldly, on those unknowable stairs. "We are already dead."

"Hush," said Diomedes. "Do not tempt the gods of Hell."

Perhaps it was that rash statement, but soon enough old Hades himself appeared to us, at the place where the staircase ended. He appeared to us as Pluto, Persephone's husband, and Pluto we recognized him to be. He had Pluto's golden chariot and four huge black horses that made Bucephalus seem small. He had black armor on his huge chest and black greaves and a black stare that stopped us in our tracks.

"Tartarus, is it, for you two?" he said in a thunderous voice.

Tartarus, the sunless abyss, was not the destination I had in mind. I said, "We're looking for Theseus."

"Ah, two more rescuers for my wife, Persephone, is it?" The laugh came again, this time making Bucephalus snort. "Well, you want the Elysian Fields then, but don't get too comfortable: once she's decided against you, you're mine."

Diomedes elbowed me before I could say any more, and we started to edge forward, each of us with a hand on Bucephalus' bridle, in the direction that Pluto pointed.

Only, as we passed him, a great spider dropped on each of us, and spun one length of web about each of our waists, and then scurried up into the dark vault again.

I tugged at the loop around my waist. It was sticky and strong.

"So you don't get lost," chuckled the huge voice of Pluto. "When your time is up, we can't have you loitering where sinners don't belong."

I had been thinking that perhaps Bucephalus could be loosed in those fields, but now I knew I shouldn't do it. I must have Bucephalus to get me out of what I had walked into, bold and brazen, with Diomedes by my side.

So we traveled, seeing not one damned soul, down a long corridor that lightened at its ending.

We traveled until my feet grew blistered and my lips parched, for we had used up all the provisions Bucephalus was carrying. And we traveled more, for there were only the spiders and Pluto behind us, and that staircase which might or might not still be there.

Eventually we came to the end of the tunnel, and there before us were the fabled Elysian Fields, where sweet zephyrs blew all the day.

But as Bucephalus snorted at the clovery fragrance in his nostrils, the fields disappeared, and in their stead was a daunting citadel on a sheer mount of grassless rock.

Here too were stairs. These were climbed, Bucephalus tight in between us, because we would not leave the horse behind, and yet there was barely room for the three of us to climb abreast.

When we reached the pinnacle, we were exhausted, and no one would come to answer our pounding on the door.

The descent, when we turned the horse around, made Bucephalus squeal with trepidation.

Diomedes said, "I'm sorry, Alexander, but we'll have to blindfold him." And I knew he was sorry for more than that—for involving me in a trip to even darker Hells that seemed to be neverending rock and awful loneliness.

"Do you think this is a trap? We cannot go down with this tired horse; we cannot get into the castle. What shall we do?"

In answer, Diomedes drew his sword. "There is no building that cannot be entered, no wall that cannot be breached, if you have the stomach for it."

I did. I got out my own sword and we prepared to storm unknown battlements, but as I was laying back for my first stroke, the door opened, and Persephone herself stood there.

"Rescuers, is it?" she said in exasperation. "I keep telling Father Zeus, it won't do any good." She stamped her foot. Her hand went to her girdled hips. She pouted.

Then a man came to stand beside her, if that is what he can be called. He was great and wide, and full of scars. His face, once handsome, was now grizzled from war and cares. His locks were long and once golden, but now like straw. Only his eyes were young, and these were full of challenge.

But as he looked from me, to Bucephalus, who had flattened his ears and bared his teeth, to Diomedes, those eyes changed. He said, "Dear, I think these are not the ordinary rescuers. We'll have them, and their steed, as guests. Tell the stablemaster to come up and get the horse."

"That won't be necessary," said Diomedes. "We have come to the wrong place."

"I think not," said the faded man who once, by his stature, was truly godlike. "I think you've found just what you were looking for. Dear, get those silly cobwebs off them."

The woman came over her threshold toward us, and as she did, the landscape around us changed. Instead of barren rocks, there now were glorious fields once more, and fair sky above, and birds that sang came swooping low.

"I'm Persephone," she said, "I hope you enjoy your stay with us." Her fingers touched the spider-rope around my waist and it fell away. She touched Diomedes', and it did the same.

More, it changed to golden rope which she picked up and handed to me. "For your magnificent horse. Make him a proper halter for tonight. And do come in, come in. This my good and noble lover—"

"Theseus, the ancestor," said Diomedes. "I know."

"And we," I said as we all went through the high doors, "are Diomedes," I nodded to my companion, "and Alexander, men lost in Hell and seeking friends."

"Seeking what?" Theseus laughed. "There are no friends here, young gentlemen, but only lovers." He squeezed his woman's waist and kissed her high-piled hair. "I am here, you know, of my own accord. I spend half my time here, with her, while her father, Zeus, sends endless rescuers to sweep her out of Pluto's domain, a task I failed."

"We know," said Diomedes quietly, his eyes misty, for now he looked upon a hero of his youth. "But I thought you had made a final peace."

"That's legend. The underworld is real. This is our

home," he said and spread his hand. "And I am content enough with it."

"What do you do the rest of the year?" I asked the foolish question.

"Suffer," said Theseus, "like any other damned fool. And think of her, in Pluto's arms . . ."

"But let's not talk of that," smiled Persephone brightly. "When we're together, it doesn't matter."

And her lover said, under his breath, "When we're apart, it breaks my heart."

So we spent a night with Theseus, in his castle, and from every window we could see a different sight of Hell, depending on whether Persephone was in the room, or not.

"In the morning," Theseus said, "I'll see you safely out of here. But you must promise never to return, and never to recommend this trek to others. You have caught us on a good day. Above, mosttimes, there are Amazons and beast-men, and there is Medea, the witch, and there are perils you know not—"

"We came by all those, even met Pluto," Diomedes interjected.

"Who are you again?" said the grizzled veteran.

"Kings," I explained.

"Warriors of small repute," Diomedes said.

"Which is it?" Theseus asked with a wistfulness in his voice I heard but did not yet understand.

"A bit of both," said Diomedes.

"Tell me more," said Theseus with undisguised longing in his voice.

So we did. We told tales in turn until our throats were raw, and every tale we told made Theseus thirst for more.

Finally Diomedes asked, "How is it you are so

starved for news of the country? Do you not go abroad when your half-year here is done?"

"Ssh," said noble Theseus. "She might be listening." Then he leaned forward and revealed the sorriest secret I have ever heard in Hell: "When I leave here, she goes to Pluto's bed and I go to my tomb. So many men have bound me to it with prayer and sacrifice, so many have touched my bones and moved them, that I am the servant of the petitioning damned. I lie half a year in my tomb and there I hear their cries. And I remember everything I've heard, lying in the earth, until I rise again. While I'm here I do the best I can for those who've asked me to intercede for them—with her husband, Pluto, who has cursed me so."

It was horrid. Neither rest nor torture, life nor death, being or nonbeing, for half of every year? Just because his love would not let him forsake the maiden, nor her eyes turn upon another.

"Surely," Diomedes said, "no woman is worth that."

"Perhaps not," said Theseus. "But better a half a year of love and kisses than a year lying in that tomb, without even the strength to close my eyes. Have you ever listened to your hair grow? Your nails? I do not recommend it. Only she keeps me sane, and only I keep her from rebelling against her husband. It serves us. Now, tell me more of the myriad Hells in all their profundity. And, on my way to my tomb, I will spread the glad news of variety and activity to all of those like me, who cannot go abroad but must bide in the personal hells they have made."

So we told Theseus everything we could remember, about every place we'd ever been, and soon we realized that another day had come and gone, and it was night again.

That night he said to us, "Tell me more tales of the

many Hells you have seen, and of the people you have met who are damned for different reasons, and what those reasons might be."

So we told him all of that, until the night was done again.

This time, in the morning, Diomedes scratched his beard and said to me, "Get the horse."

I did not argue, but obeyed. When I came up into the central court from the subterranean stables, I saw Persephone weeping and Theseus barring Diomedes' way.

So I went up to them with Bucephalus in hand and I said gently, "Your name is hallowed, Theseus. You are an example to men of all epochs. Men revere your bravery, your wisdom, your kindness. Do not despoil all of that, simply because you are lonely."

He did not acknowledge me, but stood with glaring eyes before his gate, arms crossed. So I turned to his woman and I said, "This man has given up so much for you; don't let him give up his legend, his honor."

Then I smiled at her pleadingly, so that her heart softened unto us, and she went to her lover, who nearly wept when she begged him to keep his word and bring us safely by her husband and out of this land of his.

"But Persephone, I will lose you, until next year. I will not be able to get back, but must go straightaway to my tomb. Your husband will come to you and caress you, and this time will be lost to us forever."

She said to him, "Real love is never lost, Theseus. You of all men know that."

Thereupon the hero crumbled under her onslaught, and kissed her all over, before he opened the gates and walked away with us, not looking back, his eyes full of unshed tears.

With Theseus as our guide, Pluto did not obstruct us. No spiders came down from the vault to entangle us as we found the staircase.

When we had climbed it, only the witch, Medea, waited on the scoured plain under a scarlet sky. She held out a gnarled hand, much older than her face, and said, "Ah, early this year, Theseus. Come, come, your cozy grave is waiting. And I've longer to tuck you into it."

Theseus never looked back, or said another word to us, but walked, stoop-shouldered, with the witch across the steaming plain.

I wanted to go after him, to offer to help him escape his fate, but Diomedes said this to me: "No man escapes his fate. If he loses his tomb, he loses his half a year with his love. It is a choice only he can make."

And we parted there, where the grass began to grow again, Diomedes on foot and me with Bucephalus, although I offered to go with him.

"No," he said. "Alexander, our fates are not the same. I must seek my wife, and my friends ensorceled into birds. I have spent long enough avoiding my duties. Theseus has reminded me that a man is a man as long as he acts like one, even be that man in Hell."

We clasped hands and wrists and he walked away, toward Italy, I can only guess, calling back, "Take care of your Judge and await your moment, Alexander. You're the only man I know whom the gods love despite all that Hell can do."

I have not seen him since.

Having finished, Alexander took a drink and then

said, to me only, as if there were no others present. "I didn't understand what he meant then. Now I think I'm beginning to."

"That's why you think we'll come to the Thebes of your acquaintance?" I asked softly.

"If not on this trek, then on my next. I am bound to go there, one way or the other, before eternity has its final day."

"Ain't no such thing," said Nichols positively. "If I had a chopper or a sub here, I could prove it to you."

"Your word—and its comfort—are good enough for me," said Alexander, who rose and stretched.

As he did, I noticed that the sky was lightening. So I stood up and squinted around me. There I saw no great river, but a shrunken one, barely more than a stream.

Alexander was looking too, and Nichols rose up. "What the hell?" said the American.

"Thebes, I believe," said Alexander.

"Which one?" Welch had risen too.

Alexander looked at them as if the Amerikanoi had turned into donkeys, and said, "We will know that when we get there, will we not?"

Chapter 18: Six Against Thebes

Thebes lay against the river, and over it hung a pall of years. On the Nile side is Egyptian Thebes, where we entered, strolling up the avenue of sphinxes, and beyond, to the Temple of Amen, where the pylons are decorated with scenes from the battle of Kadesh. Here were palms and fragrant cypress, and here too was Karnak, the temple city of the priests, where we wandered among the giant columns and Alexander read out the ancient names of kings and queens and gods in their multitude.

At first no one remarked us, among tourists from everywhere, worshippers of every station, and the white-linened stream of priests.

Alexander wanted to stay right there, among the monuments. "This is Karnak, but not as she was in my day," he objected when Welch pulled him firmly into a shadowed niche.

Welch replied, "These are other days, Alexander. Remember Ptolemy? How will he feel, to see you?

And your other enemies. There are Romans here, can't you see?"

"Pharaoh or not, Ptolemy would never be my enemy. He will fall down before me and kiss my feet with joy. He will offer me my kingdom back, and—"

"You pushed all that bowing and scraping on your lieutenants in Asia," Welch said with cruel implacability. "Don't delude yourself; you made them kings, after you died—they're kings in Hell, not caretakers. If we ran across one, it would be you who did the bowing."

Alexander argued, saying Karnak was not the place for living Ptolemaic kings, and that Welch's little bit of knowledge fell far short of the hearts of men he'd only read about.

The passing Roman soldiers Welch had pointed out looked at us uneasily. They treated the Egyptian priests like rivals. Men were jostled. Men pushed back. There was too much tension in the air at Karnak for Welch to be persuaded we should stay.

So we left the temple city and went among the teeming streets, where there were every sort of Arab and Ethiop and Greek and Roman, leading camels and elephants and zebras and cats of divers types.

There were more cats in Thebes than even in Akhetaten. There were giant striped cats and giant spotted cats and giant black cats. There were lions with manes and lions without manes; there were crates of cats eating ibex and fish on every streetcorner. And there were snake charmers and wine-vendors and fortune-tellers and purveyors of amulets to make a man the favored son of whatever god of the underworld he chose.

And these gods, in the pantheon-ridden city of Thebes-near-the-river, were uncountable of face and form. The Underworld had changed throughout

Egypt's centuries, and local gods had met distant gods, bearing the fruit of melded gods. So we found a temple of Isis, and we found a temple of her son, Horus, and her husband, Osiris, right beside a mosque of Mohammed, and that next to a Roman shrine to Hadrian, some benefactor god who was once a king.

This was dizzying to me, and Confucius, who understood the worship of ancestors better, explained that many different races had set their ancestors' shrines on this hallowed ground.

"But this is Hell," I protested, as we walked in a group clustered close around Tanya, who looked nothing like any person we had seen.

"Exactly so," said Confucius, his hands once again thrust into his sleeves. "What better Hell for the devout than a Hell over which their own progenitors preside? But I think you will find there are no gods here, living or dead."

This brought Nichols' head around, for he had been listening to Welch explain that Osiris/Isis/Horus was a trilogy like the Christian one that Nichols had put his faith in, when Nichols was a man.

Thus Nichols, in his unfriendly manner, told Confucius, "The Devil's going to show up and bust our butts because we haven't found Enkidu or got our report written—that's god enough for me."

"Surely," said Alexander, stopping in his tracks, aghast, "you are not telling me—now—that you worship the Devil? That foul and fallen entity that spreads misery like a plague among the damned?"

"Worship, crap," Nichols retorted. "I know what power is, and who holds it. No, I don't cross H.I.M. if I can help it. So I'm sayin', let's bunk in somewhere and get our work done. Right now, let's start asking this bunch of stiffs if anybody's seen a guy who's hairy all over, name of Enkidu. There's six of us, let's find a place to crash, split up, and do some recon."

"Crash?" asked Alexander, looking at the sky.

"Sleep. Lodgings," Welch interpreted. "That's not a bad idea, but let's do it in the latest quarter we can find—Roman Egypt ought to be the most comfortable . . ."

Confucius, all this time, had been thinking about what Nichols had said, and what Alexander had said, and now he asked this question: "If these pharaohs claimed to be living gods, and were buried like gods, and had temples and have worshippers still, then why do they not qualify as true gods of the netherworld, to be ventured and respected like any others?"

"Because, Charlie," Nichols said through clenched jaws, "this here's a pagan city full of skirt-wearing crazies like I've had lots of trouble with in New Hell. Give me a bunch of Romans and a gaggle of Babylonians, and I know what to do with 'em." He bared his teeth and I remembered that, in New Hell, the Romans and Egyptians and Assyrians had power that made the Devil's Children step cautiously. "What these fools believe ain't nothin' to worry about, long as we don't get caught up in it."

Welch said, "Nichols is right, Confucius, though I'll ask you to excuse his bad manners. This is nasty territory, and we just keep moving until Tanya, Nichols or I tell you we think it's safe."

So we did that, stopping the occasional passerby who did not look too rich or powerful, to inquire about this Enkidu who had hair all over him.

But no one we asked remembered seeing or hearing about a hairy man from Uruk, not in any menagerie of any potentate, and not loose on any street in Thebes.

Through the maze of narrow lanes we went, among

the houses built against one another and atop one another and within one another, and eventually we came upon a royal thoroughfare, broad and wide. When we crossed this, we barely avoided being run down by men in chariots, racing, and Nichols cursed the Romans with an upraised fist.

Welch caught that fist in midair and wrestled it to Nichols' side. "That's enough, Nichols. You want trouble, we'll find some. But not here, not now."

"Yes, *sir*," said Nichols snidely. "Anything you say, sir," and subsided, seething.

I could not understand this sudden discord between two who usually seemed so comfortable together. As we walked I sidled in beside Tanya, and I asked, "What is wrong with them?"

Her eyes slid sideways and fixed me with a stare of surprise and calculation. First she said, "Nothing, Homer." Then she said, "Well, yes—something. You see, they're used to dealing with Romans and Egyptians—there are a number of such nationals in Hell's power structure. But they can't pull rank here, and that's easy to forget. They don't have their equipment, and they don't have air support or backup. Remember, this trip is a punishment for them—for us. It's meant to be humbling. Nichols wants to check in with the Roman powers, announce ourselves—get mission support. He's not entirely wrong. It would be quicker. But Welch is sure that the Devil's expecting us to do just that, and he doesn't want to risk it. We're here without sanction, sort of . . . oh never mind. It's modern politics, and Hell's are Byzantine." She bit her lip and looked away.

I patted her cheek in comfort. "Do not despair. That was a good answer. Remember, I was among the Dissidents. I know something of New Hell. So does Confucius. Perhaps Welch should confide to us his plans, how he wishes to find this Enkidu, and enlist us—beyond asking chance-met men on streets, I mean."

She spat an unladylike laugh, and choked it off. "He can't do that. It's against his religion."

"Religion?" Welch, of all the Amerikanoi, was the most clearly agnostic.

"He doesn't trust anyone with his game plan, Homer. It's no reflection on you, or the quality of the team. It's just . . . Welch." She smiled and I could see concern there.

Then it struck me. "You expect to fail, is that it? You expect your Welch to fail? Not find the hairy man, and bear the Devil's wrath for that."

"He's not *my* Welch," the woman protested huffily, which of course was an outright lie. She thought he was. She wanted him to be. Her next words proved it: "My guess is that the Devil's set him up to take a fall on this, yes. I've known it since New Hell."

"Then why did you come with us?" I asked, wondering whether the Devil's retribution would extend to everyone in the party, then reminding myself that I had my own task, set me by the Devil, which was no surer of success.

"Come with you? I came with him. *He* wanted you along, because he doesn't know how to fail, because you're special to him. You, Homer, have been the best thing about this journey. You and Confucius have taken our minds off the worst of it."

"And the worst is?"

"Here. Now. What happens if we can't turn up the hair man." She smiled again, this time wanly, and twined my fingers with her own as we walked in the center of our party. "You've made the trip . . . rich, I guess. Less punishment that it otherwise would have been, that's certain. But you know what Nichols says: 'it ain't over till it's over.' "

"What's over?" Alexander wanted to know, now that he'd noticed us with our heads together.

"The pleasant part of our journey, Tanya thinks," I answered.

"Pleasant?" Alexander rubbed his jaw and then he chuckled uncertainly. "Oh, I see, a New Dead joke. Well, the joke's on all of you—look around you."

As I did what he asked, I realized that the streets, on this side of the thoroughfare, were different. The buildings here were more ornate. Stone and thatch were more prevalent than mud brick, and yet the quarter looked much poorer. Also, there were less folk about, and these were fairer-haired, more unkempt, in wooly chitons and long capes that swirled when they rushed past us. The breeze no longer smelled of cat and eucalyptus, but of onion and garlic and overcooked mutton.

"*My* Thebes," Alexander whispered theatrically, rolling his eyes. "A trick of the gods, no doubt—the spite of the underworld upon my head, that we've missed the Roman quarter and stumbled into Boetia."

It was a true miracle of the worst kind, I had to admit. If the land had been folded, if the maps men paid so dearly to make had all been wrong, then it might be that the Thebes of Alexander's youth should sit across a thoroughfare from the Thebes of the Nile.

It should not have been, and when I looked back the way we'd come, the thoroughfare was misted, as if steam arose from its pavings.

Nichols, too, looked back, and elbowed Welch. "Shit," said Welch, and turned us all around with economical haste. "Let's see if we can get back over there."

But we could not. The mist was as thick as a velvet

curtain. Once within it, we got lost. Each of us was suddenly alone; I could not see my hand before my face.

Nichols swore and Welch yelled, "Don't panic. Everybody stand still. One at a time, until we're together, count off!"

Nichols counted first, to show us what Welch meant.

I stood still in my prison of white, daring only to stretch out my arms in case I might brush a companion. But no one did I touch, though I turned a full circle in my tracks.

I have been blind, remember. Though words in thick fog are bounced around and may seem to come from anywhere, the series of numbers that Nichols dependably uttered brought not only Welch, but me as well, to his side.

"Welch, is that you?" demanded Nichols. A man had to be nose to nose to see another's face in this posset of mist.

"Yeah, yeah," said Welch's voice. "See?" And Nichols pulled me close: "Then who's this?"

"It is I," I said.

"Damn you, Homer," Welch said in anger, "I told everyone to stand still. How do you think we're going to find them, if we're all blind as bats and go wandering—"

"I who have been blind, know the light of sound as well as the light of day," I rebuked him, and after a long silence, a hand came down on my shoulder and squeezed, and Welch's voice became intimate and low: "I'm sorry, sir; I'm just trying to do my job."

Welch had not called me 'sir' for many days, and I judged it a measure of his distress.

"Do not be worried," I told him. "We have not come so far to be confounded now. We will find the other Thebes again, if you think it is truly a better place to bide."

"Alexander," Nichols called out, "count like I did—steady, loud, until we find you."

"In Greek or in English?" came Alexander's response.

"Don't matter, fool. Just count."

And as Welch held my shoulder, and Nichols, I suppose, held his, I led them unerringly to Alexander through the opaque mist.

Next we found Tanya, and Welch let go of me to enfold her. Thus I had a moment to ask the Macedonian if there was anything I could do to help him, should we find ourselves back in Boetian Thebes.

"Stay near me, Homer," came the boy king's voice. "And watch my fate unfold. I, too, am being punished on this journey—the Devil knows that for a few days I thought to give the Dissidents a worthy leader, be their lord, and teach them the ways of winning wars."

This I had forgotten, and I felt a pang for the boy king, who was so lonely in Hell without his armies or his beloved horse. So I told him, "Alexander, get behind me. We will find Confucius, and then we will make an accommodation with our fates." My voice shook, though I'm sure that Alexander did not comprehend the reason.

I had just realized that every one of us, from Tanya who harbored a purer love for Welch than Hell could forgive, to myself, who with the help of Confucius conspired with my muse to trick the Devil and write a true tale of the horrors of Hell—all of us were guilty of hubristic, recent sins against the Devil.

But I told myself, as Confucius chanted and I led the group to him, that there were no innocents in Hell, and this was as it should be. I have never shrunk from duty, nor had any of these around me. This we had on our side of the ledger: none of us were the sort of fools who thought we were unjustly here, and none of us the sort who pretended we were still alive.

If Hell were a pleasant place, we six would have been consigned elsewhere.

But here we were, among the white and unremitting fog of the thoroughfare, and none of us could guess where it was we might emerge—or if we ever would.

Once the party had been united in what Nichols called a "damned Conga line," we shuffled along until I saw a patch of color, then another.

And when we emerged, we were still on the Boetian side, but the streets of Thebes were no longer quiet.

There were Macedonian cavalry everywhere, and peltasts and archers, and there was a hail of deadly missiles above our heads.

We ran for cover as horses thundered by, their murderous hooves so close to me that pebbles spattered my face. We crossed the street and pounded on a handy door, to no avail. The door stayed shut.

Welch shouted and dragged Tanya toward an alleyway. Nichols pushed me roughly in their wake. Then I realized why both men were shouting: a great engine of war, a wooden tower with archers at its top, was coming down the street, pulled by warriors screaming battle cries. Behind it was a siege engine with a catapult, and this was flaming.

"It's the Companion Cavalry!" Alexander nearly screamed. I saw his face, contorted with emotions, where he lingered in the path of the engines, before Nichols ran at his knees, toppled him, and dragged him out of harm's way by the hair.

Welch had to help Nichols hold the boy king, who

was sure these were his own men, and wanted to join them. The scuffle between these friends was as fierce as between mortal enemies. When it was over, Alexander was bleeding from the nose, Welch's right eye was puffy, and Nichols was sitting on the boy king's back with Alexander's wrist in his hand, as if he'd pull the Macedonian's arm from its socket.

"You gonna be a good boy?" Nichols wanted to know as he jerked on Alexander's twisted arm. "You gonna use your head? You think you walked out of Hell into some demented drunk's bivouac heaven? You think these guys are going to be glad to see you? You're the fool who led them here. You ever heard of troops in Hell not fragging their general officers?" Again he jerked upon Alexander's arm, and Alexander grunted an obscenity.

"And you too, buddy. And your mother," Nichols said, astride the king in the dirt of the alley.

Not even Welch could convince Nichols to dismount until the last siege engine had rattled by, and then only when Alexander gave Nichols his word that the boy king would not leave the group at any time without Nichols' permission.

"You get me, king? You're part of my goddamn responsibility. All I need is to turn up without you. Even if I've got Enkidu, if you're lost, I'm liable to have to do this whole mission over again. And I don't want that," Nichols said very slowly, very clearly. "Capiche? Savvy? Welch, what's Macedonian for 'Behave yourself or your ass is mine'?"

"That's enough, Nichols," Welch said laconically, well after I would have said the same, if I had been Nichols' leader. "Get off him, and let's find a place to spend the night."

"A trench would suit me," Nichols said, still on Alexander. "And I ain't heard that oath yet, kingy.

Swear by whatever'll give you second thoughts. *Now*—before Hell freezes over with me using you for an easy chair."

Alexander swore by his mother, by Philip, by the oracle at Siweh, and by his kingship.

"That will bind him, Nichols," I said softly, but by then Confucius had already offered Nichols a hand.

The king was not pleased, and Alexander was quite the king he once had been, in the face of a Macedonian incursion. He walked like a king; he looked at us half-lidded like a king, and his bleeding nose sniffed and swollen lip curled at Nichols in royally promissory fashion all the time we skulked through the besieged streets, looking for an inn or an empty house.

We found neither, but we found a house that had not been burned, except for the spontaneous combustion of those who'd died there. Therein we bided, huddled in the dark, as the war for Thebes raged outside.

We ate cold, half-rotted meat and drank from broken jars of wine. The sandy dregs made Alexander rant, and only Welch kept Nichols from savaging him again.

"Just watch him, Nichols. You don't have to tie him up. He'll fall asleep soon," Welch advised.

And Alexander did begin to snore, soon after, as the fighting died down in the dead of night. Still, Welch would allow no fire, lest the Macedonians be drawn to us by signs of life.

In the dark there, we dared not even sing or tell a tale, but waited for the night to pass, and each man wrestled his own thoughts, tossing and turning, while one of us was designated to stay awake and serve as sentry.

It was on my watch that the angel came to the

half-open door and peeked inside. "Homer," he whispered, "you have come a long way." His smile lit up his face, which glowed with a light of its own so that he seemed truly heaven-sent.

I scrambled to my feet and followed where he beckoned, until I was outside in the corpse-littered street, where the wounded moaned and dogs fought over tasty morsels of flesh not yet dead enough to melt or burn or sink into the ground, as corpses did in Hell.

Looking at the fresh dead all around, the angel sighed and said, "One of the saddest things the damned do is die in a multitude, die in pieces, and die so fast that even Hell's bowels are overtaxed, trying to receive them."

"One man's death is as sad as a thousand," I said sharply. "I saw a man die of poisoning in Akhetaten, a man deserving of murder, and he sat long upon his throne, sleeping with the damned, and was not taken by the Keeper of the Corpses."

"The Undertaker? The Mortuary? They get to every soul, eventually. Sometimes the poisoned, and the comatose, and the slowly killed lie in limbo for a very long time." He turned and faced me again, and sorrow was a mask over his glory. "If you die again, Homer, make sure your death is clean."

That chilled me. "Is that the message you bring? Advice on how to face another death? I have died in Hell without you, angel, as I died on earth. No matter where, no matter when, all men die alone."

"I bring a different warning, another counsel, sweet Homer. Hear this: if you have faith and write your book, no matter how terrible your circumstance, I promise I will get that book and make sure it is not destroyed, but will live its own life, forever."

At this, all strength went out of me, and I fell down

sobbing. I sobbed with joy, and with relief, and with
thanks to the omniscient god who'd sent the angel.
For although Tanya might love Welch, and Alexan-
der his horse and kingship, and Nichols order and
his own prowess, and poor Lawrence all the suffering
Hell offered, and Confucius the wisdom of tradition,
I loved the book that lived only in my mind, my
Little Helliad, more than a mother her favorite child.

It was the book that had sustained me, the book
that had made every trial endurable, the book that
made sense of all Hell's misery, as the books I had
written in life had made that life worthwhile. This
was all I had ever wanted to know since I conceived
it: that my book would live its own life, that my
songs would find a thousand singers, that the eye of
the muse and the word of the muse and the love of
all things that through me the muse expressed—that
none of these could be destroyed, even though I
lived and wrote in Hell.

I looked up from my weeping to thank the angel
more properly, in prose, but he was not there
anymore.

Before me, a cur with glowing eyes was sniffing
around me, hoping I was weak and bleeding, a warm
and sepulchral feast for her and her pups.

I shooed the dog and turned back to my sentry's
duties in the house, standing that watch until dawn,
so exhilarated was I by the angel's visit.

And Welch, when he woke with the first light, was
angry that I had let him sleep. Outside, there was
pitched battle in the streets again.

Alexander looked out the door, stepped back, and
said in a low voice, "That's the Sacred Band, out
there. If they find me, friends, I will have to leave
you. I will go to them alone, and you will not dissuade me."

So again, Nichols wrestled Alexander to the ground and we trussed him up in a shroud as if he'd died, in case the Band should see him, and huddled there all day, pinned down by the vicious fighting.

When night fell, Welch said, "This is doing us no good. We're going to try to make a break for it."

"Across the road of mist?" Confucius wondered.

"We have no choice," said Welch, implacable with Nichols to implement his orders.

"We've got rope, Welch," Tanya offered, pointing to the corner of the hut. "We can rope ourselves together."

And this we did, with Alexander fettered in between us and gagged, before we snuck through the bloody streets and stepped into the mists once again.

Chapter 19: Devil His Due

I don't know how the men of Ptolemy found us. Ptolemy was one of the rulers of this Thebes, having become a pharaoh after the division of Alexander's lands subsequent to the boy king's death.

We were out of the fog in Egyptian Thebes not half a day when the tramping troops came to our inn and called for us, and the circumstances of our parting with Alexander was full of awful omens.

Before the knock came upon our door, Welch was trying to keep an uneasy peace, and had just taken Nichols aside, telling him, "Alexander never forgets a slight," and urging Nichols to make amends as best he could.

Alexander himself, at that moment, was asking me if I remembered how he'd chosen the site for Alexandria, a wistful look upon his handsome face.

So I said I did not know that story, ready to hear another tale.

At this, the boy king's face hardened as if I'd

struck him or become a bird before his eyes, and he
turned away from me without a word.

These moods of the conqueror were legend, I had
learned from Welch during the interval just before
we untied Alexander from his shroud; and after, the
boy king's behavior underscored the truth of the
American's observation—Alexander had been aloof,
distant, sullen and burning with that cold fire of
anger that smolders in men of a certain sort.

So I went after Alexander, in our small, whitewashed apartment with its low beds and weird hard
pillows shaped to hold a man's neck, and found him
lying on one.

These pillows reminded me of sacrificial stones
and made me nervous.

"Sit up," I said brusquely. "Lay your head not
upon that thing, for it is as if a man might lose his
head on one."

"Heads are lost in many ways, sir," said Alexander, stiff and formal, as if I were a stranger.

After all we'd shared, this made no sense. "You
were going to tell me of how you chose the site for
Alexandria," I reminded him, hoping the telling would
unbend him.

"No, I wasn't. You mistook me. I had thought to
affirm the oracle, but now I see it was mere delu-
sion." And the gaze he fixed me with had something
akin to hatred in it.

"Oracle?" I was dumbfounded. Confucius heard
the word and came to see what prognostication was
under way.

"Oracle?" he repeated, sitting down crosslegged
by Alexander's bed.

Alexander turned his head away from us on that
pillow, and faced the wall. Every sinew in his neck

was tense and he said, "A false prophet you were to me, Homer, by your own admission."

"When?" I said, monosyllabic in my surprise.

"How is this?" Confucius' doubting tone might well be all that caused the boy king to explain himself.

But explain himself he did: "You said, when I asked, that you did not remember how Alexandria came to be founded. You called it a 'story.' "

There was hurt and accusation on his face, as if I had betrayed him. "It is this English," I temporized. "It is unwieldy."

"It's not the language. You don't remember the oracle you gave me. Therefore you did not give it. Thus, I was wrong, and that makes sense. Even then, you were a pawn of this Devil who brought me to Boetian Thebes, and cast me out again. I would rather die at the hands of the Sacred Band a thousand times than travel with you mummers and sorcerers one more day." His lip curled.

Confucius withdrew his hands from his sleeves and there were reeds in his fist. He opened his palm and said, "These reeds are our party. Two are bent, but none are broken." He handed them to Alexander. "Tell me what, exactly, you mean by an oracle that was false."

"Homer is false, the false oracle. He flees from honest warfare; he uses the Devil's Children to do his handiwork. He tortures me by being here. He is nothing I thought he was. He is a fraud, this man whose *Iliad* I carried everywhere, even put in the most valuable box I took from Darius, and slept with it under my pillow."

"Tell the oracle," Confucius said, and his chins trebled in severity.

Now Alexander's words were hushed and tortured; his jaw grew square and tight and barely let these words come forth: "When I had Egypt in my power, I thought to found a great city here, to be called after me, as was my custom. My architects chose a site, which we were measuring and marking when, one night, I had a dream." He stabbed me with his stare. "You, Homer, came to me, or I thought it was you—gray-haired and noble, and recited these lines from the *Odyssey:* 'Out of the restless sea where it breaks on the Egyptian beaches/ an island rises from the waters: the name men give it is Pharos.' And now you tell me it was not you, that you do not remember any of that. Do you know, we found the isle, and saw all sorts of value in it: defensibility, spacious harbor, a fine lagoon. And I declared you were a mighty architect, and made my architects bow to your prophecy and remake their plans. We marked the site with barley; we were out of chalk. But the site demanded a certain kind of layout, and this resembled the *chalmys*—our battle cloak—so I read it as confirmation. Birds came and ate up the barley, and that was an evil sign I would not hear. Like you, my craven diviners lied. They said it was no evil omen, said it meant that the city would nourish men of many nations. So I told them to proceed, while I went trekking to the shrine of Amen and got lost. Ravens aided us when we were lost in the desert, so I was further fooled by that. But from then on, all we did was fated."

It was a good thing Confucius was there to say, "If Homer came to you in a dream, it was his dream-self that spoke to yours, and the results are history, not error. The past cannot be changed, Alexander. It is not Homer's fault that you read the oracle as you did, or put your faith in its advice—from which a great city rose. The town may be changed, but the well may be not be changed . . . What is important is not whether you are reunited with your past, but how you live in your present. No man is king who does not rule his own heart."

Before Alexander could reply with more than downcast eyes, the knock sounded, and the Ptolemaic guard came shouldering in among us. "Alexander of Macedon?" said the first, who wore a linen kilt and gilded weapons belt and a flaring helmet upon his head.

Alexander rose up from the pallet and my eyes seemed glued to the pillow where his head had lain.

Behind me, the guard was saying, "Please come with us, Alexander. My lord, Son of the Sun, Ptolemy wishes your company. Alone."

Nichols stepped in front of Alexander just as I tore my gaze from the pillow. "We're together, pal." And repeated that in halting Greek. And: "What do you want him for? He's a king, your boss is just a local warlord."

This brought out whetted blades, and Nichols' slingshotting rifle. He slapped it and it made that clacking noise, though its stock did not extend.

"They don't know what you're threatening them with, Nichols," Welch said from one side. Then, to the guards as Alexander put a hand on Nichols as if to push the other man from in front of him, Welch said: "You gentlemen have some reason for this summons? We've broken no laws here."

The chief of their party wheeled upon Welch and said, "I was told to say only that Alexander might wish to see his tomb, and for that he needs royal permission."

"My . . . tomb?" said Alexander in a voice like death.

Welch said, "Hold on, Alex. Your body was interred in Egypt, if I remember my classics. But in

Memphis. Later moved to Alexandria. Caused a bit of a fuss between Ptolemy, down here, and Perdiccas back in Macedon. Ptolemy insisted you wanted to be buried at the shrine of Amen. But none of this means anything more than Ptolemy doesn't think you'll come without false pretenses."

"My tomb," said Alexander again. Now he did shoulder Nichols aside, who looked to Welch for guidance and received only a headshake.

"I will come with you," Alexander told the guard.

"Then we're all going," said Welch in his quiet, commanding way.

"One must be invited," said the guard, firm but aware that he was into more than he understood.

"Then go back and get a proper invitation," Welch said: "Alexander will be right here, with us, when you do."

But Alexander would not listen. He looked around at me, and said, "This is my fate, and these are my Hells—here are my friends and enemies, not false prophets and ghosts from a future I don't wish to understand." His eyes were blazing. "Nor do I need protection from you Amerikanoi, creatures of evil."

"He wants to sneak back across the big road and let the Sacred Band tear him to pieces—he'll feel better for it," Nichols muttered loud enough that Alexander was sure to hear.

Tanya had her knuckles jammed against her lips and her eyes pled eloquently with the boy king not to leave us.

But nothing we could do would dissuade the Macedonian, who went off alone with those Egyptians, and I have not seen him since.

I knew then, in the way of men who live with muses in their heads, that Alexander was lost to us the moment the guard told him his tomb was near. It made me sad; it made my flesh heavy; it made me think of how far we'd come and how far we had to go. There is no rest in Hell, no sleeping peacefully, and there is no end to worry over the safety of one's friends.

Everyone was morose, that night. Nichols said, "I can feel the noose tightening," and no one argued.

I kept thinking of the battle in the streets across the thoroughfare, and hoping Alexander would not contrive to go there. But Hell is wide and full of traps, and each man finds the one set just for him.

Welch said, "I don't know about the rest of you, but I have to write up my report, especially now," and retired to a corner with a candle and his lapcomputer. "When the Devil shows up, I want to have this Alexander incident nailed down."

I went to another with my stylus and the new papyrus I'd bought in the bazaar, to work upon my book. But try as I might to get a start upon an Ode to Satan, every line I wrote was for my *Little Helliad*. None of it was fit to read to the Devil, when he arrived.

No one doubted now that we had reached "the end of our tether," as Nichols put it. In my head, an ephemeral Ptolemy abused a heroic Alexander, and I saw what it might be like to look upon your tomb. Would the body be there? In my mind it was, embalmed and within a great sarcophagus, the way Welch had described it lying in Alexandria.

The worst was not that Alexander had left us gladly, without fond leavetakings or tears of parting, but that he was disappointed in me, and in himself, when he did. When I tell the tale, no matter how he may suffer at the hand of the Ptolemy he made a king, someday he will find Bucephalus again, when all his sins are expiated, and the great black stallion will carry him to high Olympus, where I myself, some-day, will greet him.

I hadn't forgotten the Devil's promise of Olympus. My logical mind wanted to write a book to please the Lord of Hell and make him keep his promise. I had seen the pinnacle. I could write my way out of Hell. Who else has such a choice?

But a man with a muse is not merely a man with a talent. My muse was not at all interested in a book making a hero of the Devil. My muse wanted to show the suffering of mortal souls in Hell, and the glory of their courage, and the heroism which is ours that never dies or flags in the face of unending travail.

My muse thought life in Hell was no different, no worse, than life on earth, except for the ending. No man, Welch said to me that very night, gets out of life alive. Therefore if no man gets out of Hell, why is it worse?

But I knew that men did get out of Hell. I recalled that Heraclitus had. I had seen Achilles burn on the beach, and the Devil gather up his flesh and soul to make him new again. In Hell, my muse thinks, there is reason for hope—more, even, than men allow themselves.

So I wrote what my muse wanted, and not what would please the Devil. I wrote all night until my hand began to tingle, and my fingers grew cold and numb. I wrote beyond that point, until I could not hold my tools, and then I stopped and tried to focus on the room about me.

There, in slatted rays from Paradise as she rose outside, Nichols was pleading with Welch in low tones, that we must at least try to rescue Alexander, and Tanya was arguing that finding Enkidu, the hairy man, took precedence.

How long this had been going on I could not

guess, for when I write, the world grows dim and two-dimensional, and all its upheavals are like half-remembered tales to me. But Confucius had entered into this argument, and he was saying, "We should announce ourselves at the court of Ptolemy. It never hurts to make oneself known at the court of the king."

"Ptolemy's not a king, he's a raghead warlord," Nichols insisted.

"Whatever he is," Confucius said slowly, as if reasoning with a child, "you are Amerikanoi in the Devil's service. Surely that dignity can serve to get us an audience. And we can see how Alexander is faring. You cannot rescue a man who wants to die."

"Or even just somebody who doesn't know how to accept help," said Tanya, looking straight at Welch.

Welch said, "Well, we've got more chance of finding Alexander than we do of finding Enkidu, unless he's disguised himself as a lion or a tiger."

"If we see him, and he gives us a hard time," Nichols offered, "I'll whack his ass onto the Trip. Let him argue with the Undertaker about where he belongs."

"Whatever you do, Nichols, don't shoot Alexander, is that clear? If he wants to stay here, it's not up to us to force him back. Anyway, these discrete Hells have odd rules. He might not show up right away at Reassignments."

"You mean he might die forever?" said Confucius.

"No, I just mean that some of these little Hells are pretty self-sufficient. Hard to get into; hard to get out of. So let's not go blowing guys away because it's easier, that's all. Or because we've got a personal axe to grind."

I remembered Achilles on the beach, and what Welch had done. But I said nothing. If it were true that Alexander might languish here, or die here and be reborn not in New Hell, but among the streets of Boetian Thebes, what did it matter? Bucephalus would find him when the time was right, wherever Alexander chose to go.

So I went with the Amerikanoi and Confucius, and Confucius let it be known that he too saw the Americans for what they were: creatures of His Satanic Majesty's Secret Service, men concerned only with their own performance, who had no one else's welfare in their hearts.

Despite this, Confucius saw some sense to presenting ourselves before the warlord, Ptolemy, though I did not. I could feel the funneling of time itself, the catastasis of fate, and I could hear the angel warning me to die a clean death, if I would die again.

All the way to the palace of Ptolemy, I kept seeing the pillow on which Alexander lay his head, which was a solid block out of which a depression had been cut. Men's heads are chopped from their bodies on stones not so differently fashioned. That omen made everything I saw dark and pregnant.

The cats in the streets growled at us as we passed. Some fought with one another, pacing and snarling and attacking their neighbors, long-clawed paws snaking through the bars of their cages.

I have often wondered what animals did to be consigned to Hell, but animals are a part of man, and man of them, and all life belongs to the same chain, as Heraclitus knew. So the anxious cats made me more anxious, and I lagged behind our party as it approached the warlord's fortress.

This was a Hellenized place, with double walls and guardposts, much less open than the earlier palaces on the same street.

Yet it had the processional way, with sphinxes and

great stone hawks, to guard its entrance, and a reflecting pool of its own, and colossal statues by its double, gilded doors.

These were statues of Set and Anubis, and to Welch this meant something, for not only did he name them both, but he stopped and checked his pistol.

Behind us were the faithful guards past whom we'd bluffed our way with talk of New Hell power, watching curiously. Above the outer gate, men with far-shooting bows watched us as well. Then Welch, still stopped, took a step back the way we'd come.

"We can't just turn around," Tanya told him.

"I know, but something's wrong here."

"Where is it, here, that something is not wrong?" Confucius asked. "Be steadfast in your heart," the sage advised. "Show no fear, for what can befall us will befall us." The sage grinned widely, an encouraging smile that buried his eyes in fat and showed little, black-spotted teeth.

So in we went, with Welch and Nichols preening and announcing themselves as mighty lords of Authority, here on the supremely secret business of the Devil himself.

"Children of Set," said the bejeweled eunuch who announced us from the far end of a long, narrow audience hall, "bringing petitions."

Confucius started to object at that, but Welch said, "Close enough. We'll straighten it out with Ptolemy when we're eye to eye."

So we walked up the long narrow room, between carven columns, and on either wall I saw the mystery of the dead set out there, painted upon the incised rock. I saw the bird-headed Thoth with his feather, I saw Anubis, the guard dog, and I saw the great crocodiles and serpents of the underworld, ready to carry men off to their fate. And Ptah, I saw, in his shroud, and Osiris, bound up like a mummy, and the handmaidens of the black-faced lord of death were all around.

This audience hall seemed longer, once we were walking it, than it had seemed when first we started. We walked along the dark marble of its floor, and we walked some more, and the throne between its columns got no closer. We walked faster. We closed our ranks. I looked over my shoulder and saw the door through which we'd come, and it was as far from me now as the throne ahead.

Equidistant from the threshold and our destination, it occurred to me that Ptolemy, a warlord, could not have an audience hall grander than his entire palace. But by then it had occurred to the others, too.

Confucius was walking very slowly, as if in a burial procession. Welch had one arm around his woman, as if to keep fate from tearing them apart. And Nichols' slingshotting rifle swung its snout this way and that, looking for an enemy against which it could prevail.

There were no enemies of flesh and blood in this place, we soon found out.

There was only—the Devil on his throne of human bone, and he was as terrible as he'd been when first he appeared to me.

His great snout issued forth smoke and his wolf-eyes gleamed, and his barbed tail lashed as we approached.

When we were standing before him, he said, "So, we meet again, fools and sinners." His claws tapped upon the skulls that were his throne's armrests. "Where is Alexander? Where is Achilles? Where is

Lawrence? Where is Enkidu?" The questions rattled around the room like hard-flung missiles.

Welch put Tanya behind him and spread his arms as Nichols tried to come up by his side, holding the other man back. "Enkidu's wherever you have put him. He's not in Thebes, or anywhere along the way—not where I can find him with the resources you've given me."

"Some dignity would be appropriate, some salutation," said the Devil in a voice that made my teeth water.

"Sir." Welch stood up taller. "My lord. Your Majesty."

From behind him, I could see how his body trembled to speak these words, and I remembered that the Amerikanoi suffered no kings to rule them. Nichols was holding Tanya firmly, keeping her quiet with an unflinching glare.

"You have not told me of the others, sinner," said the Devil to Welch.

"I have it all in my report, back at our rooms, on disk—"

"This?" The Devil held out his black palm and Welch's lap-computer appeared in it. "Excuses. Drivel. Whining and self-justification." The computer burst into flame, and then exploded.

Pieces flew. Welch threw up a hand to guard his face. Tanya screamed and hid her head against Nichols' chest. Only Confucius and I, in the rear of our party, did not flinch.

Confucius' reasons, I cannot guess; but mine were simple enough: my turn had not yet come. It was coming, but nothing so mild as a hurtling piece of wire or glass could preclude it.

The Devil dusted the charred and smoking remnants from his palm and then leaned forward. "Few men see me, Welch. And when they do, there is a reason. Do you know why I appeared to you in New Hell?"

"Poor performance," said Welch very low.

"Oh no," said the Devil. "Not that. All performance is poor in Hell. Treachery—it lies in your heart. A definite lack of allegiance. An overbearing sense of responsibility to your . . . countrymen, let's say. Your allegiance is only to me, only to my benefit, only to my will. Not to these—" The Devil indicated Tanya and Nichols. "Not to Alexander, in whose fate you interfered on your own recognizance, when you made him a friend and 'helped' him. So now you have delivered him to the fate that he deserves. And as for you—those who misuse their power, lose it. Is that clear?"

"Yes, sir," said Welch, rod-straight and taut with discipline.

"Good. You have failed to find Enkidu. You will stay here among the nether hells, until you do. And you will have no help from Authority—no technology, no power. You are a damned soul of no repute, until either the hairy man is found, or Egypt herself sends you back to me. Now, what do you say, Harvard man, classics student, traitor, lover, fool?"

"Yes, sir," said Welch. And then: "My subordinates don't deserve any blame for this. It's my mess. . ."

"Ah, you would sacrifice yourself for these." The Devil was not pleased, even I could see.

"I don't think they're out of bounds, is all," said Welch. "They just took orders. The quality of those orders is my responsibility."

"Ah, but they too indulge in affection, in loyalty,

in friendship and in love. Begone, all of you, and learn the lessons Hell provides."

The Devil merely pointed, and Welch, Nichols, and Tanya disappeared.

I was heartbroken for them. I forgot my place. I forgot my vulnerability. I stepped forward and said, "And what will happen to them now? It is unclear to me that they did anything wrong."

"Exactly," said the Devil, and then his glowing eyes narrowed. "Nothing wrong enough. I hope you understand better than you pretend, Homer. Those souls are full of self-sacrifice and pride in their humanity. They care for one another. They are companions of the heart. This cannot be tolerated. Surely you understand what I am saying, you who must write the book of Hell?"

I mumbled that I did, but I did not. "Are you going to separate them?" I demanded.

"They will separate themselves, when they have disappointed each other long enough and well enough, and suffered enough on Welch's account. Don't worry, I need all of their kind I can get. It's just training them that takes time. They must learn fear, and humility, Homer." The Devil yawned, then snapped his jaws shut. "Confucius, what are you doing here?"

"Learning," said the sage.

"And what have you learned?"

"That your will is inscrutable. The past cannot be changed; the future cannot be changed; only the present can be changed."

This syllogism pleased the Devil, and he nodded. "Good. Have you questions for me?"

"No question seems appropriate at this time," said the cautious sage.

"A perfect answer, once again. Shall I put you among your ancestors, where you belong? Or back in

New Hell, where wise counsel is sorely needed by these stubborn, uncomprehending damned of mine."

"Whatever you choose. A man does not choose his own fate. The winds blow, and a man does the best he can."

The Devil frowned, perhaps perceiving that Confucius was not sincere in his humility, that such surrender is in itself a form of arrogance.

But my wise friend bowed very low, his hands in his sleeves, and when he pulled them out, he dropped from one clenched fist the six straws he had shown Alexander. I looked at them there, on the marble. All were bent, but none were broken.

Confucius cast a surreptitious glance at me and I nodded, to signify that I had seen this good omen, and understood.

Then the Devil came down off his throne and bade me tell him of the beginning of his book, and I was struck mute with stagefright.

I opened my mouth and nothing would come out of it. I gestured that I was thirsty, and I croaked as best I could that I had only taken notes so far, that the book would be long in its writing.

By now the Devil was bearing down on me, and he was hideous and huge. His great snout came close and his jaws opened wide and he breathed upon me all the fetidness of every corpse that had ever rotted, before he said, "You trifle with me, scribbler. I have your notes. I can make nothing of them."

Again came the outstretched palm, and my scribe's kit appeared in it. "You are mine, Homer. You will write this book to my satisfaction. And, since you are meddlesome and canny, you will write the rest of it where I can keep a closer watch on you."

He stepped back. He began to fume. He started to

flare. He dropped my parchments. I scrambled to pick them up.

The Devil said, "Go you, both, to the courtyard, where your disposition awaits. Look neither to the right nor to the left, or you shall spend eternity as statues in this parched and angry land."

Upon that last word, with a gout of flame and a belch of smoke, he disappeared.

So did the great audience hall; so did the majestic colossi outside, and the inner courtyard as we had known it.

In its place, there was a wide and sandy desolation, broken by tumbled walls, with only unforgiving dunes beyond. In these dunes I saw the glint of bones, but only from the corner of my eye.

I did as I was told, quaking in every limb. I looked neither to my right nor to my left. Confucius, at my side, brushed my arm and we grasped hands, lest we lose one another somehow, and we strode forward. We put foot before foot in that desolation, thinking of the city around us and the palace around us that were not anything at all now but parched remains.

Had it always been thus? I do not think so. Nor do I think the bones we saw were any of our lost companions. I think the Devil is a master of rending hearts, of stealing humanity from man. Of bringing out of us what is truly the worst.

For I was frightened for myself, then, for my book unborn, though I had my own notes under my arm, grabbed up from the floor where the Devil had dropped them before he flamed away.

I was frightened that nothing would ever be before me again but this desolation, that Confucius and I were doomed to a sandy wasteland.

Then the 'courtyard' where we walked erupted in a storm of sand and dust. Noise inundated us, like the bellowing of the Minotaur. My ears pounded with it. My eyes closed from the sand that whipped me. I lost hold of Confucius' hand because I feared for my manuscript, which I clutched to my breast with both hands.

I stopped walking, so fierce was the gale. It screamed like banshees; it wailed like the Mourning Fields; it pulsed like a heart dying.

From everywhere, pebbles and sand pelted me, and then a giant black insect came out of the maelstrom and alighted beside me.

Out of it, before the roaring gale had even stopped, jumped Achilles, who hurried me into its maw. I tried to tell him that Confucius was out there somewhere, but he wouldn't listen. His orders said nothing about Confucius, or the Americans, he yelled as he strapped me into the seat beside him.

There was no use protesting. He had muffs on his ears and the gale was all around us, and into it the great metal insect was already lifting.

And I had my manuscript, after all.

Chapter 20: My Fate

What *is darker than the dungeons of New Hell? The Devil's wrath.* Thus ran the opening lines of my *Ode to Satan*, but my heart was not in this writing, as shown by the fact that I could not bring myself to ask my muse to sing of the Devil.

This one and solitary riddle I composed, during the whole long ride through the maelstrom back to New Hell with Achilles in the belly of the insect. Not enough by far, I knew, to stave off my evil fate, but there were other riddles obsessing me, and bold Achilles was one of them.

He gave to me a pair of muffs, which were like a talking crown, and with them on my ears I was free to ask him questions, speaking into the depending diadem. And he was free to answer.

"Achilles," I said, watching all of Hell speed by below, "where did you go, when you left the beach?"

"When Welch iced me, you mean?" said the man on whom the whole *Iliad* had turned, who now controlled the infernal insect whose hum was as loud as damnation. "Back to Reassignments. Suited me. All they were in for was trouble and I've got a perfect record."

I did not understand any of that. I said this, and Achilles snaked a look at me, quick as a serpent's tongue. Then he laughed in my ears and said, "Look, old fella, just don't you worry about them others. You got enough troubles, all by your lonesome. Big troubles, or else you wouldn't rate a personal pickup by somebody like me." His chest puffed out. He sat up tall.

"I am not concerned with myself. What of those we traveled with? Do you not care for them at all? Do you not worry for Alexander, in Thebes? For—"

"Snot-nosed brat," sniffed Achilles. "Caesar thought we shared a soul—him and me and Alexander. Put the three of us together, and weird stuff happens, even for Hell. Yeah, I care not to be around Alexander too much. But don't worry about him. He'll find Thebes amusing." A nasty chuckle came and went. "Wait till he runs into Herakles. I wouldn't mind seeing that. Talk about clash of the titans . . ."

"You truly do not care about the fates of fellow sinners?"

"Look, you senile old hack—I work for the Devil, capiche? I like my job. I got all the access and all the clout I need. I got the best equipment, anything I ask for. I don't worry about nobody but myself. Ever. Never did, in fact. If you thought different you were wrong."

This was my Achilles, jealous of everyone and everything around him, desiring only supremacy and to appear to be a man of stature. But not even a loving Devil could—or would—give him that.

"Not even Confucius thought you a creature of evil

so foul," I said, my temper lost. "How could you betray your heritage, your—"

"Legend? You wrote that, not me, buddy. Teach you to drink too much. Men never were like you wrote 'em; nobody on that beach was any nobler than me, though there were some high and mighty airs being put on. And they ain't no better now. One thing you got to learn about Hell, old man, is if you play by the rules, things go better. Like how old you are when you're reborn next. And how much grief you get, and generally the quality of life." Now sly Achilles winked at me. "You could have it a lot easier, Homer. Since you did so much for my reputation, let me give you some advice. Write the book H.I.M. wants; do your job, and I'll personally see to it that New Hell's a real revelation to you. Nice apartment. Good food. Women, boys, prepubescent girls—whatever you want. Just toe the line . . ."

I listened no more to the tempter, creature of the Devil's pleasure. I waited until he had finished, and then I said, "I will consider your offer. But it troubles me about my friends, those with whom I traveled. Confucius, most of all, did not deserve—"

"Everybody gets what they deserve, Pop. You gotta realize, that's the first rule of Hell. As for Confucius, he could be a Judge, for all I know—or care. I ain't turnin' this rig around; I ain't pickin' up no hitchhikers. I got girlfriends waiting for me back home, and missions to fly. I'm just delivering you, that's all. You got a last chance to play along, why don't you take it? You be a good old fella, you'll go to nice digs. You keep on like you're goin', you'll spend your time in a hole on bread and water."

This was the truth, but a warning given by Achilles I could not credit. Nor did I have control over my muse, where the Devil's book was concerned. Nor could I write in the shivering insect that buzzed so angrily. I tried to take some notes, and the motion made me sick as I sought to watch the words I wrote.

Soon I was learning the lesson of the "airsickness bag," as Achilles called it. And then, over a place of flame where the river Cocytus writhed like a sacrificial serpent upon the land, I fell asleep.

When I awoke, we were on solid ground in the great and top-heavy city of New Hell, where unsound buildings clawed the sky and from everywhere came a wind that wailed with the suffering of its multitude.

I was dazed, awakening there, for I had been dreaming. In my dream, I was walking with Confucius again, and he was my Judge, as Achilles had teased me. The sage was taking my hand to lead me out of Hell, but I had to let go of him to grab my manuscript before it fell into the flaming Cocytus, below the bridge on which we were suddenly walking. When I looked again for him, Confucius was gone.

I never wrote a sadder tale than that dream, but in the way of dreams, it was only the mood that stayed with me, that of hopelessness, as Achilles helped me out of the insect's maw and handed me over to my jailers.

Just before they took me away, these men with crooked crosses and lightning bolts upon their gray uniforms, Achilles asked once more: "Sure you won't change your mind, old man, and recite a Devil-pleasing verse or two right now, so's I can help you out?"

"I am not ready," I said quite firmly.

Achilles took off his helmet, tugged on his red pigtail, and squinted at me in the bright lights shining from the prison wagon into which I was bound.

"You're a fool, you know. Want me to check you out in a week or so, in case you change your mind?"

"I'm sure any company will be welcome," I said stiffly, wishing Achilles was a better man than I had made him, not worse than I ever thought he might be.

So without trial, without evidence of wrongdoing more damning than procrastination, I was to be incarcerated in New Hell's dungeons, far below the miserable streets.

I watched through the chickenwire on the wagon's window as I was taken to my cell, in the basement of the Pentagram where special prisoners are often kept, and I saw nothing, outside, to make me change my mind.

New Hell is the most scurrilous of places, lawless and convoluted, where every sort of depredation is encouraged, and every sort of thug and cretin makes his home. On the ride to my cell, we passed estates belonging to Romans and Assyrians and Babylonians, each worse than the next, for these citizens of the ages were all here to serve the Devil, cogs in Hell's bureaucracy.

I saw the towering Hall of Injustice, with its unfinished pinnacle and bulbous tip. I saw the ravaged Decentral Park, where slant-eyed men fight a hopeless war from tunnels that do not lead out of Hell, but only deeper into it.

Then I saw, I thought, the very corner where this adventure had begun—the noodle shop was there, at the entrance to the Chinese quarter. And I felt tears well, thinking of those I'd left behind.

Beyond that, the ride remains a blur to me, for I realized what I should have said to Achilles. I should have told him, I knew then, that the Devil had not fulfilled his part of our bargain yet, thus it was too early to condemn me for not keeping mine. Had I not been promised leave to seek my heroes? I had found only Odysseus, and Achilles himself. I had not interviewed Diomedes, or Menelaos, or Agamemnon. Not a single Trojan had I met.

When Achilles came back, as he had promised, I would send that protestation to the Devil, who would certainly hold to his word if he meant to punish me for not keeping mine.

So I deluded myself that this was just a temporary misunderstanding, and chided myself that my wits had been too addled to face the Devil and remind him of our bargain. But I had been afraid, and mourning the misery of Alexander, I told myself. There would be time to set things right. In Hell, there is always time.

A man who is sent to prison is not a man who is in control of his faculties. The heart shrinks. The soul rages. The outer world fades, and the inner world grows urgent. I underwent all the indignities of a newly-arrived prisoner as if in a dream to which I was only half committed. Men stripped me, handed me a bar of soap, looked between my legs and cheeks and stuck their fingers where men's fingers do not belong. All this I withstood stolidly, holding firm to my certainty that my time in jail would be short. It was a mistake, a misunderstanding. There were many mistakes in Hell, I knew, and for once this comforted me.

My mind seemed to float on a tether, far above my senses, which endured the catcalls of the other men in the showers, and the scalding heat of the spray, and the whistles and kisses which greeted me as I was marched down to my cell.

Although in that cell I found my writing kit and my notes, that whole first night I did not write a word. I spent my time rejecting my confinement. I did not even pace off my cell. There would be plenty of time for that.

In the morning, guards hustled us out of our cells for breakfast, which was a feast of maggots. I eat little in any case; this offal I did not eat at all, though the prisoner next to me warned me I should take what I could get.

Then we were sent to the exercise pen, where demons with whips put us through grueling paces. I could not climb the ropes up and down to the pits where the damned dug for the sake of digging, and I was beaten.

No one lifted a hand to help me, though other prisoners were all around. When at last I fell to my knees, I was carried back to my cell. I remember, in my delirium, telling those who bore me on a stretcher, "But I am Homer. I am here to write the Devil's book, not to dig holes like a common laborer."

No one listened, or no one cared. I dug with the others every day, and tried to write at night. But this proved impossible, for I was given no candle, no lamp, and when the lights in that pit went out, its darkness was complete.

Blind men write, I told myself, and tried to relearn old and half-forgotten skills. I composed the Devil's preamble within my mind, making a memory house for the work, so that each room I visited was a chapter, and I could go from one chapter to another by walking through the mansion in my mind.

For I was frightened, now, of spending eternity without writing either book, and I wanted to be ready for Achilles when he came. But my muse betrayed me one night, unbuilding the mansion in which the Devil's book resided, and putting the house of the *Little Helliad* in its place.

Consequently, when Achilles finally arrived to see me, I was not bold in my recitation. I was not brave, I could not find the door behind which the *Ode to Satan* resided, but stumbled through a few halting phrases, and ended up synopsizing what I planned to do.

This bored Achilles, for primitive men like only stirring rhythms, and bold songs neatly sung. It is the form, not the content, that holds them, and the Ode had no form, without me finding the doors behind which I had locked away the poem.

So I said, near tears and with quivering lips, "I need a candle, I need peace and quiet—time to write. Achilles, for the sake of what I made your name, have pity. They march me out to dig in holes. My hands are blistered, too stiff to write. And when I come back, out go the lights. If the Devil wants his book, he must give me a chance to write it. I need the proper circumstance."

"You've got the circumstance you wanted, remember? You were more interested in your buddies than in doing the sensible thing." Achilles liked to see me grovel. He paced before me, his head dipping like a cock before hens as he made his stiff-kneed way around my cell. "I'm no critic, but I'm not impressed with what I heard just now. Still, because of the *Iliad*, I'll help, yeah."

"Oh, thank you, thank you," I heard my weakened self say.

"Don't thank me yet, Pop. I'm just getting you off work detail, that's all. And I can't guarantee how long that'll be for—I'm leaving on a mission, day after tomorrow."

"Leaving!" I was terrified. Achilles was my only link to the outside world. "But how will the Devil know of my progress?"

"Don't sweat it, Pop. He's got his ways."

Achilles turned to go, and I protested: "You cannot leave yet. Tell the Devil for me that he has not kept his own part of our bargain." And I explained about not meeting the heroes whom I needed to interview, and asked him to take my message to Satan.

"You expect me to tell H.I.M. that he's screwed up? You've got me confused with somebody who gives a damn for your smelly old hide." Achilles left then, taking with him my last and best hope for clemency.

But he did get a candle to me, and my days digging in the pit were at an end, though I could not say for how long.

Now I was moved into a solitary confinement, where no daylight ever came and no sound was ever heard but an occasional moaning, as if the stones of this jail were themselves alive.

There I wrote, and wrote, and wrote, but always I wrote the *Little Helliad*, for my muse had locked me out of the place where the Devil's book languished. Every time I would try to go there, my muse would seduce me with remembered stories, of Alexander and Bucephalus, of Achilles himself, of Odysseus and Lawrence, of lonely-hearted Hesiod, of Theseus and Persephone and the heretic king of Akhetaten. Oh, I had plenty to write, and write I did.

And all my tales I swung around the pivotal one that I had heard from Heraclitus, that tale of the Devil and the Trojan Woman, for it reechoed through all the others. It was the lynchpin, the cornerstone, the wellspring from which all the Hellish tales I learned had come.

There must be more tales in Hell than any man could tell, but all of those I learned were tales of love and its transmutation. For in Hell, love is the only weapon against the Devil. And like all potent weapons, it can hurt the wielder, and innocents standing by. Yet it hurts the Devil like nothing else can, by Satan's own admission. Proof, if I had needed it, was all around me, not just in every tale, but in my cell, and in his punishment of those who'd traveled with me.

My muse's book went well and fast, and though it brought me to the verge of tears, it never pushed me over, into self-pity or shameful lamentation. Only when I would break away from it, to write the Devil's book, did I feel despondency creep upon me like a pall.

Then would I sweat, and shake, and bewail my fate and everyone's. Then was I bitter and cold and old and full of woe. I became resentful of my fate because writing without a muse is like plowing without a dray beast, like singing a song with no melody, like studying a nonsensical lesson.

But I got it started. I found the place where the story turned; I made my way into its horrid middle. And then the lies of it heaped themselves upon me like a rock wall falling, and I stopped writing altogether.

This, in all the years I had lived on earth and wandered in Hell, was a punishment never before visited upon me. I felt like an empty vessel, without joy or purpose. No line I wrote could keep its rhythm, for every time I thought to coin a phrase, the Devil's visage would appear before my eyes; his claws would tap the yellow skulls of his throne, and I would be frozen with the fear of his displeasure.

How can one please Evil that does not recognize its cause as malignant? The Devil thought he could be a hero; he did not know how repugnant he was, with his lust for power and his love of conflict for its own sake. He who must triumph over mankind for the sheer joy of it, who would force his ways upon the world, who nurtured selfishness and had no thought for any being but himself—how could this creature be enfamed? How could any consciousness who will tolerate no thinking but his own, who listens only to those who agree with him, who perceives all not subservient as enemies, who seeks to stamp out or suppress any who oppose him—how could such an entity be made laudable before man?

For is mankind not diversity itself? Is progress not the oversweeping of the old by the new? Is freedom not inherently superior to order, which can only be stagnation and entrenchment in the end? Mankind's weakness is not the Devil's strength; the Devil's weakness is the forcing of his will upon the weak.

Hell, I now realized, was the Devil's punishment, more than man's. His task of ruling over men in Hell was impossible. And when I saw this, I trembled. To let the Devil know I knew him for what he was—the most damned sufferer in Hell—would be foolhardy. His only response to any who saw him as he was, must be harassment and destruction. In his soul, there was nothing but a thirst for domination, and those who saw him as less than the lord of Hell, he would stamp out at any cost.

I remembered the trial of Hesiod, and its foreshadowing of my fate. I went back carefully through my secret book and worried over what would happen when the Devil found my *Little Helliad*, which was full on every page with the insights that had helped me learn the awful truth of the Devil's personal torment.

He who cannot love those he does not totally control is more damned than the weakest under his sandal; he who demands blind allegiance is sure he does not deserve any; he who boasts of his magnificence is the meanest of us all. The Devil, I had finally realized, was miserable, loveless and afraid.

Only those who had no other choice respected him; only those he could make totally dependent upon him could he ever trust—for whether they knew of his unworthiness or not, *he* knew. Though none of the souls in Hell might ever grasp it, the Devil knew he was a fraud, a pretender, and no amount of power would ever heal this flaw, for it was in him to the bedrock. It made him what he was.

I should have seen it in the tale Heraclitus told me, but hindsight is always clearer. Now I saw it in that tale's retelling, and every other.

And I was saddened, though not for the Devil, for he who surrounds himself with evil and purveys evil, is in truth evil. No ends justify such means as the torments all about me in every nook and cranny of the underworld.

Time and again, I went back to the *Ode to Satan*, but I could not keep my revelation off those pages. I meant to write of a mighty power to be feared, but I wrote of a vicious coward to be pitied, shunned, and despised. This creature cast down from heaven hated everything better than he had become. He hated acuity, and intellect, and honor. He hated knowing sacrifice, and generosity, and friendship. And most of all, because he had none, among all the teeming fools who served him, he hated love.

No allegiance of convenience or necessity is love. No price can buy it, no willfulness can deny it, no soul who is without it can ever hope to force it to his will.

Thus did I run up against a wall I could not scale in the writing of the Devil's book. And I remem-

bered the warning of Altos, and of Confucius, and of
Hesiod. And I was glad that I had tried and failed to
subvert myself, for so little a thing as freedom for my
body. Though I did not know it then, my soul was
free, the day I put the *Ode to Satan* to my single
candle's flame.

As for my *Little Helliad*, I began digging once
again. I dug at the mortar between the stones of my
cell, to make a niche where I could hide it. I dug
with my fingernails, but I would have gnawed with
my teeth.

And I admit, despondency overcame me, for my
songs were meant for others' lips and ears. Like any
parent, I wanted the *Little Helliad* to have its own
life.

In my dual tribulation—of loss of hope for the
book I loved, and loss of the book I hated, which
might have saved my body but made me despise my
soul—I had forgotten the angel's promise.

I had forgotten more than that, you must realize.
If you have never been a prisoner, you must consider what it is like to be denied the light of day, the
vagaries of chance, the profundity of fortune. In my
cell, nothing happened to me that I did not engen-
der. In my heart, I was living in a grave, alone. My
muse had nothing to look upon to excite her, and she
was quiet.

This quiet, for a man like me, was twice the burden that blindness had ever been.

So when the angel came, I did not look up. I
thought it was a guard come to replace my low-
burning candle, or to bring my daily bread and mag-
goty posset.

I slumped where I was, protecting the stone behind which my secret book was stashed. I had chewed
the mortar I'd scraped away, having carefully saved

every bit of stony powder, and replaced it in the cracks when it was wet enough. But it would not stand close examination. My back firmly against that stone was the only way.

I saw the sandaled feet first, and the light that comes with the grace of God. But any light beside my single candle's was bright to me, in those days, and I did not raise my eyes.

So the angel came down on his knees to look at me, and then I knew him. I knew the whiteness of his robes. I knew the sweet smell of his skin like fresh air, a smell I had not breathed for far too long. I heard the rustle of his wings like the soft murmuring of a mother to her child.

"Homer," he said to me in a voice so gentle I cannot describe its beauty, "Homer, look me in the eye."

I did that and it was painful. So bright was he and beautiful, so full of care and empathy. "Altos," I said, and the voice I had used so little for so long was but a croak.

"I have come to keep my promise. Give the book unto me." He held out his beautiful hand.

I blinked. I rubbed my eyes. I said, "Do I dream this? Are you real? If you are a Devil's trick—"

"The book, Homer. Fear not." The hand before me was steady.

"It's . . ." I was going to make excuses, say it was rough; say it was unfinished; say it suffered from the weakness of my spirit; say it had within it the seeds of my destruction, and more—that it was the Devil's greatest enemy, the truth as seen through the uncompromising eyes of a mortal man with nothing personal to gain. Instead of all that, I said, "It's . . . here."

Then I got up on my own creaking knees, with all

my joints protesting from so long in damp and inactive confinement, and I began digging at the mortar my spit had helped to pack against the stone.

I heard him say, "Good. Do hurry," as I was digging.

When I turned around, I was afraid he would be gone—so afraid I closed my eyes. If this was a deception of the Devil or some social-climbing demon, I had fallen right into it. I held the *Little Helliad* in both my hands with a death grip.

Not until the angel tried to take it from me did I dare to look, to see if it were truly he.

It was that shining countenance, those eyes of infinite understanding and patience, that godhead better than any Phidias ever sculpted.

And down on me that angel smiled a smile of fatherly pride, and selfless joy, and then he took the book. He brought it to his forehead. He closed his eyes against it. He opened them and said, "Thank you, Homer."

And then he walked away, without another word, right through the walls of stone as if they did not exist. No word did he offer me of where and how my book should live, no comfort beyond those few words.

There I sat, long after he had gone, empty, with nothing left to protect, drowning in my plight and my hopelessness. Twice I pulled out the stone again, and twice I replaced it. All that remained there were my notes. The *Little Helliad* was really gone, and I was but a husk.

I slept too long, I do know that. Perhaps I'd hoped the angel would take me with him. Perhaps I cried out at my awful fate.

The next day, when I woke, I demanded of my guard more parchment. I could not sit there, unmoving. I would try the Devil's book again, I told myself.

But I did not. I worked on this, my notes—my journal—for my soul's sake.

I wished I'd told the angel that I wasn't going to write the Devil's book. I told myself that that was why he'd left me, because I might yet sing my song in praise of evil. But then I thought better of it: I was hurt, and lonely; I had lost my book, my passion, my child of love, that was all. The angel who had looked at me like a mother had not found me unworthy. There was simply nothing even a handmaiden of the greatest god could do for a sinner such as I.

When the commotion started outside my cell, I paid it no attention. Noises came and went. None of it had aught to do with me.

But when men came running down the hall, and someone called my name, I yelled back hoarsely. And when my door was forced open from without and men stood there, not guards, but men in blotchy clothes with weapons, I blinked and rose, and pushed back against my cell's unyielding walls.

"Homer? Homer?" called a voice I did not recognize. "Come on, man. Come with me. Freedom awaits, but we must hurry."

I did not know the voice; my blurry vision could not make out the face. But I saw the hand outstretched to me, a strong hand of a strong man. And I took it, stopping only long enough to grab my notes from their niche.

I leaned against this rescuer, who put an arm around me. With his help, among his bold compatriots, I stumbled through confusion, down the corridors, out a door into blinding brightness, and then into a van waiting beyond.

As the van pulled away, my head jerked back and hit the metal, and I was stunned. As I slid to the floor, I heard men laughing and congratulating one another on a job well done.

But it had been too much for me. Try as I could, sleep came and stole over me, with her velvet cloak, making all the men and their brave celebration into a welcome dream of freedom.

Chapter 21: My Hero

Even before I was fully awake in the jouncing van, three men among my rescuers caught my attention— proof that what poets write about real souls is inherent in them. One was the strong man with the strong hand, on whose shoulder I had leaned.

This man was built like a god, tall and straight and with a harshness to him that overrode his beauty. Ares might have been his name, but it was not. This man had an eagle's stare, and hair with golden glints, and a close-cut beard he stroked whenever he would look at me. And at such times, his mouth would quirk, but never smile.

Along with him, huddled in war council as the van sped through night-dark streets, was another bearded man—shorter, swarthy, and in his prime. This man had a round face and dark deep eyes like coins, in which the hardness of a fighter gleamed, matching all the armaments hung from his person like trophies of well-won wars.

And with these two fighters, the great and the

small, was a gray old man, with a sharp nose and a pale glance that had seen too many such councils, but would not look away.

They whispered and they glanced at me and they whispered once again. All the others in the van—a dozen fighters with faces painted to match their clothes, and heavy boots, and New Dead weapons—gave these men room, and deference, as befits strong tribal leaders.

The troops themselves were jubilant, and it was from their bursts of nervous victory chatter that I gleaned my first hints of what had befallen me.

These soldiers were the men of the short young warlord who sat in council, and him they called Bashir Gemayel. They told me our destination was a camp of the Dissidents, who would be pleased beyond measure to have "the great bard"—myself—back among them.

It was their strike against the Devil that made these men so nervous, yet so proud. And I further learned, from listening hard and listening well, that this Gemayel was not a Dissident himself, which was why I did not know him. He had done this deed which none among the Dissidents dared do, to prove it could be done, to set a strong example of resistance, to galvanize flagging spirits among the rebels. For Gemayel was a man who loved all rebels, if not their causes.

But his men were not sure of their welcome; this I knew by how extravagantly they reassured each other that it would be a glorious one.

And I knew it by the way their eyes strayed to Gemayel, like a pack of hounds denied the eating of the fox they'd run to ground, who long for their master to pet them and feed them and croon to them of how well they'd done.

All of this I learned, before the three leaders made their way to me, stooped low in the jouncing van.

When they sat beside me, they asked me of my health, and of my faring. They were respectful, even the old man, who spoke first to me.

And when I'd said, "I am forever in your debt, but curious. Who are you, and why are you helping me?" it was the gray-beard who replied: "You don't know me, grandson? I am Nestor, your maternal grandsire. Under the circumstances, it was, we think, the least that we could do."

"Nestor?" The man at whose hearth I'd learned so much. He looked different to my old soul's eyes than he had to the eyes of Homer, the curious child. He was not so old, now; his lined face was not a map of inscrutable adventures. But I was glad to see him, and bubbling with questions as I always had been, hearing stories at his knee. Then I thought of his words, and the thrill of reunion left me. All questions telescoped into the burning ones of present need. "Circumstances?" I asked, reminded of Achilles, telling me my 'circumstance' of a prisoner was one I'd chosen.

"Of blood relationship," he means, said the one called Gemayel, who introduced himself by name and said, "These men of mine, Maronites and Christians, aren't Dissidents. Our blood debt was personal, to your countrymen. Do not be tired, Homer. Do not worry if the Dissidents fear to shelter us. It's a temporary stop for you, like most in Hell. Whatever happens, we've chosen freely, remember that. As for us, we're proud to fight the Devil, whenever we are able. And especially when a friend asks us for our help." His round eyes flickered to the big man, who watched me possessively.

His was the deep voice and the helping hand. His

was the command of this expedition, I had no doubt. "And you, sir?" I asked. "It seemed it is to you I owe my debt of gratitude."

He ducked his head, and nearly smiled. He raised it and in the intermittent light of the speeding van, he looked on me again with unmistakable fondness and pride. "You don't recognize me? There's no reason that you should. I sailed from Troy with your grandfather, here, in those days when we were living men. And I've heard much of you. It was fated that we two should meet." He was teasing me, giving hints, playing a game that trivialized my debt and his victory.

But that was his way. I had finally met a hero whose song I had rightly sung. I met his hand with mine, and mine was trembling. "Diomedes," I said with certainty, no hint of question on my tongue or in my mind.

"At your service, far-seeing Homer," he said quietly. And then that voice grew terse. "We have far to go to bring you home, and I need to know that you desire it."

"Home?" I said. "Welch, Odysseus, even Alexander bade me stay away from Troy."

"Welch is a creature of the Devil. Odysseus meant well; he told me you were wandering; he has troubles of his own. And the Macedonian is a man with a torn heart. He knows only himself, forever." The big man shifted and his eyes probed mine. "Your choice, Homer: I will take you with me, home to Argos or to Nestor's Pylos, such as they are in Hell, or leave you with the Dissidents, or you can choose a place. You didn't write my war the way I fought it, but you wrote it well enough for me to owe you that."

This man was proud and careful not to be too kind, mindful of all the ancient codes of manliness and

reciprocity. "No need to endanger yourself, Diomedes.
I have longed to meet you. I am honored. Grandfa-
ther Nestor and you both must consider that the
Devil hates me more than all the Dissidents in
Hell. . ."

"The book. We know. Odysseus told me; I told
them." He indicated Gemayel and Nestor. "Of all of
us, before you and after you, Homer, you were the
greatest warrior. Your words endured where no pan-
oply or conquest triumphed . . . over time itself. No
man who knows war as I do can blame you for
writing what you did, but only praise you. We are in
your debt, every soul among us, for teaching the
lesson of Ilion. If men mistake its nature, or read
what is not there, what matter? The truth is in the
lines."

The truth is in the lines. In life, all over my world,
I had been lauded as I went from place to place
reciting my poems. I had been given a silver bowl by
Midas' sons for composing their father's epitaph. I
composed the Iliad in fifteen thousand verses and
the Odyssey in twelve thousand verses, and gave my
bowl and my poems to the oracle at Delphi. I recited
my works in Athens, in Corinth, and on wind-whipped
Argos, home of the hero who had just given me the
greatest compliment that ever I received.

And now he said to me, oh so softly, quoting from
my *Epigoni*, but doing more than quoting—giving,
as he was wont, sage advice: " 'And now, muse, let
us begin to sing of men of later days.' "

Wise Diomedes was full of guile, as I had drawn
him, to choose those lines and challenge me to live
up to them. There was more work for me to do, his
rich eyes told me; there were songs to sing as yet
unmade; there was a wealth of souls whose spirits
waited to be raised.

Clearly, there was more in Diomedes' heart than such a man would reveal here and now, but I trusted him. He had saved me from the jail; I had my notes, and in his company, I would maintain my freedom. His eagle's glance made me sure of it, and willing to die again and again, if I must, to live again and sing again and fight again against rampant evil.

For the first time, I thought of my travail in terms of triumph. I, Homer, a mere mortal poet, had thwarted the Devil and reaffirmed my worthiness to my muse.

So I nodded gravely to Diomedes, here in flesh to prove to me the Iliad was not composed in vain, or in error, or in foolishness, and put to him this question: " 'What is the mark of wisdom among men?' "

He gave back to me my ancient answer, " 'To rightly read the present, and to march with the occasion.' "

So I added: " 'In what kind of matter is it right to trust in men?' "

Then he responded, as I had in life when Hesiod asked me, " 'Where danger itself follows the action close.' "

Nestor laughed, and the spell was broken. And Gemayel took the words at face value and agreed that this, exactly, was our present situation.

Though the magic of that moment was gone, I had felt at one with the mind of the Iliad's best man, and all the misery of my spirit and my muse, which had afflicted me since we had stumbled upon Achilles and Odysseus and found them wanting, now disappeared.

If there was true death in Hell, I might have died then and slept easily. For I had not been wrong, in the eyes of this man who knew I had misjudged the war—not wrong in the truer sense a poet strives for.

Later, he would talk to me of the misery I had not told, but never with accusation in his voice.

He had been there. I had not. In Hell, I was learning that many events of the sort that make a man a hero are purely travail when one endures them; that there are things in men's lives that are only grand after one has survived them. While they happen, they are merely misery.

Thus Diomedes, Nestor, and I came among the Dissidents under the protection of Bashir Gemayel, who never admitted to having more than a dozen men, Diomedes said, but always had that many, no matter how many he might lose in skirmishing.

The Dissidents were encamped deep in wild country, under great fishnets strung on trees and intertwined with leaves to make a concealing canopy. They were not pleased to see us, being hard pressed and fearing that the enemy might follow us here.

Diomedes pulled me aside and said, "See? A temporary lodging, only. A gueststead, nothing more," and clapped me on the shoulder as if I were a fighter before he went off among the militia leaders of the camp.

We were there three days, while men sat in council and exchanged news with those who'd rescued me, before I realized how long I'd been shut away in the Devil's dungeons.

By the fire one night, a ragged little Semite with curly hair was reporting on things in New Hell to the chieftains, and he said, "Oh yes . . . I forgot. Welch and his team came back empty-handed from some secret mission. Got demoted. They'll be assigned to harass us." He meant the Dissidents. "If it was a bad enough falling out, between them and Authority, they might be right for recruitment."

This I doubted, but I said nothing. I was relieved

that they had not been eternally consigned to the Nile, where Amerikanoi did not want to be. I would have questioned this spy further, but it was not my place. And the next day, Diomedes, Nestor and I, with our Maronite bodyguard of exactly one dozen men, left the Dissident camp by night.

Another of the growling, whining insects of metal came down to swoop us up, and this one was controlled by Gemayel himself. "Hurry," he flashed us a grin. "I've got to get this back to the armory before anybody realizes it's missing."

And hurry we did, into its echoing maw, where we sat among the raucous Maronites and made our plans.

Diomedes wanted to take me to Argos, windwhipped Argos, which he said was enough like home to make me glad. This I wanted to see, and Nestor was anxious to return to his homelands, where life was simpler.

"And then," Diomedes said with that look of his that always pierces me to the soul, "when you're rested, Homer, perhaps you'll come with me on a journey."

"A journey?" I was tired, but not so tired as I once had been. And this man, of all the heroes of my *Iliad*, had the most tales to tell which I wanted to hear. And the most right to my eye and my muse, if further tales needed writing.

"A . . . search," said Diomedes. "You see, there were these companions of mine, who were turned into birds . . ."

I knew the story. I knew the look of eagles in Diomedes' eyes. And my muse was rustling in my head, getting out her golden harp already, which she plays when the rhythms of the words start to form.

Thus I found a new beginning, another tale to tell, to replace the emptiness left when the *Little Helliad* was done and I put it in the angel's bright hand. I had harbored thoughts, till then, of finding the angel and making sure all was well with my book, but I knew it would be.

Stories are god-given, and once in a great while, a poor bard like myself gets the opportunity to give a story back. So where the *Little Helliad* goes, and who sings it, will not trouble me.

Though I miss Confucius, I have another tale to learn, a bold companion who is a great hero, and a destiny to let unfold. Like Alexander, who stayed where his fate was, I have found my place.

In the great insect called Helicopter, by Diomedes' side, with my muse softly singing and grandfather Nestor's Pylian citadel in the cloud-fleeced distance, I took out my notes and began trying to capture the moment that I first caught sight of high-walled Pylos, with Paradise rising from the Sea of Sighs at her back.

Authors' Note

The *Little Helliad* takes its inspiration from what remains of the post-Homeric and pre-academic poetry, especially from *The Epic Cycle*, which contains *The Little Iliad*, "in four books by Lesches of Mitylene," and where the original contest between Homer and Hesiod can be found in its entirety. Structurally as well as texturally, these fragments have been our guide not only for the shape of the book, but for Homer and Hesiod's tone and the occasional quote.

Where we have paraphrased or altered existing text or bent myth and chronology, as well as genealogy, to suit our purpose, we did so in full awareness of conflicting academic theories, other contradictory versions in the Homerica and elsewhere, and the expectations of the casual reader.

When myth and scholarship are purposely blended, when what is history serves as a basis for what is not, the end must justify the means. Our hope is that this volume, created with the greatest affection and respect for those souls we have cast into Hell in order to bring them the rebirth of a new readership, will remind the erudite reader of treasures perhaps forgotten, while introducing new readers to the wealth that lies in our literary past.

All of us working in the framework of the *Hell* project are aware of the unique opportunity it offers: to let us write new stories about the greatest historical and mythical personages of mankind's past, not simply reinterpret a finite series of anecdotes on which, in many cases, the individuals involved have themselves written the definitive works.

Thus, for Hesiod and Homer, we went to the men themselves and to their early chroniclers, such as Democritus. The account of the Pythia during Hadrian's reign was our choice for Homer's geneology. For Heraclitus, we used his cosmic and common fragments as preserved by his school and others who succeeded him. For Diomedes, we used primarily the *Iliad* and *The Returns*; for Alexander, Plutarch was our final authority; for T.E. Lawrence, Lawrence's own *Seven Pillars of Wisdom*; for Theseus, Hesiod, Homer, and what exists in folklore, some of which is commonly ascribed to Theseus himself, and some to Herakles—an example of the compaction which is traditional in such myths and which tradition we hoped to follow in this text.

The mixing of Herakles and Theseus in ancient texts nowhere matches the Theseus legend we have pieced together—purposely; in mythic tradition, he escaped from Hades, leaving a companion behind; in most versions, other men stayed with Persephone. In that case, as everywhere else in this volume, we have chosen our own path to create stories suitable for the *Little Helliad*. Sometimes this was accomplished by restating or clarifying existing history or mythology, but more often by extending it—composing new vignettes that are constructed upon the foundations of the literature but go further, in the spirit of the old.

The revelations produced by the discussion of Odysseus' fidelity, and the matter of his relations, or lack of same, with various women and what his wife did and did not know are supportable by a close reading of the text of the *Odyssey*—Victorian attitudes promulgated the more familiar, and yet clearly wrong, conclusions that Odysseus told his wife of his sexual exploits or, equally unlikely from the original data, did not engage in extramarital relations.

In contrast, the "King of Wen" piece is entirely apocryphal; there is a 'King Wen' who appears in the Chinese texts, most familiarly in the *I Ching*, but our story is not a new version of any existing King Wen story. Thus we have purposely set it apart by installing the "King of Wen" convention. In this way again we have attempted to convey the spirit of the ancient authors and their tales, while fashioning pieces from whole cloth to convey the message specific to the *Little Helliad*. For Confucius we have used the man himself, and his commentaries and studies of the *I Ching*.

In matters of history, we have been stringent. Where Near Eastern studies are concerned, especially in the second millenium b.c., we are sufficient authorities unto ourselves. With a narrow specialty in the Amarna Letters period, we are thoroughly familiar with all the Near East material; thus our Akhenaten draws from our own work on texts standard in the field, and a list of sources—some of which have never been translated into English—would serve no purpose; many facts about Amarna Egypt are still hotly contested and may always remain mysterious. Our Nile pieces, latterday as well as 18th Dynasty, in this text draw upon twenty years of study, and beneath the Hellish conventions are many truths.

The story of the Devil and the Trojan Woman is a myth that might have been, but never was—or, if it ever existed, was lost. One familiar with first, second, and late third millenium b.c. texts will recognize those elements which define wisdom literature, and those from religious texts, which, we hope, we have used to the same effect as did those ancient authors whose students we are.

We have done, we hope and believe, what we set out to do: take Hesiod's advice and present, through our own muses, a song not of things that are, or shall be, or were of old; but another. If we have been successful, some credit is certainly due to the other writers in the shared project that is Hell in all its manifold volumes, especially to Carolyn Cherryh and David Drake, whose towering scholarship and enthusiasm buoyed us whenever we despaired at the task of making this material amusing not only to the historically sophisticated, but to that new generation who must be convinced, somehow, by some of us, that history relevant to the human condition does not begin with the invention of the 8088 chip.

—Janet and Chris Morris,
Cape Cod, 1987